Shugra's gaze narrowed and her mouth set as she unleashed the storm.

A bitter wind tore through the forest, whipping black ash into a blinding, swirling cloud. Thunder rolled and rumbled.

"Buffy—" Joyce started toward her. Giles pulled her back.

Xander struggled to his feet, his hands raw and bleeding from the wooden pikes he had pulled out with his teeth.

"Imperium iussu una!" Angel strode forward to stand by Buffy.

In the sky, streaks of red lightning coalesced into a single bolt. Shugra glared and sent the deadly shaft of primal magick driving down toward the Slayer.

"Reversus pravus unde iacia!" Buffy gasped the last word of the spell. Out of oxygen, her heart no longer pumping, she slumped into Angel's arms.

"Buffy?" Angel lowered her to the ground and put his ear on her chest. "Giles! She's not breathing!"

D1332799

Buffy the Vampire Slayer™

The Harvest
Halloween Rain
Coyote Moon
Night of the Living Rerun
Blooded
Visitors
Unnatural Selection
The Power of Persuasion
Deep Water
The Angel Chronicles, Vol. 1
The Angel Chronicles, Vol. 2
The Angel Chronicles, Vol. 3
The Xander Years, Vol. 1
The Willow Files, Vol. 1

Buffy the Vampire Slayer

Child of the Hunt
Return to Chaos
The Gatekeeper Trilogy
   Book 1: Out of the Madhouse
   Book 2: Ghost Roads
   Book 3: Sons of Entropy
Obsidian Fate
Immortal
Sins of the Father
Resurrecting Ravana
Prime Evil

The Watcher's Guide: The Official Companion to the Hit Show
The Postcards
The Essential Angel
The Sunnydale High Yearbook
Pop Quiz: Buffy the Vampire Slayer

Available from POCKET BOOKS

BUFFY

THE VAMPIRE

SLAYER™

PRIME EVIL

DIANA G. GALLAGHER

An original novel based on the hit TV series created by Joss Whedon

POCKET BOOKS

New York   London   Toronto   Sydney   Singapore

POCKET BOOKS, a division of Simon & Schuster Inc.
1230 Avenue of the Americas, New York, NY 10020

ISBN: 0-671-03930-X

First Pocket Books printing March 2000

10 9 8 7 6 5 4 3

Printed in Great Britain by Omnia Books Ltd, Glasgow

For Lloyd Dixon,
with affection and gratitude
for all his support across the Atlantic

Acknowledgments

The author gratefully acknowledges the following people for their assistance: my agent, Ricia Mainhardt, and her partner, A. J. Janschewitz, for always being there when I need them; my mother, Beryl M. Turner, and Betsey Wilcox for proofreading and keeping me on track; my husband, Martin R. Burke, for providing foreign language translations; my editor, Lisa Clancy, for her guidance, support, and confidence; and Lisa's assistant, Micol Ostow, for answering questions promptly and efficiently. I am especially grateful to Joss Whedon and the cast and crew of *Buffy the Vampire Slayer* for their creative efforts and inspiration.

Diana G. Gallagher
October 8, 1999

Chapter 1

BUFFY'S WANDERING MIND SNAPPED BACK TO THE PRESent. Cornered and blindsided by the low, husky voice, her throat constricted with an oppressive dread. All eyes were on her. She wasn't ready and cringed under the penetrating scrutiny.

How could she be prepared for this unexpected peril when she was coping with so many other distractions? Vampire attacks, demons with delusions of universal omnipotence, the verbal state of war between Xander and Cordelia, Oz's monthly episodes of hairy-hound guy syndrome, and the heartache of loving Angel combined with a grueling training schedule and nightly patrols had become matters of routine, but the cumulative effect was wearing. Even more so now that she was determined to improve her GPA. She rarely slept more than four hours a night, which made it difficult to study and even harder to concentrate in school, especially since surviving her Slayer duties often depended on catching a few daytime Zs.

And now this!

The new menace was female and attractively packaged in a tall, slim body with classic facial features, bruising brown eyes, and blond hair cut stylishly short.

Buffy's hopes of graduating with the rest of the senior class dwindled as Crystal Gordon's stare bore into her. The pressure in her throat spread into her chest and her heart lurched as though shocked by an electric prod. The realization that she was experiencing the symptoms of a major anxiety attack was more unnerving than the antagonistic source. She was the Slayer. She didn't panic, was *not* panicked now.

Then again, how to escape an embarrassing situation instigated by a belligerent authority figure with the power to pass or fail her wasn't covered in the Slayer manual. In the classroom, Mr. Pointy was as useful as a limp noodle against an undead mob.

Buffy breathed in slowly, convinced the new history teacher was a protégé of Principal Snyder, whose stony glare could petrify a student at fifty paces. However, whereas Snyder openly despised all teenagers, Ms. Gordon's animosity had been focused entirely on Buffy since her arrival at Sunnydale High two weeks ago. Or so it seemed.

"Whenever you're ready, Ms. Summers." Ms. Gordon made no effort to mask her annoyed impatience. She looked at her watch and sighed.

The pressure in Buffy's throat eased and her pounding pulse slowed, but the sound of shuffling feet, the stares, and the collective anticipation gripping the classroom kept the tension level at a crushing high.

Willow winced, sympathetic with Buffy's plight but helpless to assist with the academic emergency.

Xander studied the ceiling as though how many dots there were in a twelve-by-twelve square was guaranteed to be a crucial question on the next exam.

Anya raised her hand to answer. For a supernatural being who had suddenly been trapped in the body and persona of a teenaged girl, she was adapting remarkably well. Although her inhuman longevity and power to grant the vindictive wishes of jilted women had been lost, she was quickly catching on to established methods of mortal survival specific to teens, like being the teacher's pet.

Anya's enthusiasm solicited a warm smile from Ms. Gordon, but the frosty female in charge was not about to let Buffy slip from her grasp. The teacher impaled her with another scathing look, a perfectly plucked eyebrow arched in challenge.

Buffy straightened and coughed to clear her throat. "What was the question?"

"Article Nineteen," Ms. Gordon said flatly.

"Gave women the right to vote. Nineteen-twenty." Buffy silently thanked the forces of fate that had prompted her to read the assignment on the Constitution of the United States before she had finally dozed off at three A.M. last night.

"Yes. Quite so." Ms. Gordon held Buffy with her barbed gaze a moment before abruptly turning away.

Buffy knew her answer was correct. What she didn't

know was why the young woman had taken an immediate dislike to her. But she could guess.

Snyder sabotage.

The principal had hired Ms. Gordon to replace Dan Coltrane, the history teacher who had been killed by the jaguar incarnation of the Aztec god, Tezcatlipoca. Snyder had obviously warned his newest faculty member about Buffy Summers, the notorious troublemaker he had expelled and then readmitted under duress. Then, in spite of her sincere desire to do better, she had missed several classes and barely passed last Friday's test. Habitual inattentiveness and late assignments had cemented the unsavory image Snyder had planted in the new teacher's mind.

Ms. Gordon paused at the front of the room. Stunning in a tailored, sea-green suit that gently hugged her distinctly feminine curves, she exuded a commanding confidence that arrested adolescent rebellion before it started. With the possible exception of Xander, whose mouth often operated independent of his better judgment, no one even contemplated disrupting her class. She held everyone's silent attention when she started to speak.

"The Nineteenth Amendment was the most important legal affirmation of women's rights since the seventeenth century, when Ireland was incorporated into the United Kingdom and forced to abandon the ancient Brehon Laws in favor of a male-dominated English judiciary."

"What were the Brehon Laws?" Michael Czajak asked.

"Excellent question, Michael," Ms. Gordon said. The

boy flushed as her approving gaze swept over him. "The ancient Celtic legal system isn't covered in most history courses, but it should be."

Buffy watched and listened attentively, but not because she was inspired by Crystal Gordon's impassioned discourse. She had had to cope with hostile teachers before, but none of them, including Snyder, had ever bullied her into a breathless bundle of jangled nerves.

"Brehon Law was unique in many ways," Ms. Gordon continued, "including the right of women to own property and divorce husbands who humiliated, lied or in any way dishonored them."

"Since when is male-bashing part of the curriculum?" Oblivious to the danger of cutting rebuke, Xander huffed indignantly, then glanced at Anya. "No wonder she likes you."

"Those were the days." Anya withered Xander with a superior smile.

Unable to let a slings-and-arrows moment pass, Xander countered. "Plenty of fodder for the revenge mill, huh?"

Anya just nodded and sighed.

The teasing exchange did not prompt the disciplinary retort Buffy expected. Instead, Ms. Gordon's eyes mirrored Anya's wistful look, giving the impression she shared the girl's longing for the past. Except, Buffy reflected, Anya had been around for a thousand years and had probably lived in old Erin at one time or another. Unless Ms. Gordon was centuries older than she looked, she had not.

Since nothing supernatural registered on her Slayer

sonar, Buffy had to conclude that Crystal Gordon was human and merely felt a wishful attachment to events and times she could study, but never experience. Even so, her uneasiness was not dispelled. History teemed with unspeakable horrors conceived and perpetuated by evils that were wholly human in origin.

"So women were equal with men?" Willow asked. "Back then—in Ireland, I mean."

"Almost, but not quite. It wasn't until the Civil Rights Act of 1964 that—" Cut off by the bell, the teacher surrendered control to the unstoppable stampede of students fixated on food and the midday break from educational tedium.

Buffy leaned toward Willow as everyone began stuffing papers and books into bags. "Did this period seem longer than usual to you?"

"The class before lunch always seems longer." Xander loomed over them with one hand shoved into the pocket of his baggy pants and a quirky grin on his face.

"Especially when you're famished." Pulling a blue denim hat with a turned-up brim over her auburn hair, Willow stood up as Buffy eased into the aisle. "Which I am."

"Not hungry, but I can use the break," Buffy said.

"I'm free." Anya shoved between Xander and Willow's desk.

"And since one always gets what one pays for—" Xander wrinkled his nose. "—I'll pass."

"I meant for lunch." Anya slumped despondently. "I hate sitting in the cafeteria by myself. Everyone stares like I'm some kind of freak."

"You are. Were," Xander corrected himself.

"Not that we hold that against you, Anya," Willow quickly interjected. "It's just that after you almost, you know, condemned us to a Sunnydale that was overrun by vampires—"

"Including yours truly," Xander said pointedly.

"Right." Willow shuddered. She had had the distinct displeasure of meeting her vampire self when Anya, hoping to retrieve her lost wish-necklace, had tricked her into trying a temporal-fold spell. Fortunately for all concerned, Willow the vamp was returned to her proper reality and Anya's power center was not recovered. "So it's not easy to just, well, forgive and forget."

"That was Cordelia's idea, not mine." Anya shrugged self-consciously. "Believe me, if I could take back that wish I would."

"And believe me," Xander added emphatically, "the male half of the species is *so* glad that's not possible."

Buffy had misgivings about Anya, too, but the grounded Patron Saint of Scorned Women had seen, heard and experienced a lot over the past millennium, some of which might prove useful. Besides, she knew what it was like to be singled out and ostracized for weirdness and felt a certain empathy with the displaced entity. She waved Anya to follow as they fell into line behind the student horde pressing toward the door.

Xander whispered in Buffy's ear. "Why do I have the feeling I'm going to regret this?"

"I don't know," Buffy whispered back, amused. That was a lie. Although Xander hadn't noticed or was in denial, it was obvious to everyone else that Anya was developing a serious interest in him.

7

"Excuse me—"

Buffy halted as Rebecca Sullivan shoved into line ahead of her.

Xander bumped into Buffy and muttered, "Some people think they own the aisles."

"Sorry, but I've—" Rebecca glanced back, her voice muffled with a sob. Short, with straight dark hair and a round, freckled face, she nervously adjusted her glasses.

"Forget it, Rebecca." Xander shrugged apologetically. "Just pre-lunch classroom rage. I'm over it now."

Rebecca's smile was as lame as Xander's joke. She sighed and started to cry.

"What's wrong?" Buffy had hardly spoken to the shy girl during her three years at Sunnydale, but she couldn't ignore Rebecca's distress. Not when it was dripping on her notebook.

"Nothing. I just—" Rebecca's gaze darted toward the far front corner of the room where Kari Stark and Michael were speaking with Ms. Gordon.

There was nothing unusual or sinister about the conference huddle, and yet, Buffy's apprehension intensified as she watched. Michael, who practiced witchcraft and wore heavy make-up to ensure his isolation from the mainstream, and Kari, a plain but pleasant and intelligent girl with no occult connections that Buffy knew of, were *not* uncomfortable. They nodded in response to something Ms. Gordon said and waved as they turned toward the door. The warm sparkle in the teacher's brown eyes hardened as her gaze followed them out of the classroom.

Buffy shivered, disturbed by the malice evident in

the woman's shifting demeanor. Or was she imagining trouble where there wasn't any?

"Kari!" Rebecca called out.

Kari cast an annoyed glance over her shoulder, rolled her eyes, then took Michael's arm and turned down the hall.

Hurt by the blatant snub, Rebecca shoved through the student bodies ahead of her, bolted through the door, and ran in the opposite direction.

"What was that all about?" Anya asked.

"Being human hint for the day," Xander said dryly. "Never ditch your best friend since fourth grade for a guy."

"Kari and Michael?" Willow frowned, then sighed. "Not hard to understand, I guess. Considering what happened to Amy. I mean, they were pretty close, but—"

"Rodents with naked tails aren't exactly a turn-on," Xander said as they filed into the corridor.

Buffy elaborated for Anya's benefit. "Amy Madison turned herself into a rat so she wouldn't be burned at the stake."

"Which perfectly illustrates the old saying 'the lesser of two evils,' " Xander added.

Buffy nodded. "But Willow's taking good care of her."

"Only until I figure out how to change her back," Willow added. "Which isn't as easy as I—"

"Willow!" Ms. Gordon appeared in the doorway. "I'd like to speak with you for a moment, please."

"Uh—sure." Willow hesitated, obviously bewildered.

"Wait—" Suddenly anxious when she caught the

teacher's eye, Buffy moved forward as Willow stepped into the classroom. She stopped just as suddenly, her frantic gaze shifting from Willow's questioning baby blues to Ms. Gordon's curious, brown-eyed stare. "Never mind. It's . . . nothing."

But it wasn't nothing, Buffy thought as the teacher smiled and closed the door. She had no idea why she had been overwhelmed by another surge of chilling dread.

Or why she wanted to run.

"Are we going to the cafeteria or not?" Anya's patience bottomed out thirty seconds into Willow's impromptu conference with Ms. Gordon.

"As soon as Willow comes out." Xander answered without looking at Anya. He watched Buffy, waiting for her to do or say something, anything to assure him she hadn't totally and inexplicably checked out.

Anya fixed him with a petulant pout, silently intimating that her gastric cravings were somehow his fault. "I was *never* this hungry before I . . . changed."

While Xander was thrilled to the bottom of his nifty new high-tops that Anya was powerless and preoccupied with her stomach rather than him, Buffy's vacant stare was a troubling development. The odds of surviving Sunnydale would plummet from fighting chance to not a prayer if the Slayer went over the edge. He leaned closer, ignoring the subtle traces of scented shampoo that teased his deprived male hormones via his nose. "Xander to Buffy—"

"Hmmm?" Buffy blinked, then turned to stare blankly at him. "What?"

"Well, either you're into some kind of Zen meditation involving the spiritual depth of classroom doors or something's wrong," Xander pressed. "I'm guessing something's wrong."

"Just tired." Buffy's wan smile amplified the worry in her eyes. "Whoever decided teenaged girls should burn the midnight oil dusting vampires didn't take modern lifestyles into account. Like homework, having to graduate from high school, getting into college, not to mention the occasional date, which I don't have . . . much. Anyway, there's only so many hours in a night, and I don't spend enough of them sleeping."

"Right." Xander nodded, opting to be relieved. Even with her enhanced strength and reflexes, he often wondered how Buffy managed to function without suffering the debilitating effects of sleep deprivation. "But take my advice, Buff, and *don't* take your morning nap in Ice Woman's class again."

"Ice Woman?" Anya looked at him askance. "Are you referring to Ms. Gordon?"

"As in gorgeous with a heart of cold? Yes." Xander faked an exaggerated shiver. "If looks could freeze, Buffy would be an icicle."

Buffy's expression clouded again, and Xander instantly regretted the remark. The fate of the world rested on her shoulders, a responsibility she accepted and managed against outrageous odds with no recognition from the student body or faculty. Not surprising, since no one knew about the sacrifices she made to keep Sunnydale safe. Relatively speaking. Crystal Gordon was no exception. It was bad enough the stern, new teacher had stewed her on the humiliation hot plate and then served her up as an example for class consumption. Although Buffy had handled it with cool and collected Slayer aplomb, she could have done without the sting of his thoughtless reminder.

"Well, I like her," Anya said defensively. "Mr. Coltrane didn't even know my name. Crystal offered to help me work out my problems. Adjusting to—whatever."

"Crystal?" Xander gave *that* a surprised two eyebrows up. "On a first name basis with the teacher, huh? I guess ice water is thicker than blood."

"It is?"

Xander hid his disappointment when the slur zoomed over Anya's head. He was just grateful the uptight, humorless Ms. Gordon neither favored nor despised him. Not often, but sometimes, being nondescript and easy to ignore was a good thing. He wished Anya would take the hint. Cordelia's sarcastic rejection was a balm for the soul compared to the prospect of being the object of Anya's affections. He was romantically desperate, not emotionally suicidal.

"Crystal is a strong, independent woman who has total control of her life. She's an ideal female role model. Right?" Anya looked to Buffy for support, which was just more evidence that she hadn't quite yet tuned in to the subtleties of teenaged trauma.

"You're asking me?" Buffy hesitated, incredulous. "The creepy lady's designated victim of the day?"

"Who's creepy?" Oz sauntered up looking casually freaky in faded jeans, a plaid shirt, and platinum blond, spiked hair. It was a look only a musician could wear without fear of being laughed out of school by the fashionably correct.

"Attention shoppers!" Xander jerked backward, his hand shielding his eyes from the imagined glare radiating off nearly-neon hair tint.

"Crystal Gordon." Anya tentatively reached up to touch the gelled points covering Oz's head, then pulled back with a grimace. "Only she's not creepy."

Xander made a mental note. Icky hair was an effective Anya repellent.

"And Crystal Gordon is?" Oz asked.

"Is what?" Willow popped back into the hall. The perpetual perky sparkle Xander had foolishly taken for granted since kindergarten brightened several degrees when she saw Oz. "Hey! Cool hair!"

"Blinding even," Xander quipped for cover, just in case anyone had noticed his momentary lapse into Willow lust.

"Yeah." Oz winked at Willow. "It clashes with everything but your eyes."

"That is so sweet. Just makes me goose-bumpy all over." Willow blushed.

"So what did the ice maiden want, Willow?" Xander asked.

"Ms. Gordon? She just wanted to recommend a book on Brehon Law." Willow shrugged. "In case I was really as interested as I sounded in class. Not that I was *that* interested, but I thought it was, well . . . a very thoughtful gesture. She's actually kind of nice."

"To anyone with an IQ over one hundred and

forty—" Xander started when Buffy grabbed Willow's arm.

A bit too roughly, Xander thought uneasily. He didn't have the Slayer's ability to sense approaching evil, but his human internal warning system jumped from all's well to major alert in nanoseconds.

"Let's walk." Buffy started down the hall with Willow in tow.

Matching Buffy's hurried stride, Xander moved into place on her right leaving Oz and Anya to bring up the rear, which gave him two definitive advantages. Distance from the ancient, love-starved stalker that talked and walked like a girl, but wasn't—not really—and eavesdropping proximity to Buffy and Willow's conversation.

"I know it's none of my business, Willow, but—" Buffy scowled. "—you *like* Ms. Gordon?"

"Like?" Willow hesitated. "Well, maybe not exactly like, but she was nice—to me."

"How nice?" Buffy asked sharply.

"She just offered to lend me that book tomorrow." Willow's expression phased from confusion to irritation to concern. "What's the matter, Buffy? I mean, well . . . you're a little tense. A lot tense, actually—"

"Brutal interrogation does seem like overkill," Xander interjected.

Buffy started, her stricken expression saying volumes more than her words. "No, it's— Sorry, Will. I didn't mean to put you on the spot. Just forget it, okay?" She instantly withdrew.

Willow cast a helpless glance at Xander behind Buffy's back.

Xander fielded it with a helpless shrug, his own anxiety mounting. They all got a little testy now and then. Who wouldn't with the Hellmouth as a hobby? But it wasn't like Buffy to take her frustrations out on her friends. Not without a damn good reason. "Am I the only one missing something here?"

"We're all missing lunch." Anya's eyes narrowed accusingly.

"I can walk faster." Willow latched onto the change in subject with a grateful glance at Anya.

"Please." Anya sighed, exasperated.

Buffy stopped when everyone else turned toward the cafeteria. "Look, I'm gonna pass on lunch."

"Want to talk about it?" Xander asked. "Whatever it is that's bugging you, I mean."

"Not now, Xander." Buffy shrugged. "Maybe later. After I talk to Giles."

"Giles!" Willow gritted her teeth, closed her eyes, and drew her shoulders up slightly, a sure sign she had forgotten something important. "I forgot to tell him I finished programming the database last night."

"The one for indexing and cross-referencing hundreds of years of Slayer info?" Oz asked.

"Yeah." Willow sighed. "He's been on me about it for days, like *I* don't have a life or . . . or things to do or . . . anything."

Oz grinned. "I'm rather partial to the anything part myself."

Xander looked up sharply. "Define anything."

Willow grinned. "Well, not exactly *that*—but close!"

"I'll tell Giles about the program, Willow." Buffy's mouth tightened into a poor imitation of a smile. "Later."

A dozen explanations for Buffy's odd behavior flashed through Xander's mind as she walked away. None of them inspired a funny comeback.

Giles leaned back in his desk chair and removed his glasses to rub his weary eyes. The quiet of the noon hour was a welcome respite from the seemingly constant comings and goings of students who had recently discovered that Sunnydale High had a library. He desperately hoped the sudden interest was just a passing fad and that the general student population would return to the public book depository without undue delay. Although he begrudged no one the chance to broaden their educational horizons, the high-school library was woefully deficient in acceptable references, and the presence of anyone outside the Slayer's circle was highly inconvenient when they were embroiled in a demonic crisis, which was the case more frequently than not.

Pushing an eighteenth-century manuscript aside— carefully, so as not to damage the fragile, yellowed pages—Giles rose to make himself a fresh cup of tea. At the moment, there was no crisis beyond the routine business of eliminating vampires. This afforded him the time to comb through the obscure *Watcher's Chronicles* the Council had neglected in favor of those pertaining to the more successful, adventuresome, or notorious Slayers. However, while he worked, Buffy and company had taken advantage of the rare opportunity to "goof off," an appropriate colloquialism given the circumstances.

Giles sighed as he opened a box of gourmet Irish

Breakfast teabags and dropped one into a stained cup. Perhaps he was being too hard on them. Except for Buffy, who had had no say in being chosen as the Vampire Slayer, Willow, Xander, Oz and even Cordelia, on a surprising number of occasions, were all volunteers. They deserved a holiday from the life-threatening pressures of fighting the dark forces intent on destroying the world. It was incredibly callous to expect them to spend their free time entrenched in the tedious process of gleaning facts from boring old texts. Still, their lives might one day depend on how quickly they could access vital information.

Tossing the teabag, Giles stirred and fretted over the dilemma. At the present rate of progress, the project, although ongoing in nature, would not be completed within the next century, which rather defeated the purpose of the undertaking—helping Buffy. He didn't even have the option of hiring a data-entry person when Willow finally finished setting up the cross-referencing program.

"How would I explain the data?" Giles raised the cup to take a sip.

"The same way you explain talking to yourself?" Buffy asked from the office doorway.

Startled, Giles jumped, sloshing his hand with hot tea. "Buffy. I do so wish you wouldn't creep in like that. It's quite—unsettling."

"Sorry." Buffy flopped on the chair in front of his desk and dropped her books on the floor.

"Yes, well—" Setting the cup down, Giles dried his hand on a handkerchief. "I don't suppose you dropped by to assist with reading the *Watcher's Chronicles?*"

"No, but Willow finished setting up the database."

"Did she?" Giles nodded. "Good."

"And my . . . problem is related. To the *Watcher's Chronicles*. Maybe." Buffy sighed, her brow knit in troubled brooding.

"Is it?" Giles softened his tone when he realized she was genuinely distressed. "What problem is that?"

"How many Slayers have totally lost it?"

Chapter 2

"LOST WHAT?"

Buffy didn't laugh. Giles's question was not posed in the Xander tradition of trying to be comically cute. The oh-so-British librarian really didn't understand what she meant or the disturbing significance, which made talking about the problem even more difficult. Communicating with adults about personal matters wasn't easy *without* having to translate.

"It!" Buffy made a circling motion around her ear, which caused Giles's frown to deepen but did absolutely nothing to enlighten him. "Bonkers, wigged out, off the deep end—crazy? As in nervous breakdown?"

"Oh. Yes, I see." He hesitated, still frowning.

"If the furrows in your forehead get any deeper, we'll be able to do the spring planting early." Despite her inner turmoil, Buffy smiled. Giles was charming when he was totally befuddled, in a stuffy, tweed and sweater vest with slightly rumpled hair sort of way.

"The question hardly suggests levity." Giles replaced his glasses and sat down. His starched bearing was noticeably more rigid, his tone cautious when he spoke. "Why do you ask?"

"Answer first. Then I'll explain." Buffy held his eyes, serious and braced. "How many?"

"Well, uh . . . I'm not quite sure, actually." Giles shrugged, a dismissive gesture intended to diminish the impact of his admission. "A few . . . here and there over the centuries."

"But it happens."

"Yes." Giles nodded. "Not often, however . . . considering."

"Considering that they put their lives on the line every night to keep the world safe for humanity; only, since nobody knows that's what they do, they're still expected to do whatever young girls are supposed to do?" Buffy didn't pause to breathe or give Giles a chance to respond. Stress disguised as anger poured out of her in a torrent of vehement words that seemed preferable to breaking something. "All of which can be a bit much, depending on the century and how many major demons decide to make a bid for domination over an evil universe, which usually requires the total annihilation of the good guys. Does that about sum it up?"

"More or less," Giles said calmly. "There are numerous variables, of course."

"Of course!" Buffy's flaring temper waned when she realized she was shouting. "See?"

"Buffy, you don't think—"

"That I'm having a nervous breakdown? Nooo." She waved away the ridiculous notion, then jumped to her feet. "I *know* I am. I just gave Willow the third degree about Ms. Gordon because I didn't want to believe it and needed someone to blame, and now I'm shouting at you! And I can't seem to stop babbling—"

"Crystal Gordon? The new history teacher?" Giles sat back, clearly surprised. "What does she have to do with this?"

"I, uh—" Buffy lowered her gaze and sighed. This was harder than she thought it would be. Aside from taking quiet pride in being the Watcher for a Slayer who always got her demon, Giles really cared about her. Telling him she was falling apart for no apparent reason was almost as bad as confessing to her mom that she had slept with Angel. "I . . . had an anxiety attack in her class."

"Do tell." Giles remained unruffled, absorbing the news with no outward indication of what he was feeling inside. "How would you describe this—attack?"

"Basic basket case, I guess." Folding her arms, Buffy started to pace. "Constricted throat, pounding heart, couldn't breathe—"

"Those are physical symptoms associated with a panic episode, yes, but—what made you panic to begin with?"

Buffy explained again, slowly, annoyed at having to repeat herself. "I felt like I was being strangled, I couldn't breathe and my heart rate jumped off the chart."

"I meant *before* you experienced the physical effects," Giles reiterated patiently.

"I know, but—" Realization smashed through the fatigue and worry clouding her thinking. Buffy sank back into the chair. "I wasn't panicked, Giles. Not until I *thought* I was having an anxiety attack."

"You're quite sure?"

Buffy nodded. "Absolutely positive."

"Then it's quite possible anxiety did not cause the effects."

"Then what did?"

Giles didn't answer. He had slipped into deep thought mode, one hand covering his mouth, the other tapping the rim of his teacup, his eyes focused on a stack of musty old papers.

Buffy waited, perched on the edge of her seat, her thoughts a jumble of relief, confusion, and concern as she watched his impassive face. She took little consolation in knowing that her nerve may not have suddenly unraveled. But if that was the case, then something or someone had messed with her emotional stability, creating a debilitating physical state of panic that could, under different circumstances, be deadly.

She felt violated.

"I'm afraid I'm at a loss for an explanation, Buffy." Giles looked up and smiled, trying to put her at ease. "But there is one, I'm sure. Perhaps if you tell me everything that happened in the class, in as much detail as you remember, we'll uncover something relevant."

Giles listened without interrupting as Buffy recounted the events of last period. She left nothing out, not even that she had retreated into a waking daze that substituted for sleep when she should have been paying attention. He more than anyone understood the hardships and pressures that had, apparently, driven a few other Slayers mad. That in and of itself was enough to give her a bad moment or two. Had they been pushed into the abyss of insanity by some evil too horrendous to face? Or had some small, seemingly unimportant incident made them snap? After she and Giles discovered the reason underlying her unnerving experience, she intended to find out. Aside from being dead—or undead—going "funny farm" was the worst fate she could imagine. Definitely not the legacy she wanted to leave for Slayer posterity.

"Say that again?" Giles asked suddenly.

"What? That Ms. Gordon looked at her watch?"

"No, after that." Giles gently prodded. "You said you felt better . . . when she looked away?"

"Well, as better as possible with everyone waiting for me to totally screw up," Buffy said. "But I started breathing again, if that's what you mean."

"Yes, it is." Giles grimaced when he sipped his tea and found it cold. "And this sense of foreboding you mentioned—"

"Foreboding? Try blood-chilling dread." Buffy shuddered and rubbed her arms, a subconscious reaction to a memory that hadn't been dulled by time.

"Dread, then. You felt it twice. Once when you realized Ms. Gordon had asked you a question you didn't hear because you were daydreaming and again when Willow went back into the classroom."

Buffy nodded.

"And Ms. Gordon was looking at you on both occasions?"

"Glaring, Giles. She hates—" Buffy's head jerked

up. "Ms. Gordon zapped me with eye contact?" She had become so accustomed to the teacher's unguarded dislike during the past two weeks she hadn't made the connection.

"Possibly. We have had . . . unusual situations involving teachers in the past." Giles took off his glasses again and pulled a tissue from a box crumpled by the weight of assorted textbooks.

"Unusual, deadly, and totally gross." Nasty beasties posing as or working in consort with teachers wasn't a novel occurrence at Sunnydale High. Natalie French, biology teacher and praying-mantis woman with a lethal mating drive, had almost stolen Xander's virginity and his life. The health teacher, Mr. Whitmore, had taken the parenting class into the Twilight Zone when he had his students adopt the eggs of a mind-controlling bezoar living under the school basement. Coach Carl Marin was the worst kind of monster, though—totally human. Pressed by Principal Snyder to win the state championship after fifteen years of losing, the coach had conspired with Nurse Greenleigh to turn the swim team into fish boys.

Buffy hadn't "sensed" anything weird about them, either, so it wasn't far-fetched to think Crystal Gordon might be something other than she seemed. However, she definitely sensed an unspoken "but" as Giles rigorously cleaned his lenses.

"Spit it out, Giles. The suspense is a killer."

"Yes, well, given what you've told me, we can't rule out the possibility that, uh, Ms. Gordon has inadvertently, or perhaps, even deliberately—"

"Done a number on my head?"

"Something to that effect, yes." Giles flinched at her mumbled curse, then quickly added, "I don't mean to imply I've reached that conclusion, Buffy, only that we might have to consider it pending what develops. A quiet background check on Ms. Gordon should reveal something—one way or another."

"That makes me feel *so* much better." The bite of sarcasm in her voice was unintentional, a buffer to cushion the fear wrenching her stomach. "I mean, either I'm dealing with an unknown evil entity that can turn me into a nervous wreck with a glance or a teacher who can turn me into a nervous wreck with a glance *and* give me an F in history."

"Buffy—" Rising, Giles walked to the front of the desk and leaned against it. "You have had rather a harder time of it than most Slayers, especially this past year."

"Yeah. Most Slayers don't fall in love with a vampire or use their best friends as backup or come home to find a lovesick undead guy crying his heart out on her mother's shoulder."

"And finals are coming up," Giles said dryly.

"Giles!" Buffy grinned. "Was that a bold attempt at humor?"

"Yes. Quite effective, too, it seems." He bent forward slightly. "The point is that you've handled all the Hellmouth horrors and mundane daily problems with astonishing composure and courage. A bit of anxious concern does not mean you've . . . lost it."

"Okay. I'll take your word for it. For now." Still dismayed, but somewhat relieved by Giles's supportive assurances, Buffy relaxed. "Are there any doughnuts left? I missed lunch."

While Willow installed the Slayer database program on the library computer, Giles went in search of Crystal Gordon. She was not in her classroom but in the teachers' lounge, where a casual conversation under relaxed conditions would not arouse her suspicions. He simply wanted to meet her, to get a personal glimpse of the woman who had made a Slayer suspect that she was losing her mind.

Giles nodded to Mr. Moran as he entered the faculty's haven from teenaged turmoil. Buffy's young history teacher sat alone on a sofa against the far wall pouring over a lesson planner. He had only seen Crystal Gordon in passing. Her tailored wardrobe, short, no-nonsense hairstyle, and poised manner left the casual onlooker with an impression of unyielding severity. He was surprised to see that she was rather attractive and wondered if the stringent façade hid a softer personality.

Or malevolence.

"Mr. Giles, I've been meaning to ask you—" Mr. Moran paused, rubbing his salt and pepper beard. "Is there a copy of Howard's *Roman Conquest* in the library?"

"Yes, I believe so. Would you like me to set it aside?" From the corner of his eye, Giles saw Crystal Gordon look up.

"Yes, thank you. I'll pick it up later." Mr. Moran smiled as he darted into the hall.

Feeling a tad self-conscious, Giles returned Ms.

Gordon's smile as he walked over to the coffee station.

"You're British."

"Yes, quite." Grateful for the opening, Giles nodded, then cast a perturbed glance at the double coffee maker dominating a neat array of mugs, disposable stirrers, sugar packets, and powdered creamer. A half-full pot of aging coffee occupied each of two warmers. "And as usual, there's no hot water for tea."

"I didn't see any tea." The teacher craned her neck to scan the counter.

Giles pulled a plastic sandwich bag stuffed with a variety of flavored teabags from his pocket. "I bring my own, proving once again that hope does spring eternal."

"Ah!" Her smile broadened and an unexpected twinkle shone from her dark eyes. "I like a man who doesn't give up." She extended her hand. "Crystal Gordon. American History."

"Uh, yes . . . I know. Rupert Giles. Librarian." Her grip was firm, her gaze confident as he shook her hand. A familiar flush began to creep up his neck, a sensation he hadn't felt since his initial awkward attraction to Jenny Calendar. The disturbing warmth intensified, then cooled when he turned away to turn on the sink tap. He slipped a teabag into a Styrofoam cup and filled it with passably hot water. "May I join you, Ms. Gordon?"

"Yes, of course. And just Crystal, please." She closed her planner and set it aside as he sat down on the sofa. "Have you been in the States long?"

"About three years now." Disarmed by her easygoing, flirtatious manner, Giles wasn't quite sure how to proceed. He had primed himself for a curt, uncomfortable exchange. "And you?"

"I was born here."

"In Sunnydale?" He started, almost spilling his tea, and eyed her curiously.

She laughed. "No, in the States. Ohio."

"Yes, of course." Giles pushed on his glasses as another surge of heat flowed through him and nodded, flustered by the nervous reaction.

"Cleveland," Crystal said.

"Cleveland?" Giles blinked.

"Ohio. Where I grew up, went to school—" She leaned closer, holding his gaze and lowering her voice as though confiding a secret. "I graduated from Ohio State in Columbus and then went back home to teach in a local high school for five years." She looked past him then, out the window. "California is like a different country."

"Yes, yes, it is." Giles frowned, feeling a bit dizzy. Remembering Buffy's experience, he reminded himself to beware of extended eye contact. "Sunnydale, in particular."

"Excuse me for saying so, Mr. Giles, but Sunnydale is . . . creepy." Crystal laughed again. "Sorry. That was the only word that came to mind."

"Teenage slang can be contagious." He shifted uneasily, put off by her eagerness to talk. She seemed to be baiting him with information that would facilitate looking into her past. Coincidence or manipulation? And if manipulation, to what end?

With nothing more to gain by lingering, Giles started to rise. "I really must get back to the library. If you'll excuse—"

"I understand you're quite close to Buffy Summers, Mr. Giles." She paused, then calmly responded to his unguarded surprise. "Principal Snyder mentioned it."

"And?" Snared by dilemma, Giles sat back down and waited for her to continue. The woman made him uncomfortable for reasons he couldn't define. Yet, he couldn't neglect an opportunity to alter her perceptions of Buffy, if possible.

Crystal sighed. "This isn't easy to admit, but I'm afraid I allowed myself to be influenced by Mr. Snyder's opinions about Buffy. She's not a 'disruptive, destructive juvenile delinquent with absolutely no respect for authority.'"

"No, she isn't."

"His words, not mine. Buffy's actually very quiet and seems to try hard. Her mind wanders a bit, but that's hardly a detention offense. The problem is—" The hollows of Crystal's lightly blushed cheeks puffed as she exhaled. "I've been a little hard on her."

"Well, that's easily remedied, isn't it?" In spite of Crystal's confession, her sincerity and motives were questionable and Giles didn't trust her. He played along for Buffy's benefit, as a precaution in case Ms. Gordon was just a teacher who bullied students into failing.

"Yes, I suppose so." Crystal smiled tightly. "Does she have problems at home? Anything going on that might account for her . . . difficulties? I have a degree in psychology as well as education. Perhaps I could help."

Giles hesitated, shook his head, and lied with a partial truth. "Just the usual concerns that are of immediate and critical importance to teenagers: grades, college acceptance, dating, being . . . cool. Although I still haven't figured out what 'cool' entails—specifically."

"I'm somewhat perplexed by that myself," Crystal said lightly. "So, is there anything you can tell me about Buffy that might help?"

"Nothing extraordinary, no." Even without his reservations, Crystal Gordon did not need to know anything that wasn't contained in Buffy's school records. "It's been lovely meeting you, Ms. Gordon, but I'm afraid I really must go."

"I've enjoyed it, too, Mr. Giles."

"Yes, well, good day, then." Giles raised the cup in farewell, but did not look at her as he left.

With the database loaded into the computer and her instructions written, Willow cruised the Net while she waited for Giles to get back. The period was almost over and she didn't want to be late for English, but she couldn't leave the crowded library unattended, either. Okay, so maybe three kids browsing the shelves wasn't a crowd by most library standards, but it was heavy traffic here. She signed out books for two juniors, then watched the clock. Giles finally showed up as the third student left.

"Busy, I see." The librarian walked over to the study table, hands in his pockets and a worried frown on his face.

"A little, but the Slayer database is loaded up and ready to go."

"Is it?" Giles nodded, preoccupied with something else as he slipped off his jacket and hung it over the back of a chair.

Not the reaction she had expected, Willow thought,

dismayed. Not that Giles was prone to displays of unabashed enthusiasm or excitement, but he *had* been pressing her about the fact-finding cross-reference program for days. She watched him anxiously, hoping whatever was on his mind wasn't as bad as he looked. She really wasn't in the mood for a midday crisis. "So, how was your break?"

"Intriguing, to say the least." He pulled a pen from his pocket and reached for Willow's spiral notebook. "May I?"

"No! I mean—" She quickly flipped to a blank page and ripped it out. "Here you go."

"Thank you." Giles sat down and began to write.

Taking that as permission to leave, Willow turned the notebook back to her neatly printed instructions and slipped her bag strap over her shoulder. "Guess I'd better get going because, well, Ms. Murray isn't terribly tolerant when people are late and—" She winced when Giles's head snapped up, his eyes pleading. "It's important, huh?"

"To Buffy, yes. Beyond that, I can't say." He handed her the paper. "But I'd greatly appreciate it if you'd look into this before you go. I'll give you a note for Ms. Murray."

Sighing, Willow dropped her bag. Aside from being the major brains and adult supervisor of the secret Slayer society, Giles was like a favorite uncle, kind and concerned without being judgmental or pushy—most of the time. If he needed something, she was there. He always was for her.

No way she could refuse to help Buffy, either, even though it kind of hurt that she didn't want to talk about whatever was bothering her. She had obviously talked to Giles, though, Willow realized as she scanned his notes. She wasn't surprised that he wanted her to check out Crystal Gordon.

"What exactly are we looking for?" Willow asked as she hacked into the school computer files. "I mean, I think it's a total bummer that Ms. Gordon picks on Buffy, but, well, I don't think there's anything, you know, weird about her . . . is there?"

"I don't know." Giles rested his chin on steepled hands, then gave her a sidelong glance. "I take it you don't experience anything unusual when Ms. Gordon speaks to you."

"Uh—experience?" Willow kept her eyes on the computer screen. Crystal Gordon's Sunnydale High employment application contained more specifics, but matched the information in Giles's notes. She moved on to the next step, searching Ohio birth and school records for confirmation.

"Physical effects that seemed extraordinary, out of context with the circumstances, such as shortness of breath, perhaps, or—" He hesitated, his eyes narrowing. "—hot flashes."

"I'm too young to have hot flash—oh." Suddenly understanding, Willow shook her head. "No, uh-uh. Nothing like that unless . . . well, unless comfort counts. I mean, I thought she was really easy to talk to, but then—"

"Yes?"

"It's just that I don't miss class as much . . . and stuff. Like Buffy. Not that Buffy can help it because, well, she can't, but teachers are only human, too, right?"

"Usually." Giles smiled, but it didn't appease Willow's concerns the way it was supposed to. His clenched jaw was twitching, like it always did when he was tense.

"According to this, Crystal Gordon is, too. Human, I mean." Willow scooted her chair to the side so Giles could read the screen. The teacher's high school transcript, which was attached to her application and acceptance to Ohio State, contained a complete medical record dating back to her birth in Cleveland. However, the biographical files apparently didn't relieve Giles.

"As I understand it," Giles said, "computer records can be altered with relative ease."

"They can be, but creating a complete history in this much detail—" Willow shrugged. "Possible, but not easy."

Giles just nodded and continued to stare at the screen.

Willow frowned uncertainly. If he was suspicious enough to question the veracity of Crystal Gordon's records, maybe she should be wary, too. Maybe her impression of the teacher was based on that personality reflection thingie Oz had pointed out at the Bronze the other night. Although she wasn't sure how she felt about being honest and naive, she was and so, according to Oz, she subconsciously assumed everyone else was the same way, at least until they did something to prove her wrong. So far, except for how she treated Buffy, Ms. Gordon hadn't done anything.

"So—how come you don't trust Ms. Gordon, Giles?" Willow asked bluntly.

"I can't honestly say, Willow. She seemed quite

pleasant when we spoke, and yet, I found her presence . . . disquieting."

"So it's more like a gut feeling. You can't explain it, but it's just . . . there. Like, uh, instinct!"

"I suppose, yes." He looked at her levelly. "That and my absolute certainty that Buffy's not a hysteric."

Willow's eyes widened with comprehension and apprehension. "So that's Buffy's problem? Ms. Gordon?"

Giles nodded. "I'll, uh, make a few discreet phone calls to verify the accuracy of this information before we draw any unwarranted conclusions. In the meantime, just be careful."

"Right." Willow nodded. "Can I go now?"

"Yes, of course. You'll need an excuse—" He reached for her notebook again, his eye scanning her hand-printed pages. "What's this?"

"That? Uh, well, those are, uh—" Willow paused. Stammering just didn't cut it if she was going to make a stand and make it stick. "Step-by-step instructions for the database. How to access it, enter stuff, save it. I mean, it's not like you've never used a computer before—"

"Me?" Giles looked appalled. "I have neither the aptitude nor the time for this . . . contraption. Marvelous though it may be."

"Well, uh—" Willow's throat went dry, but she pressed on—gently, but firmly. "I don't have time, either. Not a lot of time. I mean, I've got a boyfriend and, uh, homework and—patrol! Not that I won't help with the Slayer info, I will, but—" She paused to take a breath.

"Point taken, Willow." Giles sighed as he turned to a

blank page and scribbled her note for Ms. Murray. "You're quite right. I'll give it a go."

"You will?" Willow brightened as she took the paper. "A word of caution, though."

"Only one?" Giles asked sardonically.

"If you decide to cruise the Net, it can be addicting." She left quickly, muttering as she pushed through the door. "Nobody can ever call *me* a pushover again!"

"Did you have enough?" Joyce set her fork down and wiped a dot of cheese fondue off her chin with a paper napkin.

"Stuffed." Buffy's smile gave no hint that she knew what was really going on in her mom's mind. Joyce Summers just couldn't deal with being that transparent, not when she was trying to accomplish exactly the opposite of what her well-meaning actions implied.

Buffy was anything *but* convinced that Joyce had finally come to terms with being the mother of the Vampire Slayer and didn't worry every time her daughter left the house after dark. Nor did paper plates at the kitchen counter disguise the statement made by Caesar salad, boiled shrimp, and chunks of French bread dipped in cheese fondue. For the fourteenth time in two weeks, Buffy felt like she had just been served her last meal. Like her mother couldn't stand the idea that she might meet her match on peanut butter and jelly.

"You're sure?" Joyce slid off her stool and reached for a paper plate piled with shrimp husks.

"One hundred percent." Buffy set her silverware aside and stacked her plates as her mom started to clear.

"You've been awfully quiet tonight." Joyce flipped open the trash container, dumped the shrimp peels, and hesitated before she remembered the plate was disposable, too.

"It's hard to talk in the middle of a feeding frenzy."

"Everything all right at school?"

"Lunch was a bust today, but other than that, school's fine." A guarded truth, but Buffy didn't see any reason to add to Joyce's unspoken list of major woes. At least Giles was on top of things and the outlook was good. Ms. Gordon had practically promised that she would lay off the "single Buffy out to torment" tactics, and his follow-up calls had confirmed the information Willow had found. Crystal Gordon had been born and raised in Cleveland, Ohio, and except for a dramatic jump from average student to straight A Honor Society status when she was sixteen, nothing strange had ever happened to or around her.

Not that he had been able to find anyway. He was still looking.

"Are you cool with finishing up here, Mom?" Buffy placed the heel of the bread loaf back into the bag and rolled it closed. "I really should get moving."

"I think I can manage throwing away the rest of the dishes." Joyce grinned, her expression casually questioning. "Any chance you can take a break tonight? I rented this great old movie—"

"I would, but I've got a date with a headstone." She pulled two stakes out of the junk drawer and shoved them into her back pockets.

"Anyone we knew?" Joyce asked cautiously. Although she wasn't happy that her daughter was the world's chosen exterminator of the undead, being clued into the Slayer routine and jargon gave her a sense of belonging that helped her cope.

Buffy shook her head. "Not unless you've got a tattoo you didn't tell me about."

"Uh . . . no." A mischievous smile erased a fleeting frown of dismayed resignation. "Although, I've been thinking about getting one of those little butterflies," Joyce teased, paused. "On my ankle."

"Beats a skull and crossbones where no one can see it."

Joyce scowled playfully and threw a wadded napkin.

Laughing, Buffy ducked and grabbed her black leather jacket as she headed out the door.

No one else walked the dark streets, which wasn't unusual in southern California where driving down the block to get a gallon of milk was standard procedure. In Sunnydale, avoiding the sidewalks wasn't a matter of eccentric convenience. Too many people never returned from walking the dog.

Big Jack Perkins had been closing up Tom's Tattoo Emporium when he had been attacked. Now she had to stand watch over his grave to finish the job, which would be so much easier if vamp victims were laid to rest on *top* of the ground where the sun could cremate the remains. No muss, no fuss. But ritual burial was another concession to Sunnydale denial syndrome the residents wouldn't give up, not even if the town's undertakers, who thrived on the booming business of death, agreed.

Buffy darted into the woods that flanked the old Shady Hill Cemetery, a shortcut that would shave a few minutes off her time. She was running late and didn't want to lose the element of surprise when Big Jack's two hundred and eighty-seven pounds of hungry demon broke ground. Not tonight, when she was shaken and questioning her nerve.

If Crystal Gordon was only an intimidating, human teacher as Giles and Willow's research indicated, then her anxiety attack had been real and not induced by a power beyond her control. If she didn't face it, the psychological impact and lingering effects would continue to erode her confidence. She had to conquer the problem now, before it buried her, and she had to do it alone.

At least, no hurt feelings had been left in the wake of that decision. Giles was busy delving into Crystal Gordon's past and Oz and Willow wanted to cram for a calculus test. Since Oz began his three nights of monthly detention in the library book cage tomorrow, she certainly didn't begrudge them a few hours to hang together. Xander had assumed she was meeting Angel when she rejected his offer to help stand "Welcome Wagon watch." As much as she wanted to see Angel, she hoped his own patrol kept him occupied until after Big Jack became another handful of dirt on his grave.

Yanking a stake from her pocket, Buffy jogged quietly down a deer trail toward the cemetery fence. Muscles taut, her senses tuned to every nuance of sound and movement, she was in prime Slayer mode. If she flinched, she wouldn't have depleted physical prowess as an excuse.

As Buffy jumped to the top of the crumbling stone wall that separated Shady Hill from the forest, her senses jumped to full vampire alert. In the glow of a street lamp on the far side of the graveyard, a disgusted man walked away from his broken-down car. Halfway between the street and her position, Big Jack clawed his way out of the dirt and lumbered to his feet. She was on the ground and running a split second after the newbie vamp spotted easy pedestrian prey and sprang toward his first kill.

"Hey, mister!" Buffy yelled without slackening stride, her stake gripped in a steady hand. "Run!"

The stranded motorist looked up and froze.

"Get out of here! Now!" Calculating distance as she closed in on the new vamp, Buffy leaped and threw her arms around a thick leg. The massive undead man staggered and tumbled to the ground.

Coming to his senses, the motorist took off running down the street.

Buffy was instantly on her feet, her instincts and reflexes functioning without flaw as Big Jack grunted and rolled over. "Hi! Sorry I'm late."

Beady yellow eyes glowered under the hard ridges of the vampire's countenance, the ferocity of the demon undiminished by puffy cheeks, his bared fangs no less lethal though set amidst crooked, rotting teeth. With surprising alacrity given his bulk, Jack regained his footing and lunged.

Buffy stood her ground, driving the stake through layers of fat into the heart as he barreled into her. Unbalanced by the momentum of his charging weight, she fell backward. He disintegrated before she hit the ground.

"Well, I handled that nicely." Buffy stood up,

brushed vampire ash off her arms and clothes, then fisted her stake and started after the fleeing motorist. On foot in this isolated part of town, the frightened man was still easy pickings.

And still alive, she realized as she ran through the cemetery gate and saw him jogging down the middle of the road. She put on a burst of speed and stumbled to a halt when a bolt of crackling red lightning arrowed out of the night sky and struck the man.

Shielding her eyes with her arm, Buffy watched helplessly as the man's body jerked and his arms flailed within an erratic, shifting web of crimson electrical energy. Tendrils of red lashed outward, cracking the pavement and whipping the air into a frenzy of shimmering folds and violent bursts of wind. An acrid, burning stench assaulted Buffy's nostrils as waves of charged air rolled over her, staggered her with the force of billions of heated molecules gone berserk.

When the lightning sputtered and vanished, there was nothing left of the man but a blackened mound.

Chapter 3

QUICKLY RECOVERING HER WITS, BUFFY SCANNED THE area. She heard nothing, saw nothing, but sensed a solitary vamp dart out of the shadows behind her. She spun, stake raised, relaxed.

"Angel."

A storm of mixed emotions flowed through her as he strode across the pavement, black duster billowing out behind him, his brooding eyes brimming with concern. Relief, regret, fury, and love—she ran the gambit of overwhelming feelings his dark presence provoked in the space of the few seconds it took him to reach her side.

"Buffy."

So much said in the quiet sound of her name, so many questions asked and answered as his gaze met hers. Their love, so deep and without hope, was harder to bear than any Hellmouth evil she would ever encounter. She suppressed her furious sorrow at the immutable twist of fate that kept them apart. His restored soul would not be forfeited for loving her, for no torment could be greater than losing Angel to Angelus again.

"Are you all right?" Angel asked softly.

"You caught the weird barbecue, huh?" She wasn't making light of the man's cruel death, only taking the edge off the tension that always hung between them now. And cushioning her appalled shock.

He nodded, frowning as he looked up.

"I already checked," Buffy said. "There's not a cloud in the sky, no thunder booms. Any ideas?"

"No. I've never seen anything like it."

"Heard about anything like it?" Buffy asked.

Angel shook his head.

Buffy's frown mirrored his puzzled apprehension. If Angel at two hundred fifty years old was unfamiliar with the phenomenon, then chances were good to excellent that the deadly red lightning was not only supernatural in origin, but ancient. "Looks like a job for super librarian."

Crystal waited until Buffy and her tall, handsome friend were out of sight before she left the cover of the wooded lot across the street from the cemetery and started back toward the small house she had rented nearby. What had begun as a casual stroll to soothe the tensions of the day had turned into an extraordinary and valuable experience.

Dry leaves crunched underfoot as Crystal cut through the thick woods that lined the long drive leading up to the house. Neither bramble nor branch touched her as she contemplated the event she had just witnessed.

She had sensed something unusual about Buffy Summers despite Mr. Giles's protests to the contrary. Every now and then most people experienced an instant aversion or attraction to someone upon first meeting, an inexplicable feeling that often proved accurate for one reason or another. Her feeling about the Summers girl was similar to that—and just as accurate. She had watched from the trees as Buffy drove a wooden stake into a man easily four times her size in height and weight, not counting the augmented strength of the vampire.

Fascinating.

Buffy was a Vampire Slayer.

Which explained why the power she sensed within the girl was of no use to her.

Nor was it a threat.

Crystal had already proven to her satisfaction that she could kill the girl with the force of a thought. A bit more pressure on her throat to completely block the flow of air, a clamp closing off the artery to her brain, a stronger jolt to the heart, and Buffy would die of mysterious, but apparently natural causes.

And her death might be necessary, Crystal thought as the moon rose above the tree line, infusing the dark with light from an orb that was only two nights shy of being full. Although she had never confronted a Slayer, she had heard of them over the years. As with the Hellmouth, there were obscure references in old manuscripts and whispered tales among those steeped in the occult. However, as she had just seen, while the young women who fought to eradicate the undead possessed the superior strength and ability required to defeat a vampire, the enhancements were strictly physical.

A Slayer was powerless against magick.

Crystal drew her shawl tighter against a slight chill and smiled with a glance back at the smoking remains of the dead man Buffy had not been able to save.

Nothing would stop her from fulfilling the destiny she had been born to so long ago.

Shugra had no memory of her human birth or of her first seasons in the caves that overlooked the great valley. Still, there were some things she knew about her beginning, things that were common to everyone in the tribe and rarely, if ever, changed. Other things she had learned from Chit, the female who had borne her. Still others had become clear after the joining.

Clinging to the face of the high cliff, Shugra looked down on the river rushing by below. She had entered the world on the rock ledge overhanging the far bank. She could almost see Chit, alone and in pain as her time drew near, dragging herself to the favored birthing place so long ago.

It was believed that the deep, swift waters would endow a son with the skills to hunt and the courage to defend the caves against invaders and predators. A daughter would be given the strength to toil and bear more young. The other, more subtle omens that defined a new life were left to Duhn to interpret. A bird taking wing, a predator's roar, frost, fog, light, and darkness—all had significance in conjunction with the elements, which determined the tribe's fate. Usually only the wise, old Duhn understood the mysterious meanings hidden in their signs.

Everyone understood the portents of misfortune surrounding Shugra's birth.

As she had learned later, their dread was born on the ledge with her, when a howling wind chilled the afternoon air and thunder swallowed Chit's screams. As Shugra emerged from the womb, rain poured in blinding sheets from a black, midday sky and three hunters were swept into a river swollen with mud and drowned. Bolts of lightning had torched the trees with her first, enraged infant cry.

Never before had the elements attended a birth with such violence, and the warning did not go unheeded.

Shugra clenched blunt teeth as she recalled the tale Chit had told and told again so she would never forget. Duhn had refused to look upon her or name her as was the custom, and the entire tribe had agreed that exile was a wise and necessary decision. If her birth was not acknowledged, the mark of disaster she bore could not affect the tribe.

Chit called her Shugra for the angry storm.

Shugra's eyes misted as she continued upward toward a wide ledge, her thoughts sweeping back over her life.

From the moment she had taken her first breath, Chit had been her only source of warmth, food, and comfort. They had survived on the fringes of the community, ignored, invisible scavengers, tolerated without a word or a look that recognized their existence. Her earliest memories were of fear, hunger, and cold, which, she came to realize later, plagued all the people. Human life was locked into a harsh cycle of becoming, being, and ending that not even Duhn could avoid.

And neither could she.

Shugra clawed her way onto the wide outcropping through a crevice and lay down to peer over the edge. The hunters were coming, relentless in their pursuit and intent to kill her. She watched them climb with stone axes and spears slung over shoulders and backs, their eyes glinting with fear and hatred, their bearded jaws set with resolve.

She eased back from the precipice, stood, and raised her arms toward the dark clouds gathering in the distance. Thunder rumbled and lightning cracked as she called the storm to witness her death.

The people would blame her for the destructive fury of the tempest, as they had blamed her for being born and for all the trials the tribe had suffered since. They would never accept that they, in their ignorant cruelty, were responsible for her union with the power.

The irony was amusing as well as fitting.

If Duhn had not banished her at birth, she would not have known the isolation and hardships that had molded her into the ideal vessel. Dependent on no one but herself after Chit weakened and died, she had grown strong, determined, and resourceful. She had survived with a vengeance, finding comfort in the wilds and developing a fearless respect for the primal forces that had changed her life even as it began. Thus, when the power came in a cloudless storm of blood-red lightning, she had been primed to receive it.

Shugra's memory of that day was crystal clear.

While the people hid from the storm's explosive wrath, she had walked into the turbulence. She had not flinched as bursts of crimson lightning scorched the forest and turned stone to dust around her. She had not cried out when a bolt struck her in the chest, igniting the blood in her veins and fusing her mind with a vast, chaotic network of raw energy before she lost consciousness.

When she had come to in a smoldering clearing, she was still connected—and changed.

After that, although several seasons passed before she was aware, she *was* responsible for the troubles that descended on the valley.

Shugra felt the power radiating from every pore in her scratched, scabbed and dirty skin, pouring outward through her raised hands. The inner effect was as soothing as the physical effects of her emotional turmoil were devastating.

In the past, when the loneliness had become more than she could bear, the river had run dry. When she had chanted to ease the pain of Chit's passing, the wind had whipped through the valley uprooting trees. Whenever she screamed in outrage at the injustice of her exiled existence, the earth shook and split open. And the angry storm always hovered on the horizon, held in perpetual readiness by a soul forged in pain and committed to vengeance.

As thunder rode the dark clouds across the valley now, Shugra turned and placed her hands against the rough, rocky face of the mountain. The angry shouts of the climbing hunters became muted as she closed her eyes to concentrate.

Until recently her manipulation of the elements had been a phenomenon of cause and effect, a spontaneous aspect of the fusion. However, when she realized that the dark forces were responding to the intensity of her emotions, she had begun to experiment. She had observed and remembered what action created what reaction, repeated, refined and adjusted her emotional outbursts until she had learned to unleash the savage energies at will. Eventually, she would have learned to control them.

But she was about to die.

Drawing strength and courage from the cold, hard stone she touched, Shugra focused on her breathing and calmed herself with the memory of the havoc she had caused that morning.

She had encountered a swarm of colorful flying insects while gathering healing herbs as Chit had taught her. She had tried to manipulate the flight patterns of the fragile creatures with the power of her will and failed. Frustrated when the delicate insects fell dead in the grass, she had flown into a furious tantrum. Within minutes the sky had darkened with a massive cloud of ravenous insects.

The ensuing madness filled Shugra's mind.

The thunder of beating wings had drowned out the screams of people scurrying to safety in the caves. Some did not escape the horde that had swept through the valley devouring leaves and fruit, wild grasses, and the tribe's small patches of cultivated crops.

Shugra's heart swelled with the memory of Duhn, who had stood alone against the invaders on the raised rock outside the caves, threatening them with his imagined magick. None of his chanted songs or herbal potions or rattling gourds had been able to stop them.

But she had stopped the old man.

With a wave of her arm and a glare that focused the power of her hatred, she had brought forth a swirling wind that swept Duhn off the rock. Untouched by the vicious insects, she had watched with joyous satisfaction as the swarm striped the flesh from his bones.

Grunts and curses drew Shugra's attention back to the cliff.

The hunters, frightened but driven by her murderous act to erase her vile presence, fisted their weapons as they scrambled onto the high ledge. They hesitated, wary of the wild woman who pressed against the stone wall, then shrieked in savage triumph when they realized she was cornered with no escape save a deadly plunge to the valley floor far below.

Shugra concentrated on the hard surface beneath her fingers. The people had not been able to defeat her in life. They would not defeat her in death, either. As she had controlled the wind to punish Duhn for the misery she and Chit had suffered, she would command the earth to avenge her passing.

When the first spear impaled her shoulder, Shugra channeled a lifetime of rage into the stone. The rock cracked where she touched it. She did not cower in fear or cry out in pain as ax and club smashed against her body, breaking bone and tearing muscle. She called the storm. The tempest roared across the valley, blotting out the sun and charging the air with her fury. Thunder boomed and lightning split the sky as a spidery web of fine fissures radiated outward along the cliff face and into the heart of the mountain. Her tormentors screamed in terror as the ledge beneath them collapsed and the cliff above crumbled.

Shugra felt herself fall.

Her spirit was snatched from her body and swept into the roiling realm of the power before she hit the ground.

September 14, 1988

Crystal woke up chilled by a cold sweat, but she did not awaken from a bad dream. She shivered as she studied her surroundings, taking a moment to meld the old memories with the new. As usual, the realization of who she really was neither shocked nor confused her. She had left old or damaged bodies and returned in new ones countless times since Chit had first given her life and named her Shugra nineteen thousand years ago.

"It's great to be back," she whispered, drew the down comforter up to her chin, and snuggled into the warmth. She had lost count of her many lives long before, but the number hardly mattered.

She had been born—again.

Sixteen years ago, as the source-river began to converge on Earth, her essence had fled the streams of free magick that protected her after she had chosen the donor. Her needs were simple. Stable, attractive, financially sound, but in no way extraordinary parents in whatever region of the world she would have the most freedom. She did not always choose well, but that was not the case this time.

Crystal Gordon had survived her childhood.

Which had not always been the case, she mused ruefully.

For the past umpteen centuries, each of her new selves was aware that she was different than her peers without knowing her exact identity or the extent of her ability. The subconscious block was a self-imposed precaution that prevented her impulsive child selves from revealing her true nature, a dangerous and deadly inclination that had ended too many of her previous lives too soon. Instead, the formative years were spent adjusting to an unfamiliar society and gathering information essential to her ultimate goal. Her memory and power were restored when the dream completed the transition during her teenaged years.

"Crystal Gordon." She hesitated, nodded. The name suited her, as did her circumstances. It was September in the year 1988 and she was a high school junior in Cleveland, Ohio.

"Who gets Cs?" Crystal scoffed. That would have to change soon.

She stretched again, pleased with the muscular tone in her trim, athletic body and the sharpness of her young mind. At sixteen, she was physically prime and wise enough to hide the power while she prepared. Her knowledge, understanding, and control of the primal forces that permeated the universe had grown stronger in each successive lifetime.

How long has it been? She squinted, calculated. Just over three hundred years had passed since her last reincarnation, when she had almost achieved supremacy over the source from which all magick flowed, when she had almost defeated physical death.

This time, she would not fail.

Conditions had never been more perfect!

Energized, Crystal slipped out of bed to get a cold drink from the kitchen. The terrified hysteria that had seized the people and prevented her from realizing her destiny in the past had been replaced by a measure of tolerance. While some at the dawn of the twenty-first century had romantic notions about witchcraft and accepted those who practiced it, others dismissed magick as nonsense.

They were all fools.

Chapter 4

CORDELIA'S HEELS CLICKED OUT A STACCATO RHYTHM
on the hard school floor, a hurried, steady beat that
helped her to think and bolstered her determination. No
way she was going to pay another late fee on a library
book, especially one that nobody but she had checked
out for almost three years!

She hated being in the building after-hours now. The
deserted halls lined with convenient closets and empty
classrooms were too unsettling. She still couldn't believe she had fallen in love with a geek who had two-
timed her! And she so didn't want to remember too
many, too close encounters with ugly, sometimes foul-
smelling and always ill-mannered, demons that had
been drawn to Slayer headquarters for one diabolical
reason or another—all of them involving some totally
disgusting manner of death. Too often hers.

But tonight she had no choice, not if she wanted to

speak to Giles in private. Since all seemed quiet on the Hellmouth front, there was a good chance he was alone. Buffy was duty-bound to be on vampire patrol and she had passed Oz's van going toward the Bronze on her way over. Willow was with Oz, and Xander wasn't inclined to hang out with the librarian by himself—unless his social life had sunk to new lows of isolation that plagued the hopelessly uncool. She didn't want anyone, Xander in particular, asking embarrassing questions because they had heard her arguing with Giles over five bucks. Her father's financial problems and, consequently hers, were nobody else's business. Besides, there was still a chance Daddy could squirm out of his tax evasion predicament. Then she could stop worrying about a calamity that hadn't happened yet. Going broke was *not* on her agenda.

Seeing light shining through the round windows on the library doors, Cordelia set her jaw and squared her shoulders. She had a good case and intended to fight for her rights no matter what perfectly reasonable arguments about rules and responsibility Giles shot back at her.

He sat at the study table in front of the computer chewing on the end of his glasses with his shirtsleeves rolled up and his tie loosened. Replacing the glasses, he shifted his confounded gaze to a notebook, then to the keyboard. After tentatively hitting a key, he looked at the monitor, then swore under his breath and jabbed the key again. *Odd,* Cordelia thought, but nothing about the British Watcher or his assortment of watchees could surprise her anymore.

Giles did not look up as she strode forward, but

jumped out of his seat when she dropped the heavy copy of *War and Peace* on the table. "Cordelia!" He deflated as he exhaled.

"Giles." She smiled tightly. "Now that I've got your attention, I have something to say."

"I do hope it's of vital importance. I'm a bit busy." He picked up the novel and flipped through the pages as he sat back down. "Did you actually read this? It was due back quite a while ago."

"I intended to. I wanted something that reeked of literary on my reading list, but I've been so bummed—" Cordelia aborted the explanation before she totally ruined her image and took the offensive, eyes flashing with righteous indignation. "Forget the fine, Giles. I mean, it's only been a couple of months and it's not like your phone's been ringing off the hook with people desperate to read it, right?"

"A sad truth." Giles set the book aside and leaned back with a weary sigh.

"Right!" Cordelia nodded and perched on the edge of the table. "And it's not like I haven't contributed more than my fair share to the Slayer expense fund. I mean, think about it. Has anyone ever volunteered to reimburse me for gas and cell phone charges after *my* car and *my* phone helped save the world? And let's not forget lives! No. Not once. So I think we should just call it even and—"

"Yes, all right, Cordelia," Giles said impatiently. "The fine is waived."

"Really? Great!" Pleased, Cordelia slid off the table to leave, then paused when she noticed Giles's wretched expression. "Okay, I know I'm going to regret asking this, but is something totally horrendous going on I don't know about?"

"That's a matter of perception." Giles smiled as he looked up. "You wouldn't have any idea how to operate this monstrous modern marvel, would you?"

"The computer?" Cordelia shrugged when he nodded. "Enough to balance my checkbook. Why? I mean, if there's a big demon disaster going down, why isn't Willow the Whiz here?"

"She would be under those circumstances, but this—" He waved at a pile of notes and old books on the table to his right. "—is rather too lacking in emergency status to warrant her valuable time."

"I'm definitely hearing nose-out-of-joint sarcasm, Giles."

"Yes, well . . . a bit, maybe. And quite unfair to Willow, to be sure. She did leave me precise instructions on how to transfer information, but—" He threw up his hands in frustration. "I simply don't have the patience or the time, and since the information concerns Slayer and demonic activities, hiring someone is out of the question."

Cordelia's interest suddenly perked. "We're talking basic data-entry?"

Giles nodded, frowning.

"How much does it pay?" Cordelia quickly qualified her reasons for asking. "Not that I need the money, but my time is valuable, too. And having a job might help—look great on my transcript."

Giles didn't hesitate. "Eight dollars an hour."

"Ten," Cordelia countered. "And a glowing reference. After all, *I* already know about Buffy and the

Hellmouth and everything, which makes me the only qualified person available. That's got to be worth something."

"Done. When would you like to begin?"

Cordelia slipped off her sweater. "What do you want me to do?"

Buffy and Angel breezed through the doors as Giles set a steaming cup of Earl Grey on the table for Cordelia. The vampire hung back as Buffy strode forward. She seemed intent, in control, but when she looked at him, he detected a lingering hint of the uncertainty that had haunted her dark eyes earlier.

"Hey, Giles." Pulling up a chair, Buffy cast a quizzical glance at Cordelia, then raised an eyebrow at Giles. "You're letting Cordy cruise the auction sites for designer bargains?"

The real question—whether his investigation into Crystal Gordon's background had uncovered anything suspicious—hung between them, unspoken and not for discussion in public. He would speak to her later, alone, when he could offset the lack of incriminating evidence with a recounting of his own intuitive reservations about the young woman.

"Actually, no," Giles said. "She's working—on the Slayer database."

Cordelia looked up sharply. "Only so I can honestly say I have job experience. Not that I need job experience, but *someone* has to fill in for Willow."

"What's with Willow?" Buffy asked, suddenly concerned.

"Nothing serious." Giles smiled. Now that Cordelia

had taken the burden of computer duty off his shoulders—although her hunt-and-peck typing style would be costly—he felt a tad more magnanimous toward Willow's inconvenient, but periodic need to assert her independence. "Just a minor bout of rebellion, which will pass as usual, I'm sure. As soon as we need her expertise for something critical."

"Which may be sooner than later." Buffy's tone, though flippant, carried an edge of urgency. "Like now."

Cordelia stopped typing. "Now?"

"A problem with Big Jack?" Pausing in mid sip, Giles eyed her over the rim of his cup.

"No, Big Jack's date with a stake went off without a hitch. He's dust." Buffy's impish smile segued into a disturbed frown. "But there was this little problem with a freaky red lightning thingie that fried a guy on the street. Literally."

"*Red* lightning?" Giles slowly lowered the cup, then set it down. "What happened exactly?" Folding his arms, he listened without interrupting as she described the phenomenon and its lethal effects.

"Lots of heavy duty electrical crackling, definitely red, and no thunderstorm. Angel said he's never seen anything like it." Buffy glanced back as she finished, trying but failing to conceal her emotional attachment to the handsome entity that was neither demon nor man, but was condemned to the dark and his own tormented past.

Angel acknowledged the statement with a nod.

"Yes, well, we can't discount an extremely rare, natural occurrence," Giles said, drawing Buffy's attention back to the topic. "Lightning strikes from clear skies have been documented, although usually a storm front is forming nearby. On the average, more than fifty people are injured or killed by lightning every year in the States, and the effects are devastating. The victims suffer severe physical trauma, from burns to massive brain damage and disruption of other internal organs."

"This poor guy wasn't just killed, Giles," Buffy said pointedly. "He was turned into charcoal and . . . there was nothing I could do."

"No, there wasn't," Giles said gently. "You most likely would have been killed, too."

Buffy nodded, but the pain of helpless inadequacy written on her face ripped through Giles like a knife—and initiated another, more sinister hypothesis. However, cautious reliance on logical scientific method to eliminate the obvious seemed necessary before moving on to more esoteric considerations. They were both too desperate to find someone or something to blame for the eroding of her confidence.

"And, well, although being reduced to cinders is rather an uncommon extreme, it's not outside the bounds of natural possibility," Giles continued evenly. "Lightning is an unpredictable and dangerous force with certain manifestations that are difficult, if not impossible, to prove."

"Such as?" Buffy leaned forward.

"Ball lightning, for instance," Giles explained, "which has until recently been received with more skepticism than belief, since eyewitness reports are not completely reliable. It lasts for a few seconds at most and has never been captured on film."

Angel stepped forward. "This lasted over two minutes."

Giles's probing gaze flicked between Buffy and Angel. "And you said you didn't see anyone in the immediate area?"

"Not that I noticed," Buffy answered.

"Nor I." Angel shifted awkwardly.

"Why?" Buffy asked.

"Well, uh—" Giles paused again, wondering if the admittedly far-fetched, metaphysical theory he had formed might explain the incident. "What you describe might also suggest . . . a magickal anomaly of some sort."

"What's a magickal anomaly?" Cordelia asked curiously, her attention on the discussion rather than his notes. Since she sometimes arrived at spontaneous conclusions that showed remarkable insight, albeit accidentally, he let the lapse slide.

"Some ancient texts contain vague references to pockets and streams of primal magick throughout the universe, perhaps even streams that are connected to a source as old as the universe itself," Giles said.

Buffy started with another quick glance at Angel. "An old source? Like the First Evil?"

Giles paused at the reference to the ubiquitous, noncorporeal entity that had, quite possibly, brought Angel back from Hell to kill Buffy. He shook his head. "No, I think not. 'The First Evil' is an intelligent being, driven by an agenda. The source is a . . . thing."

"A thing." Buffy eyed him askance.

"Yes, a thing. Rather like—" Anticipation registered on all faces as Giles searched for an appropriate metaphor. "Like a well or a mountain spring. With tributaries—streams branching out into a network across the cosmos." He paused again. "Assuming it actually exists, of course."

"Of course," Cordelia said.

Giles paced, thinking aloud as much as enlightening his rapt audience. "Given that, it logically follows that certain people, sorcerers, witches and the like, have an affinity with this elemental power that allows them to manipulate it."

"Like Amy Madison and her mom." Buffy's brow darkened. "Especially her mom."

"And Willow," Angel added.

"Catherine and Amy, yes. Most definitely." Giles nodded. "The strength of the affinity, the knowledge and expertise to combine ingredients, words, and cadence to create and execute a spell, and various other factors determine how much power each individual attains. Novice witches or spellcasters, like Willow and myself, must call on the ancient deities to act as conduits to the source because the affinity is weak or undeveloped. By comparison, Catherine was quite powerful."

"Which definitely qualifies as an understatement," Cordelia muttered. "Let's see, she set Amber on fire, blinded me, switched bodies with her daughter, and almost killed Buffy with . . . a bloody something spell."

"Bloodstone Vengeance spell." Giles hesitated. A good bit of luck had combined with deduction to counter Catherine Madison's power, specifically finding the dolls in the attic, which had allowed him to reverse the spells on Amy, Cordelia and Buffy. Even then, only Buffy's quick thinking and a handy mirror had turned another spell back on the witch, sending Catherine to some unknown, dark fate rather than Buffy.

"And a magickal tamale thing is?" Buffy prodded.

"Hmmm? Oh, yes—an anomaly." Glasses off, Giles resumed pacing. "In the absence of a sorcerer, your burst of red lightning might very well have been a bit of, uh, wild primal magick that wandered into the atmosphere and struck at random."

"Or?" Buffy asked, then clarified. "I mean, what if there was a sorcerer? Just because we didn't see one . . ."

"Then I daresay we'd have a rather large problem." Giles frowned. "All magick has dangerous potential, of course, but someone with direct contact and control over these primal energies would have cataclysmic power at their command."

"Is that possible?" Cordelia held up a hand. "Forget it. I really don't want to know." She turned back to the computer, her forefinger poised above the keyboard.

"We live on the Hellmouth, Cordelia," Buffy said. "Anything is possible."

"Yes, but—" Cordelia brightened suddenly. "Anyone with *that* kind of power probably wouldn't waste time or perfectly good primal energy roasting nobodies. Not when they had a chance to take out the Slayer, which didn't happen so—there's no problem!"

Giles stared at Cordelia, once again amazed by the pearls of inadvertent wisdom that sprang from her mind. "Unless it was a demonstration—for Buffy's benefit."

Buffy's head snapped back to Giles. "You don't think—"

"I don't know, but additional research is certainly warranted before we get carried away with unsubstantiated speculation." A connection between Crystal Gordon, Buffy's anxiety symptoms and the sudden physical manifestation of what might very well be primal magick was a stretch. However, with two demoralizing incidents involving the Slayer occurring within a matter of hours, Giles could not ignore the ominous implications.

Energized, Buffy jumped to her feet. "I'll get Willow. She doesn't need to study to ace calculus."

"Good thing," Cordelia said. "Because she's cramming at the Bronze."

Standing outside the Bronze, Buffy watched Angel vanish into the shadows, saddened by the parting brush of his mouth against hers, yet heartened because she knew he would stay nearby. If Crystal Gordon or someone else was directly plugged into Giles's universal source of magick, she would need all the help she could get. Even after three years, she hadn't forgotten the savage force of Catherine Madison's vindictive sorcery. Conquering an entity with infinitely more power seemed almost impossible.

Almost, but not quite, Buffy thought as she entered the social center of Sunnydale's teenaged set. Just as an infinite number of unimaginable evils were possible near the Hellmouth, there was also always some way to beat them. The trick was living to talk about it over a mocha cream coffee afterward.

The Bronze was busy for a school night, the energetic ambience driven by an urgency to pack as much living into the night as possible because somebody would die before dawn. The band was loud, on key and pounding out a decent beat, and the musk generated by gyrating dancers dulled the acrid aromas of spilled beer and stale smoke emanating from the floor and walls of the renovated warehouse. Laughter, the buzz of conversation, and the exuberance of a young crowd flaunting the hottest styles stubbornly defied the cancerous evils infecting the town. For Buffy, the life-goes-on attitude was a refreshing tonic after a day spent on an emotional roller coaster.

Smoothing her hair back, she ordered a soda at the bar, then wandered through the crowd looking for Willow. Her bright-eyed, effervescent friend wasn't hard to find. Oz was on stage playing with the band. Willow and Xander were ensconced at a table on the edge of the dance floor talking with Anya and Michael. Correction, Willow was talking. Rather than lounging with lanky arms and legs sprawled in typical Xander fashion, he sat stiffly with his arms crossed and his mouth clamped shut, the proximity to Anya obviously cramping his casual style. His sulking displeasure failed to dampen the discussion among the others. Even the reticent Michael looked more animated and engaged than usual.

"We've got to hang out more often." Anya touched Willow's arm, drew back when she flinched, glanced at Michael.

"Said the spider to the fly," Xander muttered.

Michael nodded, whether in agreement with Anya or Xander was unclear.

"Uh, well, we could . . . hang . . . now and then . . . maybe." Eyes wide, her smile tight, Willow didn't voice her uncertainty about pursuing a friendship with the ex old hag.

Her lack of genuine enthusiasm was lost on Anya, however. "Great! I think you'll be surprised how much we actually have in common."

Xander frowned from one face to another. "Does that thought appall anyone else as much as it does me?"

Taking the cue, Buffy stepped to the table. "Hi, guys. What's up? Besides not studying for a calculus test."

"We were. Studying, I mean, until Joey called Oz to sit in because Mack didn't show." Grinning, Willow looked toward the stage and waved at Oz. "He's doing really great, too! For coming in cold with no rehearsal."

"Has anyone heard from Mack?" Buffy asked.

"Flu. Not to worry." Xander glanced at the empty spaces on the vinyl seat on either side of him. "I'd make room, Buff, but that would put me dangerously close to you know who—" His eyes flicked sideways toward Willow, then back to glare at Anya. "—or you know who. My hormones can't take the pressure."

"We're leaving, so you can relax, Xander. For now." Anya's glance reflected the not-so-subtle warning in her tone as she slid out of her chair and tugged on Michael's sleeve. "See you tomorrow, Willow."

"Was I just threatened?" Xander's arms and legs unfolded and fell naturally into sprawled disarray as the unlikely couple wound their way through the dance floor crowd.

"Sure sounded like a veiled threat to me." Buffy took the chair Anya had vacated.

"Think so?" Perched on the end of the long vinyl seat, Willow tore her soda straw into little pieces. "But what can she do? I mean, she can't *wish* anything awful and make it happen so there's nothing to worry about, is there?"

"She's female. I'm not. That's power." Xander sighed. "Although with any luck, she'll decide a Michael on the leash is worth more than a Xander on the run."

"I thought Michael and Kari—" Willow tossed the bits of straw confetti into the air. "I had no idea Michael was so fickle or even, you know, a catch! Poor Amy."

"—is more interested in cheese at the moment." Xander picked a piece of shredded straw out of his coffee mug.

Buffy wasn't convinced romantic intent had anything to do with Anya's sudden interest in Michael. Across the room, the declawed saint and the timid warlock joined a crowded table, which included Kari Stark and a blatantly mismatched collection of companions.

"Now there's a yearbook picture nobody would believe," Xander said.

Buffy had to agree. Whereas Kari was thin with an angular face, straight, shoulder-length brown hair and a keen interest in academic excellence, Joanna Emidy was a gorgeous cheerleader who had never achieved a grade above a C in anything except Phys. Ed. Unless Joanna had gotten special dispensation from Harmony Kendall, who had usurped Cordelia's position as the last word on acceptable in-crowd behavior, her social standing was on a fast track to the bottom of the Sunnydale High barrel. Winston Havershem, a transfer from England the previous year, was heavy into heavy metal and accessorized his basic black wardrobe at the hardware store. The overall effect when he spoke his crisp King's English was startling. Emanuel Sanchez and Alicia Chow were strikingly average in every respect with nothing of note that made them standouts among the student masses.

Except the company they were keeping now.

"Very weird." Willow's gaze briefly settled on the incongruous group. "Even for Sunnydale."

"Personally, I think the social integration of the totally creepy with the totally ordinary is great." Xander grinned. "Especially whatever part is more attractive to Anya than me."

"Aren't you being a little harsh, Xander?" Willow asked. "She's just trying to fit in, which can't be easy after being, well, a rotten old woman for so long. I mean, we haven't exactly welcomed her with open arms, have we? So, well, why wouldn't she want to be with people who like her?"

"The question we should be asking is why?" Xander argued with mock gravity. "Do they like her, that is, or each other for that matter. Because that little enclave just reeks of a plot to overthrow the established system of class distinction among teens. Not that it matters."

"Speaking of matters," Buffy said. "A couple things have come up that need looking into, Willow."

"Really?" Willow straightened, suddenly serious. "Like, uh, maybe about what's been bugging you all day?"

"I love a girl who goes straight for the throat." Xander didn't smile as he turned his dark eyes on Buffy. "But she's right, Buff. You have been acting on the near side of freaked."

"That obvious, huh?" Buffy wrinkled her nose when Xander and Willow both nodded. She probably should have said something sooner. Besides Giles and Angel—her mom having a tendency to freak in the face of extreme Slayer danger despite her good intentions—Xander and Willow were the two people she could count on for unconditional support and understanding—as a rule. Xander had a problem with anything relating to Angel, but he was working on it, and she had needed time to digest the question of her mental stability. Now the time had come to spit it out. She briefly recounted the day's events, beginning with the anxiety attack and ending with Giles's various theories about the killer red lightning.

"First of all," Xander said, "you're the least crazy person with a reason to lose it that I've ever known, Buffy."

"Yeah, and just because everything about Ms. Gordon checks out normal doesn't mean it is—necessarily." Willow leaned forward and lowered her voice. "I think she gave Giles hot flashes."

"Which would be a major improvement over the no-hands stranglehold Amy's mom had on me—right before she tossed me down the hall with a mere flick of her evil eye."

"Right! Point, chant, wham!" Willow clapped her hands together, letting one slide off toward the ceiling. "Flying Xander. No potions or . . . or having to look up a spell, either."

"Library, guys." Buffy finished her soda and stood up.

"And let's not forget the invisible homework." Xander kept talking as he rose and stretched.

"What invisible homework?" Willow asked.

"Amy's! *She* gave Mrs. what's-her-name this mojo look to make the old lady *think* she was handing in homework when she wasn't." Xander cocked his head. "I don't suppose you could figure out how to do that trick."

"Probably, but I always *do* my homework. Be right back." Willow headed for the stage to tell Oz she was leaving.

"That wasn't what—" Throwing up his hands, Xander followed Buffy toward the exit. "So where do we start?"

"Helping Giles look through his musty old tomes for any references to primal magick analogy thingies. He wants Willow to search for anything weird that's happened in Cleveland during the past twenty-eight years."

Xander started. "I didn't realize Cleveland was a hotbed of weird activity."

October 31, 1988

Crystal sat on the ground in a cultivated grove of oaks, maples, and elms, her thirsty senses drinking in the sounds and scents she had not truly appreciated during the years before her awakening. Her new memories held a few precious moments of such communion, when she had felt the unique bond she shared with the elements during occasional camping excursions into the wilderness with her current parents. They adored her, which was not unexpected since she had chosen them, as she had chosen the time and place of her birth. The soul that had been conceived with their child had been easily routed when she had taken possession of its physical life. She had chosen well in all these things.

After so many millennia, the time was right.

Or would be near the end of the century.

In the meantime, she had much to do to prepare, quietly and in secret, leaving no trail for those who warred against the occult—or even those who embraced it—to trace.

This time, no one but the twelve she needed to achieve dominance over the source would know her until it was too late.

"Evan!" A male voice laced with fear barked nearby. "Where are you?"

Crystal stiffened when a boy in a pirate costume crept along the edge of the thicket and stopped a mere three feet from her position. He squatted down, hiding from his father in the shadows.

"Evan! This isn't funny." More frantic, louder. "Evan!"

What a naughty little boy, Crystal thought as she fashioned a long thorn on a smooth branch behind him. When he rocked back on his heels, the thorn poked the fabric covering his arm. Scared rather than hurt, he dashed back to his relieved, angry dad with a squeal.

"Something bit me, Dad!"

"Where? I don't see anything." The man inspected the boy with a flashlight as they moved on. "One more stunt like that and we're going home."

Crystal smiled, amused by the incident and pleased that the boy had not detected her presence. She had worn black to blend with the night in premature anticipation of becoming the dark if she so willed because of some unforeseen necessity.

She felt the ability stirring within, the power to become a wisp of smoke or whatever struck her fancy, a longing she dared not indulge. Instead, she let her mind flow freely, touching the other creatures that continued to exist as they always had on a world horribly violated by the abominations of humanity's enterprise. She loathed the insidious industry that had created a need for isolated refuges of the true world called parks, yet welcomed the small haven that had been spared near her home. Angered by these thoughts, Crystal found calming solace in the cadence of the cicada, the rustling of the leaves, and the predatory gaze of the owl. Keeping her emotions under control was imperative at this early stage.

The delighted squeals of other children rudely drew her back to her original purpose. Unseen in a dark thicket, she settled back to watch the ritual this society observed to honor the dead. Although she had participated in the charade since she was two, her perspective was now changed. The sight of fairytale witches and mutilated vegetables proudly displayed for sale at all the trading centers had been both startling and encouraging. The great fear that had stalked her long before and ever since the crushing debacle in Ephesus had dissipated into a mere, annoying shadow of what it had been.

Crystal sat for over an hour, entertained by the parade of tiny superheroes and princesses, monsters and ghosts as they joyously swindled her neighbors out of candy and apples. When the porch lights began to flick off, signaling the end of the treat supply or patience, she rose to return home and finish an in-depth study of herb properties for advanced biology. Her parents were thrilled with her sudden determination to learn and excel, which made the educational part of her preparations a simple matter, in direct contrast to the problems she had faced in past lives when female enlightenment was regarded as unnecessary and dangerous by the ruling patriarchs. The old goats had, of course, been quite right in that assessment.

A shrill laugh broke the stillness as Crystal eased out of the trees onto a wide expanse of grass. Having no interest in the group of partying teenagers on the far side of the meadow, she turned to leave.

"Leave me alone—please."

The girl's plaintive sob captured Crystal's curiosity. On silent feet long accustomed to stealth in the forest, she circled around the perimeter of the open area.

"Come on, Rhonda," a male voice sneered. "What's the problem, huh?"

"Yeah, we're not good enough for you?" The second boy laughed.

"No!" Rhonda's shriek was suddenly muffled.

Crystal watched from the darkness beyond the glow of an overhead light. An ancient anger flared as a scenario older than she unfolded: three males intent on ravaging a spindly girl who did not have the power of the elements to protect her. Crystal felt no compassion for Rhonda as she adjusted her vocal cords to disguise her voice in a lower register. She focused a wrath undiminished by time on the boys.

"Let her go." Crystal's baritone command mingled with the low rumble of thunder overhead.

The three boys looked up. The taller one did not release Rhonda's arm. "Who's there?"

Satisfied that the storm still responded to her fury, Crystal sent the gathering tempest away. The magick called forth by intense emotion was too unpredictable and this life was still too new to guarantee precision control.

"Let her go." The command was uttered quietly, but with an echoing timbre that chilled the blood, so she had been told. The telling was not false. The tall boy jumped, removing his hand from the girl and pulling a knife. His two companions frantically scanned the dark as they backed away.

"I don't like this, Ray." The stocky boy's voice shook with fear.

"Shut up, Brad," Ray snapped, his hand flexing on the hilt of his blade.

"Run, girl," Crystal said softly.

Sniffling, the rabbit ran stumbling toward the safety of the street.

Furious at the loss of his prize, or perhaps the loss of face in front of his friends, the tall boy adopted a fighting stance. "Show yourself! Come on!"

Crystal stepped into view and approached, smiling as she moved into range. Rhonda was gone and no one else was nearby.

"It's a girl!" Fuming, the third boy took position beside Ray, hands fisted. Brad moved to circle behind her.

"You're gonna be very sorry, bitch." Ray lunged toward her, his grin transforming into a look of stunned horror as he and his friends were immobilized.

Alive with the power, blond hair billowing in frenzied cascades, her eyes hard on Ray, Crystal exacted her own brand of vengeance. The boy's eyes widened with fright as his hand moved independent of his volition and slit his throat. Snatching the blade from Ray's dying hand with a thought, Crystal quickly silenced the screams of the other two.

The knife fell to the ground as she walked away.

Chapter 5

BLEARY-EYED, WILLOW GLANCED AT THE TIME IN THE lower corner of the computer screen. *3:18 A.M. No wonder all the words are blurring together.* However, she wasn't the only one having trouble staying on track. Buffy was asleep with her head on her arms at the end of the table. Xander had crashed on Oz's torn blankets in the book cage, but only because the bedding didn't smell like musty, needs-a-bath werewolf. She had just laundered it for Oz's next monthly confinement, which began tomorrow night, or rather tonight, since it was already tomorrow.

And I'm babbling—to myself. Extreme fatigue did that to her. At least, Oz had gone home to sleep after the Bronze closed. He wouldn't get much rest during his three-night furry phase because the werewolf spent most of its time pacing, roaring, and rattling the cage.

"Find anything, Willow?" Giles looked at his watch

as he wandered out of his office, cup of tea in one hand and a fragile copy of Selec's *Supernatural Phenomena* in the other.

Willow shook her head. "No thunderstorms within a few hundred miles and no reports of red lightning, except Buffy's. And Xander seems to be right."

"In regard to?" Giles blew on the steaming tea. By tacit agreement they were both whispering.

"Nothing weird ever happens in Cleveland . . . except, well, there was a bunch of UFO sightings in the late seventies and, uh, a few haunted house scares. No ghosts found."

"Hardly the caliber of weird I was hoping for." Sighing, Giles gently placed the old, bound manuscript on the table and rubbed his eyes.

"There was a triple murder that was never solved," Willow went on, "which was a little weird, but not really weird . . . by our definition. Although . . . it happened on Halloween in 1988, in a park, just a few blocks from the house where Ms. Gordon grew up."

"Weird in what respect?" Giles asked absently, squaring his shoulders to get rid of the kinks.

Willow shrugged. "Three high-school boys had their throats slit, with a knife that belonged to one of them. Nobody's fingerprints on it but his . . . no blood on the scene but the victims'. There was a witness, though, a girl. She reported that another guy was there, but she couldn't identify him because it was dark and she left before things got nasty. The police were pretty sure it was a gang thing, but they never arrested anyone."

"Terrible, to be sure," Giles said, "but not inexplicable."

"Kind of what I thought, except for the part about Ms. Gordon's neighborhood—not to be confused with Mr. Rogers' neighborhood, where nothing awful ever happens." Willow sighed. "I miss being five sometimes."

Giles smiled. "Me, too, occasionally."

"What about you?" Willow glanced at the crumbling, hand-scripted volume on the table. The delicate, finely crafted manuscript was one of the most treasured in Giles's collection, partly because he had won it from Ethan Rayne in a poker game twenty years ago. It was hard to imagine Giles as a rough and rowdy, irresponsible young dabbler in the occult, especially when he looked so seriously stiff and worried, like he did now.

"I'm not sure."

Buffy jerked awake as Giles drew up a chair. She pushed her tangled hair off her face and yawned. "Okay, what did I miss?"

"Not much, I'm afraid." Giles sipped tea, his face pensive. "There's been only one recorded instance of the lightning phenomenon you saw earlier, Buffy. In Ephesus, a city on the coast of the Aegean, three hundred and fifty-six years before the beginning of the first millennium."

"Not exactly yesterday." Shaking her head, Buffy forced her groggy eyes open.

"But, it's something . . . isn't it?" Willow's voice rose in pitch, like it did when she was feeling desperate. "I mean, killer lightning out of nowhere would be kind of hard to ignore, so maybe . . . maybe that *was* the only time."

"Exactly." Giles sighed.

"And that's a problem?" Buffy closed the book on the table in front of her and rested her chin on her hands.

"Rather difficult to say, since the text is vague." Giles paused, collecting his thoughts. "The ruins of the Temple of Artemis are still there, but at the time of the incident, when a devastating storm of blood-red lightning killed hundreds, the cult followers of Artemis reigned."

"Artemis, chaste goddess of the hunt and the moon," Willow added, calming herself with hard, cold facts. "Also known as Diana. Her temple was one of the seven wonders of the ancient world."

Xander walked out of the book cage and swung a long leg over a chair to sit down facing the back. "Just how extensive is that encyclopedia of useless-to-every-one-but-us trivia you carry around in your head, Willow?"

"Irrelevant, Xander." Buffy stared at Giles. "You were saying—"

"Yes," Giles continued, "the, uh, city's population was consumed by a fervent belief in witchcraft, demonism, and astrology. They were slaves to superstition and the fear it generated."

"We can *so* relate," Xander said.

Giles ignored him. "The storm occurred when an unnamed entity with a small following challenged Artemis's superiority—on the night of Alexander the Great's birth. According to the Roman historian Plutarch, Artemis was attending Alexander's entry into the world rather than defending the monument at the center of her power base."

Willow brightened. "All of which fits with your theory about a super witch, right?" Then dimmed. "Not that we *want* to be dealing with a super witch, but, well, it would explain some . . . things."

"I'll have to research further to make a determination, but it's possible, yes." Troubled, Giles sat back and folded his arms. "Artemis's temple was burned to the ground, an act of arson history attributes to a man called Herostratus, who wanted to immortalize his name, and did."

"But?" Buffy asked bluntly.

Giles shrugged, exhaled. "Since the people of the time needed someone to blame, Herostratus may have been used as a scapegoat by the defeated entity. Artemis retained her power on Earth for another four hundred years."

"And this is a problem because?" Buffy pressed.

Giles looked at her steadily. "In the event the burst of primal magick you witnessed tonight was not an anomaly, then it was called forth—deliberately."

"By the same unknown whoever that went after Artemis?" Willow asked.

"If the entity's been dormant or exercising incredible restraint for the past two thousand years, that's a feasible assumption," Giles said, frowning. "It's also possible an incredibly resourceful, but completely modern witch has discovered how to command wild magick, although to a much lesser degree than her predecessor two thousand years ago."

"Someone like Crystal Gordon?" The idea jolted Willow from academic interest mode to alarmed attention. "Even though she has a perfectly ordinary past and no priors—in the magickal sense, I mean—or, well, even in the police sense. She wasn't a suspect in those murders."

"But definitely in the immediate sense." Buffy fixed on Giles. "Hot flashes and anxiety attacks, remember?"

"Suspicious, but not conclusive, Buffy." Frustrated, Giles rose and rubbed the back of his neck.

"Murders?" Xander's dark eyes narrowed on Willow. "What murders specifically?"

"In Cleveland when Ms. Gordon was sixteen," Willow said.

"So how can you be so sure she's innocent?" Xander asked. "Not being a police suspect doesn't prove she didn't do it."

"A remote possibility, granted," Giles conceded, "but outside the parameters of inexplicable phenomena we're looking for."

"The crime was gruesome, but not weird," Willow explained. "No red lightning or hocus-pocus involved."

"Ah, yes. Red lightning." Xander hugged the back of the chair. "I don't know about anyone else, but the prospect of being a target for random electrocution will give me a few sleepless nights. Anything we can do about that?"

"Until we *know* what we're dealing with, there's not much we can do except continue the research." Giles stared at each one in turn over the rim of his glasses. "We absolutely must not engage in a witch hunt without proof."

Silent nods agreed all around, the memory of Mothers Opposed to the Occult too fresh in everyone's mind. Willow still had nightmares. Although a demon had been responsible for the hysteria, the obsessed mob of familiar faces, like Joyce Summers's and her own mother's, had been more frightening than some of the uglier, Hellmouth demons they had faced. No one wanted to falsely accuse an innocent.

"However," Giles cautioned, "it might be prudent to avoid looking directly into Ms. Gordon's eyes."

"Right." Willow nodded. "I can stare at my book for a whole class period."

Spring, 357 *B.C.*

Shugra walked alone through the hills outside the city, aware of earth and sky, connected to the mysterious realms beyond. The setting sun was still warm on her back, the breezes off the sea cool, the grit trapped between leather sandal and skin a welcome irritation, reminding her that the natural world she had known and cherished over the millennia was in danger. Men in their pathetic need for comfort and misguided deference to the immortals of Olympus had accelerated the destruction since her last sojourn in a human body.

A resigned sigh escaped her as her thoughts wandered back. More than other peoples she had known, the Celtic tribes inhabiting the lush island land in the north had genuinely respected the true world, killing only what they needed to survive with reverence and recognition of its spiritual worth whether plant or beast. They would always hold an elevated position in her esteem, even though their Druid priests had condemned her to death by fire at the age of six after she had thrown a tantrum, drawing hail from a clear summer sky that had ruined the crops and decimated the village.

Deirdre awoke from a sound sleep with a wooden bowl pressed against her mouth.

"Drink this," the priest whispered. "It will help you sleep."

She had been asleep and was too tired to argue, but not too tired to fight when the foul brew touched her tongue. The liquid burned her throat, gagging her. She spit and scratched, but her parents held her arms and the priest forced the herbal potion through her clenched teeth.

"You must be punished, Deirdre." The tear on her mother's cheek sparkled in the glow of a candle flame. "But no one wants you to suffer."

Deirdre nodded without comprehending, her mind going numb and her body limp.

The memory was still clear in her mind four centuries later in the hills outside Ephesus. The precocious girl called Deirdre had next awakened in flames and Deirdre, now Shugra, had vowed that her mistake in childish judgment would not be repeated. Before entering the life she lived now, she had woven a protection into her unique, immortal essence—successfully. Selene, as her present form had been known before the awakening, had not been able to call or manipulate the elemental powers of the universe.

But Shugra could—with the unfettered force of her own will—and now with more purpose than mere vengeance and wrath.

Shugra did not smile as she slowly turned to look back toward Ephesus. The massive Temple of Artemis towered above the city, its white marble surface sparkling with reflected sunlight, its overwhelming size commanding the eye as was intended, for the structure itself was an integral component of Artemis's ability to wield her power. As with all her deified kin, Artemis was empowered by magick but chose not to diminish her godlike image by taking human form except to satisfy an occasional whim, and then it was simply a masquerade without substance. Shugra had no choice, not if she wished to take control of the well from which she and all the beings of the otherworld drew their power. For this, an authentic physical nature was necessary and dangerous.

Existing for the most part on a mystical plane that ebbed and flowed, Artemis and her nebulous kind were like prisms, refracting the magick and requiring mass human belief and homage to focus its enormous power. As a human born, Shugra *was* the focusing crystal, needing no one and nothing to enhance her ability to draw from the streams of magick that flowed through the cosmos. But being human put her at a disadvantage. Her human body would not be indestructible until she and the source were one.

And in order to accomplish that, she, too, needed a loyal, human following.

"So, how is, uh—everything?" Willow opened her locker and glanced at Buffy, hoping she wasn't overdoing the perky.

"You mean did I experience clogged windpipe or potentially fatal palpitating heart in history?" Buffy smiled, not offended. "To answer that—no, but I kept my eye on the books. No direct contact."

"So it worked . . . the not looking. I mean, I didn't look, either, but then, I didn't have a . . . problem. So that's a good thing, then—for you."

Buffy shrugged. "Hard to say."

"Oh, yeah, well, I guess. Kind of like a field experiment, but with no control, because we still don't know if Ms. Gordon worked a spooky mojo on you or if . . . you know."

"I know." Buffy threw her history book into her locker and slammed the door closed. "Or I wish I did, one way or the other."

"I know! Me, too." Willow nodded vigorously. "And . . . and so, we should find out . . . if we can . . . because, well, because I just don't think you're bonkers, Buffy."

"I appreciate that, Willow, and I agree—with the bonkers thing." Buffy turned down the hall, then turned back. "And you're not going to get that book, right?"

"Uh—right." Willow touched the leather packet hidden under her shirt. Ms. Gordon had asked her to stop back during the lunch break to pick up the text on Brehon Law, which she had left in her car. The brief meeting would be the perfect opportunity to see if the teacher tried anything funny with her. "But I'm wearing a protection spell, so I thought maybe—"

"No." Buffy was adamant. "Giles said ordinary spells probably wouldn't have any effect on a super witch, and that's that. Whether she is or she isn't, not worth the risk. So promise me you won't do anything stupid, okay?"

"Okay. Promise." Willow nodded. They had talked about their unavoidable exposure to the history teacher that morning after everyone had dragged back into the library with only a few hours' sleep. Cordelia, who was tackling the Slayer database project with commendable but surprising dedication, had pointed out that all their suspicions were based on conjecture and circumstantial evidence. Maybe Buffy really *had* had an anxiety attack over being embarrassed in class and maybe the weird red lightning *was* just an anomaly and maybe they were all worrying about nothing—which made a certain amount of sense in Cordelia logic.

On the other hand, Giles reasoned that if the teacher was a threat with an as yet undetermined evil plan, it would be foolish to take unnecessary chances. Giles's logic had prevailed, and none of them had met Ms. Gordon's eyes during class.

"Are you going to the cafeteria first or straight to the library?" Buffy asked.

"Eat first, then on to the library. At least then I'll have a good excuse if Ms. Gordon decides to look for me." Willow grinned. "Besides, so many kids are using the library to finish term papers they put off until the last minute, Giles really does need the help."

"Is that why he's looking more frazzled than usual?" Buffy asked.

"Could be." Willow shrugged, her worried thoughts elsewhere. What if Ms. Gordon was just an ordinary teacher who didn't like being stood up?

Crystal reread the librarian's note explaining that Willow Rosenberg's help was required in the library during lunch. Mr. Giles did not want her waiting for a student who wasn't going to appear as promised. However, if her schedule allowed, she could bring the Celtic book to Willow there.

How considerate.

Ordinarily, Crystal would think nothing of the man's decidedly British and proper communication, but on the eve of her long-awaited triumph and coming from the Slayer's mentor, the portent was highly suspicious.

The Hellmouth, a weak link in the barrier between Earth and the otherworld, was located beneath Sunnydale. Like a magnet attracted iron filings, the Hellmouth attracted the demonic elements that roamed Earth. It had also drawn the raging river of free magick connected to the source closer than it had ever been before. That proximity, combined with the power seeping through the barrier and all she had learned through trial and error, ensured her success. Not even the Slayer could stop the process once it was in motion.

Certainly, Buffy had been extraordinarily successful in containing the town's infestation of vampires and demons and had an unusual longevity for a Slayer, if the tales Crystal had heard were accurate. If so, she dared not dismiss the possibility that this Slayer was exceptional, with resources she had not anticipated.

Perhaps there was more to Willow's association with Buffy Summers than friendship, and more to Rupert Giles's involvement with both girls than educational matters. She had not had reason to risk probing his mind to find out. Although the confidence that went with maturity made the librarian an unacceptable candidate for her purposes, he possessed some spellcasting ability, which she had recognized immediately and negated as quickly. His command of the power required an intermediary to be effectual and even then, it was nothing compared to the forces she controlled.

He could not threaten her with magick, but she hadn't counted on his interference regarding Willow.

Seething, Crystal crushed the note into a ball and threw it. The paper burst into flames before it hit the wall and its ashes fluttered to the floor. Annoyed with herself for indulging the anger, she closed her eyes and breathed deeply. When she opened them again, Principal Snyder was standing in the doorway.

"Problem, Ms. Gordon?"

"No, not at all." She smiled, hiding her distaste for the insolent little man. "A canceled appointment. Nothing serious."

"Oh, I beg to differ." Drawing himself up to his full diminutive height, Snyder walked in and perched on the edge of the desk. "Canceling appointments is not a habit I want to encourage here at Sunnydale High."

"She had an acceptable excuse." Still smiling, Crystal put Snyder's insufferable arrogance to work for her. "Was it your idea to have students work in the library?"

"Work in the library? You've got to be kidding. The library is a pit of—" He hesitated, having second thoughts about whatever he was going to say, and shifted gears in midsentence. "—undisciplined ignorance."

Losing patience, Crystal reached into Snyder's mind through his eyes and took control. With the time upon her and most of the necessary pieces in place, the need for absolute caution was no longer as imperative as making certain there were no unexpected complications. She stared into the principal's blank, beady eyes, removed the mental inhibitors holding his tongue, and spoke softly. "Tell me about Mr. Giles and his young friends."

Five minutes later, Crystal erased the memory of Snyder's monologue from his mind and excused herself, leaving the principal with a slight case of disorientation and wondering if he would enjoy life as a real weasel, a whim she fully intended to satisfy once the meld was finally completed. However, since Snyder was on the fringes of the supernatural loop on both sides of the fence in Sunnydale, his information had been surprisingly reassuring. Neither he nor the evil element that ran the town were aware of her true nature, which made the years of painstaking planning and precautions well worth the effort. One nuisance to cope with was enough.

As Crystal scanned the halls searching for Willow, she toyed with the idea of simply eliminating Giles and the Slayer, but rejected it. She was more than capable of protecting herself from them, but she did not want to contend with the mass hysteria and fear their deaths or disappearances might provoke. She had dealt with irrational mobs before and lost.

Now it was critical that she probe Willow. As with the ten others she had gathered so far, she needed something to tempt her into joining the coven of her own free will, which was essential to the ritual. This, too, she had learned too late and at great expense in Ephesus.

Summer, 356 B.C.

On a rise behind the great temple, Shugra waited in a clearing strewn with large boulders and ringed by scrub trees, protected by air and shrouded by fog. She had formed the barrier by condensing the tiny particles of matter of which air was made; a simple construction that was a marvel to those who didn't know the elements as intimately as she. Although word of her power had spread in spite of her restraint, the blanket of concealing mist would prevent spying eyes from witnessing the extent of her magick or sounding an alarm until she was ready.

Soon, she thought as a thin man with a malformed foot hobbled up the rise and sprawled at her feet. "You brought word of Artemis?"

He nodded vigorously without raising his eyes. "The priests say the goddess has left Ephesus to attend the birth of a great warrior."

"Excellent." Shugra smiled. Without Artemis at hand to guide her cult, the destruction of her temple would create chaos in her human power base, shattering the resolve of her followers and disarming her empowered priests. Then, nothing would stand between Shugra and the source.

Pleased with the man's service, Shugra focused on the malformed foot that had been his curse since leaving the womb and repaired it. "Join the others with my blessing."

The pitiful man contained his overwhelming awe as he backed away, which brought another smile to Shugra's lips. He would know the joy of being whole for such a short time.

She dismissed him to watch her followers file in through a breach in the wall guarded by Herostratus, her lover and most devoted. Anyone else who tried to enter, whether spy or merely curious, would be crushed and suffocated when she compacted the air around them. An infiltrator would contaminate and weaken the union of those who were totally committed.

Shugra calmed the excitement stirring in her veins as the adoring throng gathered before her. She had cultivated them carefully, winning their adoration with small demonstrations of her skill in what they called the black arts. None except Herostratus were aware that she could kill with a thought or destroy the city in ways too numerous to name without the trappings of the craft. Respect laced with fear bolstered their loyalty. Terror would drive them away and she needed their unwavering belief to reach the source.

So the city was safe from annihilation—for now.

"Our time has come!" Shugra's voice rose in the dark, the sound unable to pierce the barrier of compressed air to the city beyond. "Let my name be heard at last!"

"Shugra!" The crowd cried. "Shugra!"

They numbered only a hundred, but the intensity of their fervor was tangible, a thing alive with their decadent desire to overthrow the cult of Artemis and rule Ephesus in her name. So she had promised and so it would be, but not as her ardent followers envisioned. She had suffered too much and come too far to place the fate of her existence in the hands of sheep. Only Herostratus would be acting entirely of his own accord. The mortal souls of the others would be absorbed into the source, enslaved to her will forever once the connection was made.

"Silence!" She commanded and they obeyed. "Each

of you must bind your resolve and gather your strength for the calling."

While the herd settled into the practiced rituals of meditation, Shugra lapsed into pensive reflection. Since the joining during her original life, she had slowly come to know many things about her unique state of being. That it was unique she had no doubt. While multitudes of humans and entities not of this world had varying degrees of ability that allowed them to utilize magick, only she was completely and irrevocably entwined with the streams, her essence preserved by the unfathomable properties of the power. She had lived uncountable lives before she had realized she could choose the circumstances of each new earthly sojourn by exerting the force of her will on the streams, much as she had learned to control the raw, unfocused power of her emotions to refine her manipulations of the magick. More importantly, this discovery proved that the source was not governed by a sentient intelligence. Knowing that, she had spent her ensuing lives working to achieve her ultimate destiny.

"We await your wishes, Shugra of the ages." Herostratus knelt before her, his head bowed, the only human besides Chit she had loved in almost seventeen thousand years of living and dying and living again, the only human male who had ever loved her in return. This she knew to be so, for he could not hide his thoughts from her probes. He would die without hesitation to protect her and the secrets of her nature and intent. Even now, as she stood on the threshold of supremacy over all the magick in the universe, her human heart and body of seventeen years ached for him. The empty spaces of her long loneliness filled to overflowing in his presence. After tonight, he would share her eternity.

"Rise, Herostratus, and take your place beside me."

"I am yours to command." Herostratus held his head high as he stood and moved into position on her right.

Shugra raised her arms and turned her face toward the dark sky. The great stream that led directly to the well was closer than it had ever been before. Flowing just beyond the reach of the sun's invisible wind, it had a specific attraction to this place at this time, drawn, she assumed, by the concentration of magick practiced and the empowered entities of Olympus. After the threat of Artemis's magick was removed, the force of her followers' belief combined with her unique affinity would draw the river to Earth. She would meld as she had initially, when the electrifying red power had found her in the old valley, but this time her essence would expand into and join with the source to become master of all magick everywhere.

She drew on the power as she spoke, amplifying the guttural sounds of her first, primitive language so the words echoed even though the clearing was acousti-cally deadened by stone and wood.

"Ssstat a'gar shu bur!"

The ground shook and the assembly fell to their knees in awe. Though she needed no words to com-mand the elements, incantation had a galvanizing, yet mesmerizing effect on her people. Ritual heated their blood with purpose, cemented their unshakable belief, and dulled their awareness of everything but her. As their gazes converged, drawn without exception to her eyes, she captured their minds. Above her, the sky undulated with the energies she drew from the vast stream. She snapped her arms forward, releasing a hundred small bolts of lightning that branded her mark into human flesh, binding her followers with fire into a unified extension of her own will.

"When?" Herostratus asked, his skin unblemished, the bond between them stronger than fire. He tensed, his own blood running hot as she dissolved the wall of air and the fog. The Temple of Artemis loomed above and before them, blocking the view of Ephesus.

Tomorrow it would be gone.

Spotting the gathering on the hill, a priest cried out in alarm from the temple terrace along the left side of the marble monument.

"Now."

Shugra unleashed her fury.

The night sky burned with red fire as bolts of primal magick knifed through the atmosphere to strike the temple. Tiles exploded off the roof, exposing the wood covering beneath to an uninterrupted assault. Within heartbeats, the top of the massive structure was ablaze and crashing inward, turning the interior into an inferno that cracked stone. Screams from a harbor suddenly lashed by winds, rains, and swells of hurricane force rose and were lost in the thunder as marble columns and walls collapsed. The earth shook, crumbling hillsides, pulverizing streets, swallowing shops and homes.

Thousands of fanatics devoted to the goddess of the

hunt and the moon swarmed toward the temple. Priests arrayed in white robes and armed with the amulets and potions of their inferior craft swept through the collapsing columns and ran to safety on the lower terraces.

Shugra raged, aware of Herostratus's ragged, exhilarated breathing, the elation shining in his dark eyes.

The hundred watched in silence, immune to the pain of cinders and flame charring their flesh, frozen in a moment of adulation, their fears, uncertainties, and volition suppressed by her hold.

Intoxicated by the savagery of her wrath, Shugra did not notice the amassing of Artemis's followers until the sound of ritual chanting, a mere whisper barely heard in the roar of the storms, impacted the stream.

The disturbance jolted her, snapping her attention to the wave of humanity moving toward the hill. Wrapped in protective wards and sprinkling their magick potions before them, the priests led an army of men intent on avenging their defiled goddess. Neither their faith in the dark arts nor their unconditional devotion to the deity had been shaken. Rather than being extinguished, the power of the Artemis cult had intensified in the wake of Shugra's sabotage.

The priests called out, invoking the name and power of Artemis. The night reverberated as a thousand voices blended into one voice, repeating the incantation, reinforcing the potency of their magick.

Shugra faltered when she felt the stream shift, shoved by the unified force of the horde. Red lightning snapped and snarled around her, snatched from her grasp by the priests and rampaging out of control.

"What is wrong?" Herostratus gasped, but made no move to leave her.

"It is not done yet," Shugra hissed. Abandoning the tempest of her emotions, she concentrated her energies on the disrupted stream, reached out and hooked into it. As Shugra sent the surge of her followers' undiluted, captive belief into the ether, the stream began to bend toward her.

Holding the vast, wild flow in place against the power conjured by the priests and strengthened by the consolidated affinities of Artemis's faithful was a strain, requiring her total attention. Centuries would pass before the pathway to the source would be cosmically close enough to access again.

Her hold on the river was broken when the captive essences began to vanish.

Stricken, Shugra watched in horror as Artemis's mob slaughtered the hundred, cutting them down like sheaves, for they had no will and did not fight back. She felt nothing for the loss of their lives, for they were but tools to be used and discarded.

She mourned because this chance to attain immortal life on Earth with all the magick in the universe at her disposal was gone.

And Herostratus was gone with it.

Distracted by her grief, Shugra had been caught off guard when the blood-red bolts of primal power were suddenly set against Herostratus. While the priests were unable to call the raw power of primal magick, they had collectively managed to exert some control over the forces she had unleashed upon them. And in their collective wisdom, they had apparently realized they had no hope of killing her and had attacked her co-conspirator instead. Only the priests' clumsy efforts to tame the wild forces kept Herostratus from instant incineration.

"Shugra!" Trapped within a frenzied cage of deadly lightning, he looked toward her, his eyes reflecting the depth of her own sorrow. "I'll never betray you."

Without hesitation, Shugra drew the lethal energies away from him and took them into herself. As her body died, the violent magick dissipated and bore her essence back into the stream to grieve and wait.

She would live until the end of time.

But she would never love again.

As Crystal Gordon walked the halls of Sunnydale High, her memories of that summer night were just as vivid and painful as they had been twenty-three hundred years ago. Herostratus had not betrayed her. The priests, believing the witch had been destroyed when her evil magick turned back on her, had accused and convicted her lover of burning down Artemis's temple. The hundred had died silent, and Herostratus had not corrected their mistaken assumption.

And her name had never been spoken again.

Though she had tried and failed to meld with the elusive source twice since Ephesus, she had kept her true identity secret. She had learned much from each attempt and her mistakes would not be repeated, but most important, she had learned that the tactic of surprise worked both ways. To ensure that it worked entirely for her this time, she had done nothing to alert the world to the approaching storm and the chaotic

dawn of a new age—until she had arrived in Sunnydale two weeks ago and had begun quietly enlisting
the twelve. Sworn to secrecy and intent on having their
impossible desires fulfilled, the ten she had acquired
so far would not talk.

The Slayer was another matter.

Testing Buffy against the power had been risky but
necessary with the night of the melding imminent. Although she was certain the Slayer was not a threat, the
unusual incident might have created other problems requiring her immediate attention.

Willow would know.

As Crystal turned into the main hall, Willow paused
outside the restroom across from the cafeteria to speak
to Cordelia Chase.

"Tell Giles I'll be right there, will you, Cordelia?"

Cordelia's eyes flashed. "You're going to the library?"

Crystal backed against the wall to listen, thumbing
through her planner as though she was looking for
something.

"Well—yeah. Why?" Willow gasped. "Did something happen?"

"Not that I'm aware of, but I'll be using the computer."

"Oh." Willow started, surprised. "Why? It's not like
you're dedicated to, you know . . . the *S* stuff and, well,
the sudden interest is just . . . kind of strange."

"Do you need to use the computer or not?" Cordelia
asked impatiently.

"Not right now." As Cordelia rushed away, Willow
shrugged and ducked into the restroom.

Tucking her planner under her arm, Crystal followed. The coven had to be complete by tomorrow night. Another benefit of the great stream's attraction to the Hellmouth was the availability of rebellious, impressionable teenagers with above average affinities for magick. She would have preferred a subject who wasn't on such friendly terms with Giles and the Slayer, but Willow's abilities were too potent to exclude. As it was, she was having difficulty finding a suitable twelfth initiate.

Willow stood in front of a sink, washing her hands. When the door whooshed closed, she looked up to see who had entered. Her eyes widened. "Ms. Gordon! I'm, uh . . . I was just—" She stopped talking abruptly, afraid.

In the fraction of a second before the girl looked away, Crystal easily slipped past an impressive but inadequate protection spell and invaded her mind.

A quick probe of Willow's thoughts revealed that the librarian suspected, but did not know beyond a doubt, that the red lightning was wild magick. He was even more in doubt about her nature and motives and had judiciously chosen to do nothing, although he had warned Willow to beware. The Slayer was questioning her mental stability, a result of Crystal's meddling.

And the key to winning Willow over was obvious.

Wary of being seen with the girl, Crystal quickly imprinted a command. Willow had to commit herself and participate in the ritual of her own free will, but she had to be isolated from Giles's influence to make that decision. The implanted command was only to optimize the circumstances under which Willow would be given the opportunity to freely decide.

When Anya asks, you will go.

After erasing the girl's memory of her presence, Crystal left, confident Willow would not be able to resist her offer.

Feeling a little dizzy, Willow turned off the water and dried her hands. She hurried on to the library, dying to know why Cordelia was courting the computer as if it could vote for the coolest, most beautiful girl in the senior class.

Chapter 6

In any other town the cool, quiet night with the full moon rising would be perfect for a walk. Buffy, however, was not lulled into complacency by the veneer of normalcy as she moved past the Shady Hill Cemetery. In Sunnydale the undead stalked the dark looking for quickie meals in out of the way places. Eat and run. No matter how many sweeps she made, she couldn't serve them all a wooden stake for dessert.

Although vigilant and alert, vampires were not uppermost in her mind tonight. Aside from the minor reference to red lightning Giles had found, nothing extraordinary had happened that day. She had not experienced a single physical pang of anxiety, which wasn't as reassuring as it should be. As Willow had pointed out, since they hadn't tested Ms. Gordon's evil eye, they hadn't proved anything. When Willow failed to return to borrow the book, the teacher hadn't tried to contact her, either, which gave credence to Cordelia's theory, hard as *that* was to swallow. Maybe they were so used to finding demonic treachery behind every door, they were looking for evil doings that didn't exist. They had no hard evidence, which is what had brought her back to Shady Hill.

Buffy waited as a car sped by, she then darted to the spot where the red lightning had cremated the hapless motorist. His remains had been scraped off the street by the police and, according to a report in the Sunnydale *Gazette,* the official cause of death was spontaneous combustion. This may have raised an eyebrow or two, but little else in the way of public reaction. Case closed. Also in keeping with Sunnydale's pervasive lack of curiosity was that no one seemed to care that the fiery event hadn't scorched the asphalt. Not even a blister, Buffy thought as she studied the pavement, which threw the weight of support toward Giles's free magick theory.

She walked back to the sidewalk near the cemetery gate, mulling over Giles's response that afternoon, when she had questioned the length of time between sightings. If there were wild magick storms running rampant throughout the universe, why weren't strikes more common on Earth? After qualifying that it was only conjecture, he had hypothesized a number of possible explanations.

"Perhaps," Giles had said, "like asteroids, which were abundant in the solar system's infancy, the nearby concentrations of wild magick struck and diffused long ago. Strikes still occur, but not as frequently. Or perhaps the pockets are clumped together and the clusters are separated by immense spaces. It's possible Earth has been located within one of these vacant areas for thousands of years."

All of which might make perfect sense to that Hawking guy, but still didn't appease her uneasiness. Giles was smart, but on this particular topic, he was just guessing—except to say that the hypothetical locations and nature of wild magick didn't affect the ability of witches and the magickally-attuned to draw on the power.

Hearing the scuff of feet behind her, Buffy drew her stake and whirled. *Not a vamp.* Shrugging self-consciously, she whipped Mr. Pointy behind her back and stared into Kari Stark's shocked face.

"Sorry, Kari. I thought you were something else."

"Uh, yeah." Kari nodded and tried to push past her.

Buffy blocked her. "You know, this isn't a really good part of town to be walking around alone."

"I know, but . . . I'm not going far." The girl brushed her limp hair behind her ear and folded her arms defensively. "It's okay."

"Well, actually, it's not." Buffy shoved the girl aside and clocked an attacking vampire with a swift foot to the jaw. "We were talking here."

Kari shrieked and started to run. A fem vamp, middle-aged and modeling low-income, housewife drab, vaulted over the cemetery wall and tackled the girl as the male vamp roared and lunged back toward Buffy. She easily adjourned the meeting with a stake through the breast pocket of his grungy business suit. Before the dust cloud settled, she grabbed the fem vamp by her tangled, dirty hair and pulled her off Kari. The snarling

vamp spun, fangs bared in a face that had been lined
and bony before she acquired the ridged distortions of a
vampire.

"Hey, lady. Here's a beauty tip!" Buffy smiled and
plunged the stake into the barrel-shaped body. She
snapped it back as the vamp disintegrated and blew the
dust off the trusty point before stuffing it back into her
pocket.

Kari was on her knees, rocking and sobbing. Her
scoop-neck tee was torn and hanging off her shoulder.

"Come on, Kari. I'll walk you home." As Buffy
leaned over to help the girl to her feet, she saw the red
mark on Kari's skin in the hollow just above her collar-
bone. At first, she thought the vamp's fangs had grazed
her, drawing blood. Then she realized it was a burn.
"What's this?"

"Nothing!" Eyes flashing, Kari yanked her arm
away, pulled the flap of her torn shirt over the burn, and
jumped to her feet. "I've gotta go." She turned and ran.

"You're welcome," Buffy muttered and jogged after
her. She hung back as they left the cemetery behind,
keeping the girl in sight instead of running her down,
wondering where she was going and what was so important that her personal safety wasn't an issue.

This wasn't the first time Buffy had encountered a
mark. Giles, Ethan Rayne and their occult friends had all
been tattooed with the mark of Eyghon. Ethan had removed his when he realized the demon was homing in
and killing everyone who bore it, then had tattooed Buffy
to be his stand-in. After Angel won a quick but visually
interesting internal battle with the beast, it had cost her a
bundle to have the unattractive symbol taken off.

The mark on Kari wasn't a tattoo, but the burn was a symbol that meant something. And, now that she thought about it, Kari the bookworm was suddenly hanging out with several kids who had nothing in common, including Anya and Michael. They had different but avid interests in the black arts, and were going out of their way to be friends with Willow.

Up ahead, Kari made a sharp right turn and disappeared into the woods.

Buffy put on a burst of speed to catch up, then slowed when she saw Kari walking down a long, unpaved drive toward a small house tucked back in the trees. The girl was winded and clutching her side, but pressed on toward the lighted windows, the only beacons in the dark, dense woods.

Several cars were parked along the curb, too many to belong to the residents of the few houses on the opposite side of the street. The town proper didn't begin for another few blocks. The undeveloped wooded lots on this side expanded into a large forest. Half the streetlights were burned out and the moon wasn't high enough to improve the visibility.

Hugging the trees and brush for cover, Buffy moved down the side of the drive. If Kari lived here, then all was well. If not, she didn't want to be seen following.

Kari stumbled up the steps of a wide, covered front porch and knocked. She leaned against the log siding to catch her breath until the door opened. Light poured onto the porch as she darted inside, then shut off when the door closed behind her. Unless Kari had forgotten her key, she obviously didn't live here. Buffy didn't know who owned the house, but she was willing to bet a bucket of holy water that Kari Stark wasn't the only one who had braved the vampire jungle to get there.

Buffy moved off the drive into the trees and advanced on the house, using the windows to guide her. Dry leaves rustled underfoot and briers snagged at her pants, making complete stealth impossible. When all the lights in the house went out, Buffy stopped and looked behind her toward the street. Nothing was visible in a dark unbroken by even a glimmer from the dim streetlights.

Buffy didn't move as she assessed the situation. The occupants of the house did not want to be observed, which only strengthened her resolve to have a look. Although the complete absence of light was disconcerting, she was able to get her bearings based on her position before the blackout. The house was situated a hundred yards ahead and to her left. The drive was also on her left and the street fifty yards behind.

Buffy turned toward the drive, holding her hands in front of her to fend off branches and brush as she crept forward. Once she hit the pavement, she could follow it up to the house without fear of getting disoriented and lost in the woods. Estimating that she was probably no more than ten to twelve feet from the dirt track, she counted her steps. When she finally broke out of the trees, she stopped dead again.

There was still no light, not from the street or the rising moon.

Squatting, she touched the ground and felt the hard packed dirt of the drive. She dropped to her hands and knees, turned and began crawling toward the house. The eerie darkness seemed to thicken as she felt her way along the edge of the drive. The air became heavier, making it hard to breathe and harder to move, as though the molecular structure of the atmosphere was being condensed to impede her. She kept on, breathing slowly and deeply, inching forward until she hit a thick tangle of thorny vines. Blind in the inky blackness, she assumed she had wandered off the drive. She moved to the left, but the barrier of twisted briers stretched across the drive, barring her progress. When she tried to crawl back to the right, the area she had just vacated was overgrown with vines.

Okay, I can take a hint, Buffy thought, frustrated as she tried creeping backward toward the street. She was not particularly surprised to find the roadway behind her free of obstructions or to see a faint glow where the drive entered the street. Getting to her feet, she walked toward the light. The forces at work in the woods were not natural, but her Slayer abilities alone were useless against the magickal "keep out" signs. She needed Giles's and Willow's spellcasting expertise to counter the effects.

Still, the outing had not been a failure. She had wanted hard evidence and she had found it. Something evil had definitely established itself—or herself—in the woods.

Xander flipped through the pages of *Sorcerers: A Biographical Compendium,* published in 1784, wondering if the author had tried to make the summaries boring. Behind him, the werewolf snarled and kicked the book-cage door. The hairy guy wasn't enjoying his Friday night, either.

"Did we remember to check his water dish?" Giles looked up from the far end of the study table.

"We did, but if he spilled it, he's just gonna have to stay thirsty 'til dawn." Dust flew in Xander's face as he slammed the book closed. He coughed and waved the cloud away.

"Well, do *something* to make him stop," Cordelia demanded. She sat across the table in front of the computer. The intensity of her interest in Slayer mythos compiled by Watchers was intriguing, but since comment usually triggered a tirade of caustic sarcasm, Xander had dropped the subject. "I can't concentrate with all that racket."

"I'll tell him." Xander stood up and stretched, looking at the clock. Half an hour had passed since Willow had called to say she was stopping by the Dragon's Cove Magick Shop on her way back to the library after dinner. She was certain her protection spell had kept Crystal Gordon from harassing her about not going back to the classroom—or worse—and wanted to whip up a leather guard pouch for everyone. Good idea. Bad timing. Willow was a blossoming wicca with pockets full of holy water and crucifixes, but it was dark.

"Maybe I should go see what's keeping the Willster." Xander skipped right over Cordelia's scorching glare and zeroed in on Giles.

"Yes, please do." Giles sat back from the pile of books and papers spread out on the table. "We could certainly use her help. There must be other references to wild magick and its properties. With diligence, we'll find them."

Xander scanned the hundreds of books in the stacks and nodded. "And given the painstaking, page-turning, time-consuming method we're using to look, we'll know if there *aren't* any in a few years."

"Yes, well—that's why we need the Slayer database, isn't it?"

"Was that an insinuation?" Cordelia's temper flared. "This isn't easy, you know. I'm typing as fast as I can."

"We noticed," Xander said, deadpan. Cordelia's words-per-minute rating couldn't be calculated in double digits.

"No, Cordelia, it wasn't. Just keep . . . typing." His patience strained, Giles glanced at his watch. "I rather expected Buffy before now—" His eyes snapped to the door. "Intercept, Xander. Quickly, please."

Xander jumped forward as Anya pushed through the door with Michael on her heels. Oz didn't do visitors in his present condition, which no one knew about except the chosen few, and he depended on them to keep it that way.

"Hi, Xan—hey!"

Xander grabbed Anya's arm and propelled her back outside before she finished blinking with surprise. Michael did an about face and followed. "Sorry about that, but it's after hours. The library's closed."

"So what are you doing here?" Anya scowled. "Did you make up with Cordelia?"

"Does a black widow's mate *live* long enough to make up? I think not." Xander smiled tightly, his gaze flicking over Anya in spite of his revulsion for ex-demons who despised men. She wore a light cardigan sweater unbuttoned over a tank top with thin straps. "So . . . what's up?"

"We're looking for Willow." Anya turned abruptly to peer through the small, round window in the left door.

"When I talked to her this afternoon, she said she'd be here tonight," Michael said.

"She's not here." Xander looked through the window on the right. There wasn't a direct line of sight to the interior of the book cage and its unusual inhabitant, and Willow wasn't there. "See?"

"Yeah." Sighing, Anya stepped back. Her sweater fell open as she leaned toward him. "Well, do you know where she is?"

"At this very second? No." Xander tried not to look down, but his gaze had a libido of its own. However, he was hoping for an eyeful, not a glimpse of raw wound on Anya's shoulder. "Big ouch. What happened? Penance or payback?"

"What?" Anya followed his gaze and quickly drew the sweater closed over the injury. "I, uh, haven't quite mastered using a curling iron, yet."

Xander nodded. "And infinity curls are in?"

"Is she at home?" Normally a weird, silent type, Michael was getting downright pushy.

"Last time I talked to her. A few minutes ago." *Give or take thirty,* Xander thought. Last night at the Bronze he had been sure Anya was using Willow as an excuse to get close to him. Obviously not, which was a relief—and wasn't. If Anya had started hitting on him for real, repairing his damaged male ego might have over-ridden common sense, which degraded at an alarming rate when exposed to perfume. More alarming was that

Anya really wanted to get close to Willow. Not on *his* watch.

"Why?" Xander had to ask.

"Just thought she might want to hang out. It *is* Friday night." Anya smiled. "Come on, Michael."

Xander waved as they moved off, then eased back inside the library. He spun as the door closed. "Anya's after Willow. I really need your car, Cordy."

"No! You can't—" Cordy flinched, hesitated. "It's, uh, in the shop. Really."

"After Willow?" Giles looked puzzled. "Meaning what?"

"Meaning gotta-find-her, very-urgent, has-to-be-for-evil-purposes after. I know we hit a dead end with the wicked-witch-from-Cleveland theory today, but Anya ranks pretty high on my list of disenfranchised demons with an ax to grind." He snapped his fingers. "Oz's van. Where are his keys?"

Giles and Cordelia exchanged a glance, then both looked toward Oz's neatly folded clothes on top of the filing cabinet in the book cage.

The werewolf took that as a cue to beat his tattered blankets into submission.

"Not worth losing an arm over." Xander held out his hand. "Come on, Giles. You know it's important or I wouldn't be caught dead driving that pile of spare parts you call a car."

"Yes, it probably would be a good idea to go get her, but I doubt Willow will trust Anya again under any circumstances." Giles fished the keys from his pocket and tossed them. "Keep an eye out for Buffy, will you?"

"You got it." Palming the keys, Xander ran for the

door. Even taking the old Citroën's idiosyncrasies into account, he could be on his way back with Willow before Anya and Michael realized she wasn't home.

"Anything else, miss?" The old man squinted at Willow through the lower half of his bifocals. "I close in twenty minutes."

Willow glanced at the plastic bags on the counter, refusing to be rushed by the latest proprietor of the Dragon's Cove Magick Shop, whom she not so fondly called Grouchy. Not to his face, of course. Actually, not out loud to anyone. She didn't know his name, but he *was* cranky and the only reason she kept coming back was because there was no place else in town to buy spell supplies, occult accouterment, and other New Age paraphernalia.

"Is this powdered wort fresh?" She sniffed the bag and wrinkled her nose. "It looks a little gray."

"It's all I got." The old geezer wheezed.

"Oh. Okay. Two bottles of holy water and that'll do it." Willow smiled sweetly, which had the effect she expected. None.

"Danged kids." Grouchy teetered to the shelf of vials on the far wall, grumbling under his breath.

"Hey, Willow! We've been looking all over for you." Anya bounced through the door.

Michael came in behind her, his heavy make-up applied with precision, and nodded. "We called your house, but you weren't there."

"How'd you know I was here?" Willow wasn't thrilled with Anya's recent, almost desperate attempts to smooth over past differences. It wasn't that she didn't trust the new girl—new in every sense of the word—but, well, she didn't. The old man dropped the holy-water bottles into a brown paper bag and rang up the price.

"We just left the library and saw you through the window as we were driving by." Anya looked over Willow's shoulder as the old man put the ingredients into the large bag. "Looks like you're planning to cook up some protection spells."

"Thirty-eight dollars and seventy-six cents' worth." The old man glared. "Won't work against bog goblins, though."

"I've heard that," Anya said.

"Not a problem." Rolling her eyes, Willow slapped two twenties on the counter, picked up her bag and palmed her change.

Ignoring Anya and smiling at Michael, Willow started out the door and halted, stricken with a horrible thought. What if Anya planned to use Michael to do a temporal-fold spell? So she could get her necklace back? He wouldn't—or maybe he would. When Amy became a rat, he had lost his best friend and the only person who really understood him. He was vulnerable and Anya was taking advantage of it. She really needed to talk to him—alone.

"Willow, wait." Anya moved up beside her and opened the door. "We're on our way to a party. Want to go?"

"Go already!" The old man waved his arms. "Out!"

It never entered Willow's mind to refuse. She followed Anya to her car.

Chapter 7

BUFFY WALKED INTO THE LIBRARY, BURSTING WITH THE urgency that had driven her to run most of the way from Shady Hill.

Cordelia walked out of Giles's office with a cup of tea and both barrels loaded. She took aim with a critical eye. "Compost heap. As fashion statements go, it suits you. Kind of a carefree, I-don't-care-what-anyone-thinks, Slayer look."

Buffy pulled a length of thorny vine out of her hair and brushed leaves and dirt off her clothes, but she passed on a barbed response. A retort would just goad Cordelia to new heights of creative contempt.

"And now you're shedding all over the floor." Shaking her head, Cordelia sauntered to the table and slid into the chair behind the computer. "Just so there's no misunderstanding, Giles, janitorial duties are not in my job description."

"What job description?" Buffy took a seat and tossed the vine aside. She continued picking bits of brier off her pants as she checked the book cage. The werewolf was curled up, snoring.

"Did I say 'job?' I didn't mean *job* . . . like in *working*. For money or anything." Cordelia shot Giles a warning glance. "Right?"

"Of course not." Sighing, Giles began the ritual of cleaning his glasses, which seemed to calm him during moments of great stress. "It would appear that you tangled with a few vampires this evening, Buffy."

"Two, but it was the tangle with the woods that ruined the wardrobe. An interesting story, but I could use some of that tea first."

Giles waved her back down when she started to rise. "I'll get it."

"Thanks." Buffy took the stake out of her pocket and sat back. "I thought Willow would be here. I feel some heavy duty research coming on."

Cordelia peeked around the monitor. "Xander went to get her—in Giles's car. It could be a while. Anything I can do?"

"Maybe." Buffy scribbled the address of the house on Giles's pad and handed it to Cordelia. "Find out who lives here, if you can. My money's on Kari Stark or Crystal Gordon."

"I'm on it. I think Willow has Crystal's address in this thing somewhere. I just have to figure out how to find it." Cordelia winced and clicked the mouse.

Giles handed Buffy a cup of cinnamon-flavored tea and sat down. "I've been floundering about in the dark here, Buffy. Not much accomplished in the research department, sorry to say."

"I've been floundering around in the dark myself." Buffy sipped her tea. "No metaphor."

Giles listened without interrupting as she related the events leading up to her strange expulsion from the woods around Crystal's house, until she described the fast-growing vines. "Are you absolutely certain you were on the drive? It's easy to lose sense of direction in the dark, especially in a wooded area."

"Definitely. On the drive. These creepy crawly vines cut me off and flanked me so I couldn't get close to that house. I'm sure."

"Intriguing." Giles slipped his glasses back on as Buffy wrapped up with a quick sketch of the symbol she had seen burned into Kari's shoulder. "Infinity."

Buffy nodded. "Kari tried to pass it off as nothing, but she was wigged because I saw it."

Cordelia's head snapped up. "Kari *Stark* drives an Infiniti?"

"The infinity symbol, Cordelia," Buffy said, "not the *car*."

Cordelia was unfazed. "You're probably not aware of this, Buffy, but an Infiniti *is* a symbol—of money and success."

Giles picked up the paper, studied it, set it down. "It's rather lacking in complexity to have demonic significance."

"Hazard a guess," Buffy prodded, glad to be back on topic.

"Infinity most likely signifies unlimited or endless, but I can't say in reference to what. The circle could mean completeness, perhaps." Giles shrugged. "Sometimes it simply represents a group of people with a common interest."

"That fits. If Crystal Gordon is hand-picking kids with something in common for . . . something." Buffy was still guessing, like Giles. From the look of consternation on his face, he wasn't handling the frustration well, either. "Any luck with that address, Cordelia?"

"Yes and no. There are three Starks listed in the phone directory thingie, but none of them lives near Shady Hill. Crystal Gordon hasn't lived in Sunnydale long enough to be listed, and I can't find Willow's file." Cordelia glanced at Giles.

Giles recoiled. "I think we'd best leave Willow's files alone, don't you?"

"Not a total bust," Buffy said. "Now we know Kari *doesn't* live there."

"Oh, wait! Duh. Information has new listings." Cordelia threw up her hands, reached for her purse and hesitated. She caught Buffy's curious glance as she stood up. "There's a perfectly good phone in Giles's office. I'm tired of financing this operation."

Giles focused on Buffy. "There were others at the house as well?"

"Okay, I didn't actually see anyone, but Kari's been pretty thick with Joanna Emidy and Winston Havershem lately. And Michael and Anya, to name a few."

Cordelia paused at the office door. "A cheerleader, a brain, a metal head, a witch-guy and a desperate ex-demon. Excuse me for pointing out the obvious, but they don't have *anything* in common."

"Which pretty much makes my point," Buffy countered. "They're bonding over something, Giles, and it's not homework."

"Willow." Giles scowled. "Anya and Michael were here earlier looking for her. Since Willow isn't fond of Anya, I didn't perceive a threat, but Xander insisted on rushing off to get her."

"Good thing, in my opinion." Buffy's thoughts shifted into high gear as the pieces began to fall into place. "Michael and Anya know that Willow's a wicca."

"Which suggests that an affinity for magick may be the common denominator."

"I am good!" Cordelia returned, grinning. "Ms. Gordon has an unlisted number, but the address is a match."

Buffy watched Giles, waiting for his take on the mounting evidence that tagged Crystal Gordon as a witch. The woman could shut her down with a look or an army of vicious vegetation. All the combat techniques in the world wouldn't help if she couldn't get close enough or live long enough to combat.

The librarian contemplated the table, thinking out loud. "Manipulating the natural elements, plants for instance, falls within the realm of sorcery, and witchcraft specifically. Given that, the infinity symbol may represent unlimited magick. If the red lightning Buffy saw last night was *primal* magick, which I'm inclined to believe it was—"

"What?" Buffy asked when Giles's facial expression flicked from curious concern to grim.

"You said the mark was *burned* into Kari's skin? Like a brand?" When Buffy nodded, he stood up suddenly.

"What?" Buffy and Cordelia both asked.

"Primitive cultures relied on an oral tradition to record their histories. An amazing number of these ancient accounts include stories about young girls with immense powers, but there's a disturbing sameness that spans millennia, continents, and cultures." He stared at the book cage and his rare book collection.

Buffy followed his gaze. The werewolf was awake and glaring at them. "Can't we tranquilize him or something?"

"That may not be necessary." Agitated, Giles paced. "If memory serves, a priest in the court of Ramses II instigated the destruction of a young sorceress he believed was the reincarnation of a primitive human girl who was linked to the primal source of magick. She branded her followers, which gave her complete control over them: body, mind and—"

Xander burst through the door, out of breath and panicked. "Willow went to a party with Anya."

"And they didn't invite you?" Cordy asked.

Buffy was instantly on her feet. "You're sure?"

"Yeah. I got to Dragon's Cove just as it was closing. The old coot in charge of the place overheard them talking." Xander looked down at Buffy's sketch. "I'm thinking it's not a coincidence that Anya has a burn that looks just like that drawing."

"Good Lord." Giles sprang toward his office.

Brambles and undergrowth parted before Crystal as she led her young entourage deeper into the woods. The coven was almost complete.

"Can she do that?" Rebecca Sullivan whispered, awed. "Make me beautiful and popular?"

"If that's what you want," Kari answered.

"She can make trees walk and freeze rain," Joanna said. "We saw her. Totally weird and way cool. She can do anything she wants and she'll give us anything *we* want."

"What could you possibly want, Joanna?" Rebecca asked. "You're already gorgeous and everyone likes you."

"Yeah, well, after Crystal finishes her power trip tomorrow night, I'll be smart, too. And I'll be able to work out and never get tired. Fit and trim forever with no more aching muscles."

"I'm just so glad Crystal listened to me and chose you, too, Rebecca." Kari's tone was sincere. "I didn't want to ignore you, but no one, absolutely *no one* outside the circle can know that Crystal's a witch."

"Or that we are." Joanna paused. "Will be."

Crystal smiled. Although Rebecca's relationship with the magick was weak, she was eager to please and easily managed because of her pathetic desire to be one of the teenaged elite. Ordinarily, the insecure girl would not be an acceptable initiate, but lack of time had left her no choice. Willow, whose undeveloped abilities were much greater than the others', would offset Rebecca's magickal deficiencies.

Both girls would belong to her soon.

Anya and Michael had been instructed to take the trail when they arrived at the house. The directive she had implanted in Willow's mind would dissipate once they reached the clearing, where she would be cut off from any outside interference. If Buffy tried to follow, she would be stopped again, this time by forces more virulent than a few prickly vines.

It no longer mattered that the Slayer was aware of the new power in her territory. Once Willow pledged herself to the coven, the circle would be closed and impenetrable.

Overhead, the trees sang softly in a light breeze, their branches swaying in the dim light of the moon. The stench of decay teased Crystal's nostrils, reminding her of the valley and the ways of the first people. They had banished her, but as time passed, she had forgiven them. Their cruelty had tempered her to receive the power, and they had lived in harmony with the wilds, so unlike the civilizations of the past millennium. Some things, though, remained unchanged.

"What's going to happen?" Rebecca asked nervously.

"Nothing to worry about," Alicia said. "A little initiation ceremony and then—"

"We party." Joanna laughed softly.

The somber yet excited whispers of the nine walking behind Crystal brought back memories of others she had gathered—before she had had the wisdom to limit her childhood powers. Still, she had lived a longer life than usual in Memphis during the reign of Ramses the Great.

Egypt, 1296 B.C.

Shugra smiled, enjoying the drama her meaningless gestures and words created. The six girls she had chosen to favor watched in wonder as she wove her magick. Where there had been nothing but sand, she had brought forth an oasis.

"Tah gru da, Duhn che!" Shugra didn't laugh. Her anxious young companions would ask why and she didn't want to tell them she had simply cursed the once mighty and long dead Duhn. With a flair she was only beginning to perfect, she shot her arms up, then out, accelerating the life cycle of a date seed buried in the sand. The tree grew before their astonished eyes, eliciting squeals of delight.

"Do it again, Shugra!" Eyes shining, Yusa jumped up and down. All the girls were younger than her fourteen years and wore her mark with pride, but Yusa at ten had a particular innocence that pleased her. She had never been forced to exert her will on Yusa to command unwavering loyalty and obedience.

"I tire of making trees, Yusa." Laughing now, Shugra found a goat hair on her garment. Not even the great Ramses in all his glory knew that it contained the ingredients to conjure a thousand goats! She would settle for six. They would be female and supply milk and meat for the long siege ahead. She pushed thoughts of the impending trouble to the back of her mind and placed the hair on the ground. Mumbling gibberish in her native language and gesturing wildly, she infused the small, differentiated goat seeds in the hair with life.

The girls gasped, then cheered when six bleating kids materialized as though from nothing. Knowing they had little carefree time left, Shugra sent them to tend the herd by the spring, then sat to reflect under the palms. The desert was hot and she coaxed a breeze from the still air as she watched the girls romp with the rambunctious animals.

None of them were afraid.

But they should be.

Not of her, but of Akmontep, the priest devoted to Osiris, who had driven them into the desert.

She turned to stare across the endless expanse of the Sahara. Egypt, land without forests or snow, had seemed hostile and intolerably barren to her as a young child. She had rebelled against the burning sun at age five, growing a small date palm to maturity overnight and shrinking it again before dawn. Even these people, who believed that deities with animal heads walked the Earth, would fear a child with the power of a god.

Yet, she had flourished in a climate of superstitious acceptance as she had grown and learned. As with the primitive cultures before them, the Egyptian people were highly susceptible to ritual. She had invented clever ceremonies and used her magick sparingly to garner respect and establish a foundation of belief. Acts of kindness had kept the killing fear at bay. She had hoped to live to an old age here, for she was close to understanding how to ride the stream to the source. The dominant river of red magick was not within reach of this place or this time, but when it came again, she would be prepared.

But her studies would not be completed in this life-time.

Dust billowed on the horizon, signaling the coming of Akmontep and his soldiers.

Shugra stared at the dust cloud.

This time, jealousy would be her undoing. She had

not taken into account the priest's pride or his knowledge of cosmic mysteries. In service to Osiris, King of the Otherworld and ruler of the dead, Akmontep saw her as a threat to his esteemed position with his god and Pharaoh. He alone of the wise men she had encountered had recognized her unique life cycle. However, since her spirit did not journey through three thousand years of existence as all creatures of Earth, sea and sky before taking human form again, Akmontep called her an abomination.

"You are more than a witch!" Standing in the courtyard of her small home three growing seasons before, Akmontep had pointed an accusing finger. His voice had seethed with loathing. *"You are a primal evil that defies the natural and spiritual order of the universe!"*

She had denied it, but Akmontep knew her for the ancient being she was, knew her name—and he did not fear her power. So she would die again, but she would not surrender without a fight.

And the lesson would not be forgotten.

Rising, Shugra ran to play with her chosen one last time before she turned them into horses and set them free. Then she would summon the storm.

Willow walked behind Anya on a path cushioned with dry leaves and pine needles. She didn't consider disobeying the imperative that told her to follow, yet she was aware of certain, disturbing oddities. Like walking through the woods with Anya and Michael. That was just a little spooky. She wasn't as mad at Anya as she had been, but they weren't friends. Not do-the-danger, risk-your-life-'cause-Buffy-or-Xander—definitely

Oz, and maybe even Cordelia under certain circumstances—were-in-trouble-and-needed-help friends. So what was she doing here? She didn't know, but the Willow in Wonderland feeling got worse when she looked up.

The tops of the trees canted backward, like they were letting the moon shine through to light the path, which it did. Behind her, the trees groaned as they uprooted and moved to block the trail. Definitely strange. The vines bordering the path were growing into knotted mats so fast they hummed and creaked. She could almost feel the currents of magick gusting and wafting through the forest.

"There it is." Anya pointed ahead.

The trail fed into a clearing illuminated by the soft glow of enhanced moonlight. Fireflies swarmed on the perimeter, sparkling like glitter in the shadows. Lush moss, grass, and colorful clusters of wildflowers grew in profusion around the glen. Twelve large boulders formed a semicircle in the center.

Willow felt like a spectator in a dream, separated from reality by a mental haze as they drew closer. Several kids she knew or recognized from school were talking and laughing in small groups. She had seen a few of them with Michael and Anya at the Bronze last night, but now the ranks included Kari's friend, Rebecca, Craig Roberts, Greta Conor, and Lindsey Wayne. When Michael smiled and waved, most of them waved back. Joanna ran into the woods.

"Wait, Willow." Anya paused on the edge of the clearing, holding out her hand.

Willow stopped. When the brush and saplings on the

far side of the clearing whooshed aside, she thought maybe she should be turning on her heels and running away, but she didn't. She had to follow Anya. But it still didn't feel right, probably because Joanna emerged from the dark followed by Crystal Gordon.

Tall and regal with her blond hair slicked back and her eyes alight, the woman stood in the curve of the large stones. The long, wide sleeves of a white tunic worn over jeans slipped down as she raised her arms. The gathering fell silent as everyone quickly took seats on the rocks. Crystal's eyes settled on Willow as she lowered her arms.

"Okay, Willow. Let's go." Anya moved on, waving her to follow.

Willow obeyed, until she stepped into the clearing and her mind suddenly cleared. She halted, stunned. She had walked right into Crystal's trap.

"Hello, Willow." Crystal smiled. "I apologize for using a spell to bring you here, but it was necessary."

Willow swallowed hard. There was some comfort in knowing a spell and not stupidity had gotten her into this mess, but not much. She had seen the evidence of Crystal's magickal powers on her hike through the woods. Awesome and absolutely terrifying about summed it up. Giles and Xander would realize she was missing soon, but they had no idea where to look for her. Clear thinking and not doing anything stupid now was her best hope of getting out of whatever was going on. The first step seemed obvious. Find out the whatever.

"So, then—I guess you had a reason. I mean, if it was necessary, there must be . . . a reason. A good one.

And, well, I sure would like to know." Willow crossed her arms and lifted her chin. Maybe a defiant stance would negate the tremor in her voice.

"Of course." Crystal paused while Anya and Michael joined the others seated on the rocks.

One rock was unoccupied. Probably intended for her. Willow did a quick count. Twelve—including her—plus Crystal equaled thirteen. A coven?

Willow touched the leather pouch under her shirt, wondering if Crystal had zapped her before or after she cast the protection spell. Either way, escape didn't seem possible, not through the creeping forest. And if she fled now, she wouldn't be able to tell Giles what Crystal was planning. So it might be a good idea to stick around awhile—kind of an open-cover surveillance—especially since she probably didn't have a choice.

"I chose you, Willow, as I chose everyone here." Crystal swept her arm across the gathering. "You are of magick, charmed with a sleeping power and endowed with a sensitivity to the cosmic streams."

Nice to know for a novice wicca, but she wasn't so dense she could be moved by some heavy prose. Crystal was pushing her buttons. Trying to, anyway. Apparently, it had worked on the others. On guard, Willow tensed as the woman paused and closed her eyes.

"I am magick," Crystal intoned softly, "the heart and soul of the elements." Her eyes snapped open as she turned and extended her arm. "Water!"

Willow jumped as a suspended waterfall appeared. Foaming water flowed out of thin air, spilled to the ground, and pooled around Crystal's feet.

Okay, I'm impressed. Willow watched, unnerved but fascinated, as the demonstration continued.

"Earth and wind."

A small, swirling tornado whipped out of the opening in the trees, drawing leaves and dirt into its vortex. The ground rumbled and broke open as the dirt devil roared around the waterfall, leaving a low, cylindrical wall of perfectly fitted rocks in its wake. Leaves drifted to the ground as the wind slowed, unraveled and vanished. The pooling water was contained in the well.

"Fire!" Crystal spun back around, her eyes narrowed, her arms thrown forward. Red lightning burst from her hands igniting a fire where the bolts struck the ground. The flames remained when the lightning flashes faded.

Willow reeled with the realization that Giles's theories had just made the jump to hyper-fact. Crystal wasn't just a witch with a flair for theatrical tricks. She had primal magick at her fingertips.

Crystal relaxed her posture, smiling again as she surveyed the rapt teens sitting before her. "Please stand, Rebecca."

Rebecca flinched and glanced at Kari. Kari whispered something Willow couldn't hear, then gently nudged her reluctant friend. The girl slowly stood and hung her head.

"Look at me, Rebecca."

Don't do it. Willow caught her lower lip in her teeth when the girl looked up. Rebecca obviously didn't know that Crystal could make her do anything she wanted just by gazing into her eyes. And she wouldn't even remember! Willow swore to herself that no matter what happened, she would not meet the witch's stare.

"Pledge yourself to me and this coven, Rebecca Sullivan, and *become* the magick." Crystal spoke clearly, simply. The lack of mumbo-jumbo surprised Willow, but not as much as what she said next. "This you must do of your own free will."

Willow's spirits rose suddenly. No way she was going to freely commit to anyone—except Oz and her friends, of course. But especially not to a witch who had fried some poor guy to make a point and had tried to shake Buffy's confidence with a mental choke hold.

"Fuse your power with mine to call the river to the source and in return you will have what only I can give: beauty, poise, and the acceptance of your peers."

Rebecca just stared.

"Do you so pledge?" Crystal lowered her gaze, waiting.

"Yes, I do," Rebecca whispered, transfixed, as Crystal raised her head and released another bolt of blood-red primal magick. Rebecca staggered as the lightning struck her shoulder. She turned as the flare died, smoke rising from the burn in her flesh.

Willow didn't flinch when Crystal spoke her name and nervously met her eyes. She was standing several feet behind the ring of stones, but the power smoldering in the witch's gaze was not diminished with the extra distance. Even so, her resolve remained unshaken as Crystal repeated the pledge. She had probably promised to return Anya's necklace so her power to avenge wronged women would be restored. Most likely, Michael just wanted Amy the rat changed back into Amy the witch girl so he wouldn't be so alone, but there wasn't anything she wanted more than her independence and self-respect.

"Fuse your power with mine to call the river to the source and in return you will have what only I can give—"

Willow clenched her teeth, a "no" perched on the tip of her tongue. *Nothing Crystal offers can tempt me to join forces with evil . . .*

"—a cure for the moon malady that afflicts Oz."

Except maybe that.

Chapter 8

Buffy SCRAMBLED OUT OF THE CITROËN'S BACK SEAT carrying a bag of flashlights, cutting tools and weapons, and sundry spellcasting supplies Giles hadn't been able to fit into his kit.

Xander eyed the car with disdain. "Someone remind me to get spare keys for Oz's van tomorrow. Code-blue emergencies demand speeds in excess of thirty-five miles per hour."

"Would you please cease chattering, Xander, and get on with it," Giles said coldly.

"Right. Anya's car." Xander ran across the street.

Buffy did a quick reconnaissance of the woods along the drive. The moon was higher now, but no light broke through the trees. The house was invisible, concealed behind a wall of black that severed the driveway a few yards in from the street.

Willow is in there. Somehow, Crystal Gordon had gotten to her in spite of their precautions.

Buffy jumped when the lighted bulbs in the streetlights exploded, showering the road with sparks. "Not exactly a subtle 'get lost,' is it?"

"A bit disconcerting to be sure." Giles set down his kit and opened it. "Some light would help here, Buffy."

Buffy pulled a flashlight from her bag and tensed when she heard more breaking glass. She aimed the beam, saw Xander reaching into a compact car through a broken window. "Find something?"

"Willow's protection spell supplies." Xander trotted back with a brown paper bag. "Fair trade. I left a big rock on the back seat."

"Then she is here—somewhere." Giles motioned for Xander to drop the paper bag. "Those ingredients may prove useful."

"Pardon my lack of faith," Xander said, "but Willow's potion pouch didn't pack enough punch to protect her. How—"

"We've got company." The fine hairs on Buffy's neck bristled. She swept the flashlight across the drive, catching a moving shadow in the beam. The flashlight was in Xander's hand and her stake was drawn before she realized Angel was striding toward them, his dark brow furrowed, his eyes anxious. He raised his hand against the glare as Xander shone the light on his face.

"Well, well. What are you doing here, Dead Boy?"

Annoyed, Angel ignored Xander and addressed Buffy. "Willow's in trouble."

"We know. How much?" Buffy asked.

"Light, Xander!" Giles barked. When the beam darted to the bag, he removed a dog-eared spell book and opened it to a bookmarked page. "Please, Angel. Go on."

Angel lowered his gaze, jammed his hands into the pockets of his black duster, sighed. "I was patrolling the cemetery when she drove up with Anya and a boy."

"Michael," Buffy inserted.

"It didn't feel right. She looked dazed, so I tried to follow them—"

"Tried?" Xander asked sharply.

"The woods—" Angel shook his head.

"Are alive. I know. I lost an argument with some pushy vines a little while ago." Pocketing her stake, Buffy took the other flashlight, a knife, and a machete from her bag. She dropped the bag, gave Angel the knife, and added her light to Xander's.

No one spoke as Giles combined ingredients from Willow's bag and his kit, then separated the mixture into equal portions on four sets of overlapping leaves. He mumbled in Latin as he rolled each one, folded it over, and tied it with a length of leather thong.

"These are considerably more potent than Willow's spell," Giles said as he passed out the charms, "although not as popular now as they were in Europe during the fourteenth century."

"The odor of Black Death being more offensive." Xander held the damp, foul packet at arm's length. "Don't we lose the element of surprise if the enemy can smell us coming?"

"Surprise was never an option." Giles shoved his charm into his pocket and stooped down again.

Heat radiated from the organic mass, warming Buffy's palm before she slipped it into her pocket. Although Giles was a more experienced spellcaster than Willow, she didn't have a lot of confidence in the charm's power against Crystal Gordon's superior magick. "Any chance of backing this up with something else?"

"Yes, a Celtic binding spell to retard plant growth, which may give us a bit of an edge—if it works."

"And hopefully it won't take forever," Xander said. "For all we know, Willow may already be touring the toadstools as a worm."

"Doubtful, but do run along into the forest alone, if you must, Xander." Giles mixed a yellow powder and shimmering, green scales with gray flakes that smelled like rot in a small ceramic pot. The potion smoked when he added a pinch of sulfur and a lighted match.

"No, thanks. I'll wait for more stinky stuff." Xander gagged.

Buffy moved closer to Angel as Giles held up the pot and recited a Gaelic incantation.

"Ta' me' ag iarriadh ar Lugh, Tiarna na Solas. Let not the trees walk, nor the brier grow across the path of those who seek a lost soul. *Lugh, an airgeaduil lamh, Solas an bealachi!"*

The blackout faded into moonlight and shadow. The dark silhouette of the house at the end of the long drive dared them to enter.

"We're go for invasion," Xander said.

Giles threw his magick makings back into his bag and hoisted it to his shoulder. "Or we've been invited."

Crystal's attention was diverted from Willow when she felt the alarm transmitted through the matrix of vegetation standing sentinel. There were four intruders: the Slayer, the spellcaster, the demon and the boy. She sent a surge through the power lines to deliver an explosive message. She was aware of their presence.

She was also cautious and irritated.

They were defenseless against her power, but the pervasive great fear that had infected previous societies and had forced her to postpone the meld in her more recent incarnations was a sleeping monster in Sunnydale, too. She must not awaken it with foolish displays of power or an unexplained mass murder. The loss of Willow's close friends might disrupt the carefully cultivated harmony of the coven, raise questions better left unasked. Innocents except for Anya, the twelve had to participate in the ritual without reservation or fear. Although multiple deaths were an every night occurrence in the small town, the risk was unnecessary on the eve of achieving her goal.

Overconfidence was as much an enemy as the mob.

And perhaps, instilling a false sense of confidence in the enemy would forestall the greater threat.

The exercise might even prove amusing.

Crystal intercepted the librarian's call to Lugh and waved the darkness aside. As expected, the four quickly moved into the forest, no doubt intent on rescuing Willow. She turned back to the stricken girl, whose un-tapped abilities were vital.

"Do you so pledge?"

Willow hesitated. She had not expected to face a difficult decision. She was a white hat, one of the good guys and, well, that was all there was to it.

Except for saving Oz from turning into a werewolf three nights every month.

She loved him—not more than her parents or Buffy or Xander, just differently. She hadn't realized how much until after he caught her kissing Xander. When he wouldn't talk to her or accept an apology, she had felt cold and empty inside. Like nothing would ever be right again. Then he had forgiven her. No conditions, no lingering grudge or mistrust. He just loved her and missed her and that was all there was to that. How could she deny him a cure?

As Willow stared into Crystal's compelling brown eyes, she knew that the witch *could* cure him. Her ability to control the elements was enhanced by an understanding of how the universe worked. She could easily expunge the mysterious infection from Oz's cells.

But will she?

Probably not.

Willow had learned a lot working so closely with Giles over the past three years, and it had been proven over and over again that evil couldn't be trusted. While good derived power from truth, the power of evil was based on lies. It was that simple. The others either didn't know or couldn't accept that Crystal had made false promises to win their loyalty. Even if she made good on them, the cost would be infinitely greater than the reward.

If it was up to Oz, she was sure he'd rather be a werewolf with a girlfriend who hadn't sold out to evil, especially not for his sake. That was one of the reasons she loved him.

"Do you so pledge, Willow Rosenberg?" Crystal asked again, her voice harsher, her gaze narrowing.

"No." Willow tensed, expecting to die, hoping she didn't, knowing there was nothing she could do.

Crystal stared, unmoving.

Eleven pairs of disbelieving teenage eyes looked at her, at Crystal, back at her. Apparently, no one else had even thought of turning down the witch's offer.

Willow averted her gaze. Seconds stretched into a minute and no bolts of red lightning zinged out of the sky to turn her into charcoal. *Okay, that's a plus, but— why not?* And why hadn't Crystal simply tampered with her mind and body while she was still looking at her? Or for that matter, what stopped Crystal from just rearranging her molecular structure to transform her into a snake or a goat or something?

Maybe because the witch is keeping her options open, in case I change my mind?

"Are you crazy, Willow?" Anya asked. "I don't know what's wrong with Oz, but Crystal can fix it."

Alicia nodded. "My dad has cancer. The chemo is . . . so hard, but—" She started to cry.

Willow's temper flared. Crystal's callous use of Alicia's pain was unconscionable. "Don't you all under—"

"Grah du stit!" Crystal's dark, compelling eyes flashed.

"—dastn twah esh—" Willow stopped talking. She was thinking clearly, but her mouth was suddenly spouting gibberish. Okay, so she had a tendency to babble and, no, she didn't always make sense, but this—this was *babbling*. Like in nobody-would-be-able-to-understand-her-at-all babbling. How could she get a Ph.D. if she couldn't talk?

A more immediate crisis overrode the problems of being a permanent aphasiac. Either she was gliding backward without moving her legs or the forest was growing around her.

"Willow has made her choice," Crystal said evenly. "She's . . . dismissed."

The clearing vanished behind a mass of leaves, vines, and branches as the forest wove a dark cocoon around her.

"I gotta tell you, Giles, I didn't think your stink bomb charms would work." Xander shone his flashlight down a worn trail leading deeper into the woods from the back of the house. "But apparently they do *and* they're ecologically friendly. Completely biodegradable."

"This environment is *too* friendly, if you ask me," Buffy said. Nothing bizarre had happened, grown, or otherwise hindered their advance up the driveway or search around the house. She had vetoed breaking in since the building was obviously unoccupied. Witches liked to play in the woods. Or in Crystal's case, play *with* the woods.

"Yes, well—" Giles flicked his light to the sides of the trail. "I'm not convinced the charms are responsible for the absence of obstacles."

"I agree." Angel brought up the rear. Buffy felt his tension, sensed the vampire hovering just below the surface. "This witch *is* the woods. She's everywhere. Watching, waiting."

Xander's head jerked around. "So it's not just me? Having a severe case of scare anticipation?"

"The suspense *is* a little thick. It just can't be this easy." Buffy glanced at the bright moon peeking through the branches overhead. *One night short of full.* Major magick rituals required a full moon more often than not. She didn't know why, but if Crystal was playing by those rules, they had one more day to figure out the end game.

"Hold up a minute." Angel stopped, looked behind him, around him. "We're going in circles."

"Are you certain?" Giles yanked his snagged jacket off a branch.

"Just a feeling," Angel said. "A strong one."

"There's a lot to be said for feral instinct," Xander said.

Buffy drew closer to Angel. No music cued the woods, but something had just changed. She glanced back the way they had come. The path was overgrown with weeds and vines. "Hey, guys—"

"Buffy!" Angel threw his weight against her, hurling them both off the path as a massive tree uprooted and fell.

"Xander!" Giles snapped. "Get back! Back!"

With his arms clamped around Buffy, Angel rolled

clear as the trunk crashed to the ground, dragging dead branches and streaming vines with it.

Buffy lay still for a moment, the wind knocked out of her.

"Buffy?" Angel moved his weight off her and squinted when she raised the flashlight still clutched in her hand.

"I'm okay. Thanks." She recovered quickly, every nerve startled to attention. She tried to rise and couldn't. Vines had already braided themselves into her hair and wound around her ankles and waist, pinning her. "I can't get up—"

Angel ripped the fast growing briers from his arms, then attacked the stems holding Buffy, cutting the lifeline to their roots with his knife. The tension eased around her legs, but she couldn't lift her head.

"My hair!" She winced as the knife whacked at the vegetation around her head, reminding herself that butchered hair grew back. When she felt the vines give, she pulled free and scrambled to her feet. Her bag dangled from her shoulder. The flashlight and machete still clutched in her hands kept her from touching her hair. She didn't want to know. "Giles and Xander?"

"Other side of the tree." Angel continued to hack at the frenzied vines growing back from cut root systems. A wall of tightly woven shrubs and tree branches separated them from the trail beyond the tree.

"Giles! Xander!" When no one answered, Buffy called again, but the sound was deadened in the compact jungle of new growth. "We're cut off. Any ideas?"

"Get out of here and hope they do, too—if we can't find them." Angel was pushed backward when the girth of a small tree branch swelled to enormous size in front of him. Buffy raised the machete and slashed without hesitation, severing a broken branch from the horizontal tree trunk an instant before it jammed into his back.

"Close call with self-destruct," she explained when he shot her a startled look. "Be careful."

"Right." Angel nodded. "Let's go."

"Which way?" Densely knotted brush and timber surrounded them. Above, a new canopy of leaves and vines blotted out the moon.

"Pick a direction." Angel held his knife ready.

"That way." Buffy pointed to the right, where Giles and Xander had been before the tree crashed. The sound of rustling leaves and cracking wood straight ahead drew her gaze and the light. A hole appeared and widened.

Angel hesitated. "I'd rather blaze our own trail."

"Me, too, but—" A vine shot from the wall by Buffy's side, then retreated like an automatic cord winding back into a vacuum cleaner. She frowned, puzzled, until she remembered Giles's protection charm. She pulled the leafy wad from her front pocket and held it near the barrier. The twined tendrils and woody stalks recoiled. "Now it works. Sort of."

"Good. Maybe it'll help us get out of here."

Nodding, Buffy touched the charm to the fallen tree. The brush overgrowing the trunk writhed and withdrew. "This way."

Using the machete to speed up the process, Buffy hacked a hole in the thick labyrinth and crawled through to the other side. She paused in the opening to pan the eerie scene with her flashlight. Moonlight shone through translucent mists that swirled in frantic eddies around trees infested with hanging moss, snakes, and huge spider webs. The forest floor had turned into a swamp.

Giles's spell bag was hooked on a twisted branch within arm's reach. A flashlight bobbing on the muck slowly sank.

Quicksand.

There was no sign of Giles or Xander.

Blood seeped from several cuts on Willow's hands when she finally clawed free of the woody cage. She jumped out before it grew back around her, having no idea how much time had passed. It felt like hours, but probably wasn't. The only good thing to come out of the experience, aside from still being alive, was finding out that Crystal's incoherence spell had worn off. To keep mentally on track while she dug out, she had managed to sing a medley of songs from the Dingoes's play list without missing a syllable. Except when she couldn't remember the words. *Just like Devon,* she thought with a smile.

She couldn't see the clearing, which was weird but okay. Getting back to the library would be a lot easier if she wasn't being followed. As she picked her way through the moonlit woods, she reviewed what she knew so she wouldn't dwell on the eyes watching her from high perches or the vines that snapped at her feet.

Crystal was gathering a coven of teenagers with witch potential, but the circle wasn't complete. One of the rocks was still vacant. She was extremely powerful, but she wasn't all-powerful. She needed the combined power of the coven to call the river to the source, which might be the hypothetical source of all magick Giles had mentioned. Only it wasn't so hypothetical anymore. Crystal didn't just draw on the red lightning of primal magick. She channeled it with a natural ease— like it was part of her.

"*. . . and become the magick.*"

Willow didn't want to go where another leap in logic led. If Crystal made direct contact with the source, would she *become* magick?

Something growled in the darkness. Being threatened by a wild animal wasn't the distraction Willow would have picked, but it took her mind off the dreadful possibility that a wicked super witch was plotting to corner the market on magick. She moved faster, ignoring the gnarled branches and vines that grabbed at her clothes. An owl swooped in from behind her, grazing her head with its talons and tearing out strands of her hair. She ran then, ducking low tree limbs, breaking through spider webs strung across her path, and stumbling over massive tree roots that popped out of the ground. She ran until her legs ached, then stopped, out of breath and hopelessly lost.

She collapsed on a rock, too tired to go on without a break. She had taken the route of least resistance, weaving through the trees without paying attention to direction. Instead of moving toward the street, she may have plunged deeper into the vast expanse of forest. She couldn't tell. Everything looked the same and the only sounds were the ominous slitherings, creakings, groanings, and rumblings of the agitated flora and fauna in the bewitched forest.

"Don't panic. Think! You've been in the woods before." The clearly spoken words soothed her jangled nerves. Crystal had scrambled the signals from her brain to her mouth and she felt—violated. She had been terrorized by a lot of demons, but none of them had messed with her personal physical functions, except for threatening her life. No wonder Buffy had been so freaked about the anxiety attack that wasn't an anxiety attack.

Willow stood up and rested her hands on her hips. She was also tired of being pushed around by a bunch of plants. "Hey! How do I get out of here?"

The ground vibrated. A vine with a diameter larger than her arm broke through the dirt and circled her ankle. Willow screamed when her feet were pulled out from under her, wishing she hadn't asked. Trees and brush whipped past in a blur as the vine dragged her over the ground.

For a plant, it was making remarkably good time.

Xander tripped over a root, almost pulling Giles down with him when he dropped to his hands and knees. He had been clinging to the librarian's jacket so they wouldn't get separated in the dark. His flashlight, along with the rest of their equipment and supplies, had been abandoned right after Buffy and Angel had disappeared and the woods decided to redecorate. He liked the freaky forest motif a lot better than the ghastly swamp theme.

"Xander?" Giles paused.

"Right here." Xander was on his feet and moving forward before he became the squashed innards of a tree sandwich. Behind and around them, the forest steadily closed ranks. They had been herded like sheep since escaping the bog, forced to keep moving ahead of the timber compactor. "Watch your step, Giles. Call me paranoid, but I *know* that root tripped me on purpose."

"Yes, it probably did." Giles faltered as Xander grabbed back onto his coat. "Our witch has a nasty sense of humor."

"A little game of cat and mouse before the kill?" Xander had avoided the question, but they had been wandering too long without getting anywhere. Although Giles's spells hadn't been all that effective, the familiar accented voice added a calming touch of reality to the surreal circumstances.

"I don't believe so, no." Giles pressed on with a sigh. "Although, I'm not sure why. It's quite within her power to dispose of us without much ado."

"That doesn't ado a lot for my weakening hold on emotional stability." Something zipped over his foot. Xander deliberately didn't try to imagine what.

"Yes, well, if we survive this little adventure, it may be because she has nothing to gain from our deaths and, perhaps, something to lose." Giles batted away an overhead vine. "Until we have reason to think otherwise, it's in our best interests to believe we're simply being . . . detained."

Which is fine for us, Xander thought, *but doesn't bode well for Willow—unless Buffy and Angel have found her. Please find her.*

Where the hell are they anyway?
And what the hell was that?

"Giles?" Xander slapped at a branch clawing at his shoulder. Another branch descended and twined around his other arm. "I think there's a good reason to think otherwise!"

Xander lost his grip on Giles's jacket when he was hoisted off the ground. "Hey!"

The librarian's hand clamped around his leg. A thick vine looped around his chest. Pulled from above and below, he wondered if he was about to find out what it felt like to be drawn and quartered.

"Xander! I can't hang on!" Giles strained to keep his grip as Xander was pulled higher. He stretched, standing on his toes, his hand sliding.

"Please! Don't!" When Giles let go, Xander was whipped upward. His stomach followed a second later and almost caught up before the branches drew back and threw him. He sailed through the air like a stone out of a giant slingshot.

Buffy swung the machete mechanically. Since they had been turned back by the swamp, she and Angel had chopped and charmed their way through what felt like half a mile of stubborn vegetation. Her tank top clung to her sweating skin and she knew her hair was a rat's nest of cobwebs and brush. The ends were a little ragged where Angel's knife had struck, but at least she didn't have a mangled cut.

"Are we moving in circles again, Angel?"

"Nope." He looked back, a slight smile visible in the moonlight that suddenly streamed through the trees. He pushed aside a curtain of vines. A car sped past on the dark street beyond.

"We're out!" Buffy dashed through the opening and sank on the ground. She was tired. Not a surprise considering that the moon had arced to the far side of the night sky. They had been beating back the forest for hours. All the parked cars were gone, too, except for the Citroën.

Angel dropped Giles's spell kit and hunkered down. He frowned when he caught her staring at the bag. "We can't go back in after them, Buffy."

"I know." She glared at the woods. Giles, Xander and Willow were in there somewhere and she couldn't help. They couldn't even find them. Angel's vampire strength and her Slayer endurance plus a little luck had made it possible for them to escape, but physical ability couldn't counter the dark magick that controlled the forest.

Crystal Gordon's magick.

"She let us escape, didn't she?" Buffy sighed.

"Seems so." Angel jumped up again. "Did you hear that?"

"What?" Buffy got to her feet and into a fighting stance. Then she heard it: a drawn out, muffled cry of alarm. She jumped back when something big crashed through the trees.

Xander belly-flopped on the ground at her feet.

Giles followed a moment later, executing a deft tuck-and-roll as he hit dirt.

"Am I dead yet?" Xander moaned.

"Not quite." Buffy knelt beside him. "Glad to see you again. Any broken bones?"

"I hurt too much to tell."

Angel gave Giles a hand up and steadied him until his legs stopped shaking.

"Thank you. I'm quite all right." With a curt nod, Giles adjusted his askew glasses, stepped back, and self-consciously brushed himself off.

"Any sign of Willow?" Buffy asked.

"No, none." Rubbing an elbow, Giles limped toward the woods. He didn't go in, but stood staring as though he could will the young wicca to appear.

"Anya's car is gone," Buffy said, stepping up beside him. "Maybe Willow's still with her."

Wincing, Xander pulled himself into a sitting position. "She's better off lost, if you ask me."

"Just a minute—" Cocking his head to listen, Angel moved along the tree line away from Giles.

"Looking for a midnight critter snack?" Xander quipped.

"Shh!" Buffy inhaled sharply when she saw a dark form stumble out of the woods and collapse. "Willow!"

Angel reached her first. Cradling her head, he gently brushed her auburn hair off her dirt-streaked face.

"Hey, guys—" Willow smiled slowly as Buffy, Giles, and Xander crowded around. "What are you doing here?"

"Looking for you," Xander said. "Why else would we brave the horrors of Godzilla woods?"

"A vine ran away with me." Willow grimaced. "I think my back is one big, black and blue bruise."

"Speaking of unusual marks—" Xander leaned forward and flicked her hair back. "You didn't happen to acquire a new tattoo, did you?"

Willow shook her head and pulled down the collar of her tee shirt. No burns marred her white skin.

Giles drew Buffy back slightly and whispered in her ear. "Not to alarm, but she may still be under a spell."

Buffy nodded, pushing aside her despair for her friend.

"I found out stuff, though." Using Angel as a brace, Willow struggled to sit up.

"About Crystal?" Buffy asked.

Willow's eyes widened with excitement. "I think Ractlys nawts ot eakt ervo cimkag!"

Chapter 9

"HERE THEY COME." ANYA GLANCED INTO THE REAR-
view mirror as Giles's old wreck drove into the school
parking lot and stopped by a blue van.

Crystal sat in the passenger seat calmly staring out
the window she had fixed with a curt incantation and a
casual wave. *Good. The vampire is no longer with
Giles and his young friends.*

"Shouldn't we duck down or something?" Anya
asked.

"They can't see us."

"Oh. Cool." Anya sat back with a wistful sigh. "I
wouldn't mind being able to spy on someone without
being seen."

"Like Xander?" Crystal raised an eyebrow. Since her
demon persona, Anyanka, had waged a reign of terror
against men for a thousand years, Anya's crush on the
gangly boy was amusing, but not a problem. The girl

149

had tasted power and wanted it back, no matter the cost to her or anyone else. Her determination made her trustworthy—to a point. After they finished her errands, Anya would be sent home with implanted instructions not to see or speak to anyone except her family and Crystal before returning to the clearing tomorrow night.

Like the others.

"Xander Harris? No! How could you even think—" Anya exhaled. "Is it that obvious?"

Crystal winked. "Don't worry. Your secret is as safe with me as mine is with you."

"That's pretty safe." Anya's gaze followed the tired looking troop toward the back door into the library. "Are you sure Willow won't say anything?"

"Absolutely."

Anya leaned toward the windshield. "Xander's limping."

"I'm not surprised, the way you kids dance."

"Dancing, huh." Anya's eyes narrowed. "After tomorrow, he won't want to dance with anyone but me."

Crystal smiled, nodded. Anya had no idea that Xander was still alive or that her own fate had just now been determined by her interest in him.

An unusual find because of her demon past, Anya's experience and perspective added dimensions to her personality that appealed to Crystal. In nineteen thousand years, only Chit and Herostratus had been caring companions and she was not immune to loneliness. She had seriously considered preserving Anya's free will and personality after the ritual, to create a surrogate daughter who was totally devoted and deserving of reward. However, as she had just confirmed, Anya's affections for Xander were too strong and would always taint Anya's feelings toward her. Crystal abandoned the idea without a qualm.

After tomorrow, nothing Anya thinks or wants will matter. Her essence will be absorbed into the source, her will dissolved, and her soul enslaved.

Regrettable, but necessary.

"They're inside," Anya said.

Crystal nodded again and continued to wait. In certain situations, timing was everything. She gave them a couple minutes, then focused on the structure that confined the werewolf. If the beast maimed or killed someone, Willow's precious Oz would take the blame.

"Okay, Anya. You can go home and get some rest now."

Buffy trailed the others between the stacks on the upper library tier. She felt like she had just run the Boston Marathon—twice. Xander had developed a definite limp, and Giles kept rubbing his elbows and knees. Being flung from the treetops played havoc with the joints. With dawn imminent, Angel had gone to scout the underground hangouts for any street talk about the new witch in town, and Willow was doing her best to fill in the blanks.

"But you can shake your head and nod." Xander glanced over his shoulder at Willow. "To answer questions."

"I guess, but what if . . . you-know-who—" Willow cringed like she expected to be struck down on the spot. "—thought about that. What if my head falls off or . . . or my neck freezes stiff if I try to answer a question about—you know."

"I guess a test is out of the question then?"

Willow cuffed Xander's arm. "Hey! Maybe typing would work! I could get along with less than ten fingers—if I had to. But I'd rather not."

She was upset. *More upset than she's letting on,* Buffy realized. On the drive back from the woods they had discovered that Willow could talk just fine as long as she wasn't talking about Crystal Gordon or anything associated with Crystal Gordon's plans. So they didn't know exactly what had happened to her besides being dragged by a racing vine.

Cordelia had fallen asleep at the computer and jerked awake as Xander clomped down the stairs.

"Sleeping on the job, Cordy?" Xander wagged a finger in her face. "Any more of that and Giles will dock your pay."

"Dock? You mean *not* pay?" The blood drained from Cordelia's face as she turned to Giles. "You wouldn't—I mean, if I was *getting* paid."

"No, I wouldn't." Giles tossed his keys onto the study table and smoothed back his tousled hair.

Buffy trudged to the end of the table. Aside from needing a shower and some sleep, she was more worried than she wanted anyone to know, too. Unless Giles pulled a miracle out of the dusty pages of his trusty tomes, the big, bad witch had the upper hand.

"What happened to you guys, anyway?" Cordelia's nose wrinkled with disgust. "You look like disaster movie extras and smell worse."

"You should have caught a whiff *before* we threw

Giles' charms out the window." Swinging the spell bag, Xander started toward the office.

Willow eased into the chair beside Cordelia. "How's Oz?"

"Quiet. He's been sleep—"

Buffy idly glanced at the book cage. It took a moment for the meaning of what she saw to register in her brain when the cage door bars turned fuzzy and vanished.

The werewolf didn't hesitate. It blinked once, then charged.

"Loose!" Xander held the spell bag up like a shield as two hundred pounds of enraged wolfman sprang toward him. "Red alert!"

"Giles! Gun!" Buffy put her aches and pains on hold and threw herself into the snarling wolf.

The librarian bolted behind the book counter.

The wolf roared as he went down. Buffy couldn't hold him and jumped clear before his teeth took a chunk out of her shoulder.

"Coming through!" Xander dropped the bag and lunged for the weapons cabinet in the open book cage.

"Xander!" Cordelia shrieked. "Look out!"

The infuriated werewolf caught Xander around the waist and heaved him across the room.

Willow was on her feet, eyes wide and panicked as Buffy tackled the werewolf around the ankles.

"Giles!" The Slayer dropped the beast as Xander hit the swinging doors and slid into a dazed heap on the floor. Bouncing back to her feet, Buffy snapped off a kick as the wild thing righted itself and sprang. It staggered back a step.

Giles slipped a dart into the tranq gun.

"Okay, furry guy. Eyes on me." Buffy clenched her fists, every muscle primed. The beast charged as Giles fired and fell when a dart struck its side. Buffy sagged. "Is everyone okay?"

"Fine—for a human basketball." Xander rose on unsteady legs and leaned against the wall. "Doesn't anything use an old-fashioned punch to the jaw anymore?"

Giles reloaded the rifle. "Manacles and chains, Buffy. In the weapons locker."

"Got it."

Giles aimed the rifle toward the downed werewolf, ready to fire again if the beast stirred. "I believe a protective ward around the library is in order, Willow. On the off-chance it might dampen the effects of Crystal's magick."

Willow nodded, breathed deeply. "Nadia fo eth oomn, dnib, uh—tseab . . ." She paled. "Oh, no."

"Oh, boy." Buffy froze in the cage, chains dangling from her hands.

Cordelia frowned. "What kind of spell was *that?*"

Stunned, Willow shook her head.

"Let's secure Oz first, shall we?" Giles pointedly looked at Cordelia. "Then we'll address Willow's . . . difficulty."

Difficulty is hardly the word for it, Buffy thought as she clamped the heavy manacles around the werewolf's wrists and ankles. A speech impediment that kept Willow from casting spells was a class five disaster, considering the current crisis.

With the werewolf chained and sleeping off the drug,

Giles entered the book cage to get the Egyptian text he had not been able to access earlier.

Still in shock, Willow hadn't said a word.

Xander broke the heavy silence when Giles joined them at the table. "Charades or twenty questions?"

"Not now, Xander." The book was left untouched while Giles questioned Willow, hoping for clues that would narrow the scope of the research. His first queries were phrased carefully to determine her ability to answer without actually speaking. To Buffy's immense relief, shakes and nods did not have any harmful side effects and she could type, to a degree. The printed words became jumbled if she was too specific, but they tended to be anagrams and were easily deciphered. After an hour of deft probing, Willow had confirmed many of their assumptions and contributed new information.

Crystal Gordon not only had ready command of primal magick, she intended to take control of all magick everywhere at the universal source.

Of equal importance, however, was the possibility that the witch was not as invincible as she appeared.

"Why not?" Xander asked first. "Or did I miss an important nod?"

"Sebuace hes tle su og." Willow scowled. "Rats."

"I'll, uh, handle it." Giles smiled tightly. "As I suggested while Xander and I were stumbling about in the woods, Crystal may have something to lose. Perhaps she fears raising any alarms that might trigger mob retaliation from the town's residents."

Xander sat back. "Excessive death is SOP in Sunnydale. It's a surprise when people *don't* die."

"Nevertheless," Giles went on, "she's apparently decided not to risk it, which indicates that she's vulnerable."

"Vulnerable? With all that power?" Cordelia scoffed. "I don't think so."

Buffy focused on Giles. Brow knit, glasses off, staring at the top of the table. His mind was working at full throttle to find the chink in Crystal's armor.

"No, it makes sense." Rising, Giles shifted his stare to the floor as he paced through the deductive process. "Crystal can't draw the stream, if you will, that's connected to the well of magick alone. As powerful as she is, she's not powerful *enough*. She'll have to draw on all her resources, her own magick and the coven's. The proximity to the Hellmouth may also be a factor."

"But the coven isn't complete because Willow didn't join," Buffy said.

" 'Just say no.' Good advice." Willow squirmed. "Not always as easy to follow as it sounds."

Buffy wondered what Crystal had offered Willow that was so hard to turn down. She didn't ask. Willow would tell her when she was ready.

"Yes," Giles said softly, "but you may have disrupted things more than you realize, Willow."

"Good. Because I would really hate it if I had lost a chance to—" Willow faltered, regrouped. "—and, uh, not being able to cast spells for nothing."

"You're still on our side, Will." Xander's smile was sincere. "That's not nothing."

"All her initiates are young, more susceptible to her psychological machinations than adults would be." Giles rambled on, locked into the natural flow of his thoughts. "And I would think she's already identified and conscripted those teenagers with the greatest magickal ability—Willow being exceptional in that regard."

"*Was* exceptional," Willow said glumly.

"*Still* exceptional." Xander raised a finger for emphasis. "A tongue-tied spellcaster *has* to be unique."

Giles hesitated, a small twitch tugging at the corner of his mouth. "The point is that she probably can't replace Willow with someone possessing the same talent or potential. Not on such short notice."

"Then I don't see the problem. We just make sure nobody shows up at the party." Cordelia grinned, pleased. "We have the guest list."

"I rather doubt the solution is that simple." Giles sighed. "Although free will is apparently required for membership in the coven and the ritual, Willow was forced to attend tonight's gathering by an implanted imperative. Crystal would certainly take similar measures to ensure everyone's presence tomorrow night."

"Tomorrow?" Buffy cocked her head, curious. "Because there's a full moon?"

"Yes, of course." A puff of dust wafted from the old book Giles flipped open. "Female power is strongest during that phase."

"I knew there had to be a reason." Dried mud flaked off Buffy's arm as she leaned forward. "So what do we do about it?"

"I don't know." Giles squinted as he carefully turned yellowed pages, oblivious to the four pairs of eyes staring at him until Xander loudly cleared his throat. "Yes?"

"Not that I don't like watching you read, Giles, but

I could really use a shower." Grit and debris fell onto the table when Xander combed his fingers through his hair.

"Oh, well—yes, you do, I suppose." Giles waved a dismissal. "Some sleep would be in order as well. You'll need to be awake and alert tomorrow night."

"I'm ready." Cordelia stood up. "Who's driving?"

"I am. If Oz doesn't wake up while I'm trying to cop his keys." Xander headed for the book cage, cautiously.

"What about you, Giles?" Buffy looked at him askance. "Dirt does nothing for your proper British image."

"My reputation will survive until morning, I'm sure," Giles said dryly. "Someone has to stay with Oz, and I have some preliminary research to get past before we can devise a defense or, preferably, an aggressive offense."

"We're out of here, then. Let's go, Will."

"Just a moment—" Giles stood up and nervously folded his arms. "I think it would be wise if Willow spent tonight with you, Buffy." His gaze shifted to Willow. "Just as a precaution in case Crystal planted other suggestions in your mind."

Willow gasped. "No! I—oh. Well, I did look at her a few times, but—" She winced. "I guess I wouldn't remember if she hit me with the old evil eye, would I?"

"Probably not, since you don't remember the last time," Giles said.

"Come on, Will." Buffy smiled impishly. "I won't let you get away with anything. Promise."

"Good, because . . . if Lacstry's ginnlanp to use *me* as some kind of secret weapon, well, I'm going to be really . . . mad." Willow's eyes flashed when she realized what she'd said. "I *am* mad. And not happy."

"We'll be right back." Willow slammed the door of Oz's van, then stuck her head back in the window. "Five minutes. I'm traveling light."

"Better keep the motor running." Buffy stood beside her, scanning the street and neighboring yards. "Just in case."

"Done." Xander nodded and shifted into park. "Parking in this town without the engine running is like hitching a ride to the undertaker's."

"I'd stay with you, but I've got my orders," Buffy said. "Sorry, Willow."

"Don't be sorry, Buffy." Willow shuddered. Crystal could have programmed her to sabotage their efforts to stop her rendezvous with the source—or maybe to commit some horrible crime. Just *knowing* the witch could control her mind had her imagining little evil synaptic impulses lining up to ambush her brain.

"We're wasting sack time here." Xander leaned over to roll up the window and lock the door.

Willow followed Buffy up the walk. Cordelia had insisted on being dropped off first, but she had also promised to guard Oz again tomorrow night—as long as they barricaded the open door, doubled the chains, and tranquilized him before they left.

"Guess everyone's asleep," Buffy said. No light shone through the Rosenbergs' windows.

Standard procedure, Willow thought as she unlocked the door. She came in so late so often, she could find her way around in the dark without stumbling over anything. "Just stick close," she whispered. "And hope no-body rearranged the furniture today."

"Right behind you."

With Buffy on her heels, Willow tiptoed into her bedroom. After they were inside and the door was closed, she flipped the light switch.

Roused by the light, Amy stirred in her cage. She sat up on her haunches, front legs dangling and whiskered nose twitching.

Buffy shielded her eyes against the glare. "Guess we woke her up, huh?"

"She's probably hungry." Willow opened the cage door to remove the rat's food dish and paused. Michael had probably sold his soul so Amy wouldn't be a rat anymore. He should have known better. Willow was certain Crystal Gordon had no intention of fulfilling any of her promises.

Amy would be a rat until Willow figured out how to change her back.

And Oz would always be a werewolf.

Unless Crystal Gordon succeeds in melding with the source of all magick tomorrow night.

Then we'll just be dead.

"Yes, Willow. Oz is still out cold." Setting his cup on the desk, Giles sank into his chair. Willow had called from the Summers's house to let him know she and Buffy had arrived without incident.

He heard Joyce banging pots in the background. The noise ceased and he assumed she was cooking and not expressing anger or frustration. Buffy's domestic diffi-culties had dwindled now that Joyce knew about her daughter's irrevocable status as the Slayer. He did wish the attractive but headstrong woman was as understanding about his role as Buffy's adviser and friend. His hands-on association with the fight against evil put rather an uncomfortable strain on the relationship.

"Yes, I'll check his water." He rubbed his forehead, picked up the cup and sipped. "Actually, I am making progress. She's, uh, been defeated before. Details later. Good night, Willow."

Giles hung up and leaned back. He *had* made remarkable progress during the past hour, beginning with the Egyptian account about a young sorceress with incredible control over the forces of nature.

"Deep thoughts. Good ones, I hope." Xander stood in the doorway with a sleeping bag under his arm.

Giles started. "Xander, I wasn't expecting you. Is something wrong? I just spoke to Willow—"

"Not a thing." Xander shrugged. "Well, nothing beyond an acute fear of being electrocuted. I pulled up a lawn and couldn't sleep. Red lightning phobic."

"Yes, well, uh—here is fine." Xander's home life was far from ideal, but Giles didn't pry.

Xander tossed his gear by the book counter and settled into the chair in front of the desk. "So, judging by the look of total concentration, I'd say you're onto something."

Giles eyed him over the rim of his glasses. "I have uncovered an intriguing historical correlation. More than one, actually."

"I'm all ears." Xander propped an elbow on the desk, his hand cupping his chin. "Once upon a time . . ."

Giles smiled. "Yes, well, there was a priest in the

court of Ramses II called Akmontep and a common girl with unusual magickal powers, who was making rather a name for herself among the people. Akmontep believed the girl was a reincarnated primitive witch, a primal evil in human form that had acquired her power when history was being recorded on cave walls."

"Reincarnated?"

Giles nodded. "The Egyptians were the first to believe that the human soul was immortal and introduced the concept of reincarnation. It was thought that every soul cycled through the lower life forms before returning as a human in a few thousand years."

"So they built the pyramids and took everything they owned to the grave—like a nest egg for when they returned?" Xander asked, then added. "Not realizing they'd be robbed blind before they got back."

"Yes," Giles agreed, "but Akmontep wasn't concerned with the afterlife, but with his position and reputation as a master magician with Pharaoh. He was jealous of the girl's power and drove her into the desert. She survived a month's long siege in an oasis before he killed her."

"And this is relevant?"

"Quite relevant." Giles met Xander's intent gaze. "Akmontep only succeeded after the sorceress had been weakened by the prolonged use of her magick, an enormous energy drain. Still, she had defended herself against his army with monstrous storms comprised of sand, wind, rain . . . and red lightning."

Xander straightened suddenly.

"Hundreds died," Giles continued, "including the six

female children who wore her brand—infinity enclosed by a circle. Her name was Shugra."

"And how long ago was this?"

"Roughly thirteen hundred B.C.," Giles said.

Xander frowned. "You're thinking Crystal Gordon might be this Shugra person?"

"I think it's possible, yes." Giles drank his tea slowly. His mind raced as he connected the dots. He would have discounted the idea of a primal witch who had been returning periodically with her original personality intact for thousands of years—except he had found supporting evidence. "The same circled infinity brand was found on the dead followers of a woman called Shugra at Ephesus over nine hundred years later."

"Ephesus. Where the temple burned?"

Giles nodded and glanced at an open volume on the desk in front of him. *Chesler's Translations: Ancient Mystic Journals and Letters* contained a more detailed account of the red lightning phenomena. "A witness wrote a description of the burning of Artemis's temple to a friend accomplished in the black arts. He had heard rumors about a witch called Shugra, who was secretly plotting to usurp the goddess' prestige and power."

Xander waited, tense and silent.

Giles understood. The implications were as frightening as they were promising. "Diomesos saw Shugra and Herostratus together when the red lightning was conjured from a clear sky and set against the temple. After a small cult following was killed, Artemis's priests managed to turn the lightning back on Herostratus. He was saved when the frenetic bolts savagely attacked and killed Shugra."

"Wait a minute." Xander leaned forward. "She got zapped by her own magic?"

"Apparently." Giles rose to make himself another cup of tea. "Although Herostratus was credited with the destruction of the temple, I'm certain the power came solely from Shugra—and that the Shugra of Ephesus was the same entity Akmontep killed on the Sahara."

"But she *was* killed," Xander stated for clarification. "Again."

"And returned—again." Giles poured hot water over a fresh teabag. "Shugra reincarnates in the traditional sense—in a new body that's born of human parents and must mature. However, she retains her original identity and memories. I suspect she's been reborn several times since 356 B.C., but I've only found one reference that remotely connects a later reincarnation to Ephesus. Tea?"

Xander shook his head.

"This is a somewhat obscure collection of fifteenth- and sixteenth-century documents regarding witchcraft in Germany." Giles handed Xander a relatively new book and sat back down. "There's a mention of an 'extremely powerful and most vile witch' in a petition on page ninety-six, I believe."

Xander opened the book and scanned the page. "This doesn't say anything about someone called Shugra."

"Or red lightning. By the late fourteen hundreds the Inquisition witch hunts had been gaining momentum for over a century. I assume she was deliberately maintaining secrecy—about her activities at the time and any connection to the past."

"Covering her historical tracks," Xander said.

"Yes, so to speak. However, the same brand was found on members of a suspected coven in the village of Ulmdorf near Rothenberg in 1487, the year after a group of German inquisitors published the *Malleus maleficarum*."

"The what?"

"Otherwise known as *The Hammer of Witches*," Giles explained patiently. "Essentially, it was a handbook outlining how to identify and punish witches, using various methods of torture when the accused refused to cooperate."

"Lucky for Willow she's a twenty-first century witch." Xander cocked an eyebrow. "Did it work?"

"Always." Giles huffed with disgust. "The procedures were excessively cruel and condemned thousands of innocents to unbearable suffering. Since all evil lies, denial or silence was just as damning as admittance. The accused were tortured and terrorized until they had no choice but to confess."

"Which certainly qualifies as a no-win situation."

"Precisely." Giles sighed. "But in this particular case, the coven may have actually betrayed Shugra—known as Ilse Pfeiffer. A hundred of her followers were captured and interrogated. Neither they nor the inquisitors escaped the fires that swept through the dungeons of Castle *Aufklaren*."

Rothenberg, Germany: March 1487

Shugra drew her shawl tighter over her head as she approached the castle wall. None of her initiates would recognize the wrinkled old hag she had become as the young woman she actually was, but a demeanor of cowed humility was as essential to her disguise as the bucket and cleaning brushes she carried.

Adjusting her vision to see in the predawn darkness, she found the door in the rear wall and dissolved the interior crossbars that locked it. Rusty hinges creaked as she entered a dark, narrow stone passageway and pushed the heavy wooden door closed behind her. She paused to get her bearings. Her mark was like a beacon in the labyrinth of corridors that twisted through the massive edifice. Eyes downcast and stooped as suited her feigned age and menial position, she shuffled toward the flesh that bore the brand.

Her presence wasn't questioned when she joined the other scullery women the Bishop had conscripted to care for the castle and his needs. In their righteous arrogance, the inquisitors thought the fortress secure. No witch would dare infiltrate the bastion where they pressed the crusade against the black arts. Yet, while the King's soldiers scoured the countryside looking for her, the notorious witch Ilse Pfeiffer walked their hallowed halls.

"And where might you be going, crone?" A guard halted Shugra in an arched doorway. Beyond him, stone steps curled downward into the dungeon.

"Beggin' your pardon, sir, but his Grace is after having the filth from them wretched souls cleaned up a bit." Her voice cracked and she did not look up. His feeble mind could be easily swayed, if necessary.

The guard sniffed the stench rising from below.

"But seein' as how *I've* no mind to be goin' into the midst of them devils—" Shugra turned to leave.

"Hold on," the guard growled. "You'll do as the Bishop wishes, *alt* woman. Get on with it."

Shugra nodded and hung her head as she passed.

The lower levels of the dreaded castle were as foul as the village gossips had described, even though their reports were dredged from imagination. Water seeped through loose mortar and crumbling stone and the damp festered with tiny, infectious creatures no one but she could detect. When the invisible mites invaded the basic structures of which all things were made, the victim developed ravaging and painful maladies. Those who survived the tortures demanded by the *Hammer of Witches* would sicken and die before they starved.

Which was no less than they deserved.

Though bound together and to her by the brand, they had free will.

And they had betrayed her.

Ignorant of her true identity, they had not named Shugra, but treason against her in any name could not be forgiven.

Shugra's bare foot slipped on a patch of moss. She smothered it with a thought as she struggled to keep her balance. Her heart leaped when a large hand clamped around her frail arm.

"What's your business here?" Another guard demanded.

"The holy chair." Shugra cringed and held up the bucket with a shaky hand, grateful that he hadn't seen the moss shrivel and turn brown. Killing a guard would alert the hated Bishop and she had business to finish before she destroyed him and the traitors.

The tall, burly man nodded. "Make haste, then. His Grace will be down shortly."

Shugra scurried down the torchlit corridor past metal doors that kept the prisoners confined but did not muffle their wails or contain their putrid smell. Several of the hundred the soldiers had captured when they swept through the village keened or slept in the rat-infested cells. The others were close. She felt their minds and relished their misery.

More guards stood near the entrance to the large alcove where Bishop Steuben and the magistrate Bruer provoked confessions from the innocent and the guilty. Most were innocent, but even those with some ability were helpless. *As lambs in the jaws of wolves,* she thought. Their tormentors had no concept of true magick or understood the primal energies that empowered her. The inquisitors couldn't hurt her as Akmontep and the priests of Artemis had, but they had stolen her opportunity to meld when they had taken her initiates. The source would not be within reach again for another five hundred and thirteen years, and for that inconvenience they would die.

The guards flanking the entrance ignored Shugra as she scuttled into the chamber. Once inside, she quietly set about scrubbing the Bishop's chair. When the Bishop and Bruer entered with three men deemed to be solid, upstanding citizens of Rothenberg and a notary, she blended into the background, a nonentity invisible to their esteemed eyes.

The portly Bishop was speaking, his tone and expression grave. "I'm disturbed that we've yet to apprehend the Pfeiffer witch."

"Do not fret over the matter, your Grace." The elderly magistrate fawned, a twinge of fear in his voice. "Someone has obviously given her asylum. They will be charged with conspiracy as well as witchcraft."

The notary, pen and paper in hand, sat on a bench near the door.

The three citizens stood along the far wall. They radiated tension as their eyes darted about the alcove, then lingered on the strappado, the preferred instrument of torture among the pious. *Simple but elegantly excruciating,* Shugra thought with an upward glance at the rope hanging from a high, sturdy beam.

"They must be found first." The Bishop wheezed as he took his seat and arranged his robes. "Perhaps Herr Decker is ready to be of assistance."

Shugra seethed with anger as the small man was dragged into the room begging for mercy. She had but to catch his traitorous eye to silence him, but she was in no danger and curious. If the inquisitors followed the edicts of the *Hammer,* Decker would suffer at their hands before he died.

She hoped.

"Please, spare me, your Grace," the pitiful man cried as a guard stripped his tattered clothes off his spindly body. Shugra knew this was done as a precaution should he have a magickal charm sewn into the garment. "I know nothing of witchcraft. Nothing!"

"Then how do you explain the mark on your shoulder?" Steuben asked icily.

The man's eyes widened in terror. "An accident! At the village forge."

The magistrate chuckled. "Are we to believe that identical accidents left identical marks on so many?"

"I know not of any others—"

"Enough!" The Bishop motioned to the guards, who forced Decker to his knees on decayed straw matted with human waste. "Confess now to the crime of witchcraft and your life will be spared."

Spared for greater misery, Shugra thought, *or not.* It was rumored that death followed confession with few exceptions. The exceptions were imprisoned for life with nothing but bread and water for sustenance. Eventually, if disease didn't kill them first, they, too, were burned.

The cowering man shook his head. "I cannot confess to that which I haven't done."

"So be it." Sighing, the Bishop languidly waved his hand.

Decker screamed as the guards bound his wrists with one end of the rope strung over the rafter. When they released him to grab the other end, he bolted in panic and stumbled backward when the large guards jerked the line taut. Decker struggled, scabbed heels trying to dig in as his arms were pulled over his head.

Shugra watched dispassionately while the guards hoisted the wretched man toward the rafter. Suspended by his arms a few feet above the floor, Decker screamed in agony. The other witnesses appeared agitated, but their concern was as false as their word. Fanatic righteousness registered in their eyes when the guards suddenly let the rope slide through their hands. Decker's body dropped. The guards just as suddenly tightened their hold on the rope again, interrupting his fall before his feet touched the ground.

As Decker was pulled upward for a second drop, Shugra wondered how many falls were needed to separate his arms from his shoulder sockets. She would never know.

"Ilse!" Decker screamed. "Ilse Pfeiffer bewitched me with a potion! I thought it was mead! I swear!"

The three citizens nodded.

The Bishop glanced at the bench where the notary was penning the confession, then nodded to Bruer. "The accused has admitted to the crime of witchcraft and awaits sentencing."

The magistrate inclined his head toward the Bishop and ordered the guards to lower Decker to the ground. "Ernst Decker, having confessed to practicing witchcraft in the presence of witnesses and bearing a witch's brand as proof of his guilt, shall be put to death by burning—"

"Oh, he shall burn." Shugra removed her shawl as she stepped away from the wall. Eyes bulged as her wrinkled, brown-spotted face faded into the smooth countenance of youth. "But he will not burn alone."

"It's her!" Decker shrieked. "Ilse Pfeiffer! She's the witch who brought the evil arts to Ulmdorf!"

The Bishop reddened with anger at her audacity and sputtered, too stunned to speak.

The magistrate pointed. "Seize her!"

The two guards in the doorway jumped to obey. Shugra repelled them with a flick of her wrist, tossing them back into the passageway.

"How dare you use your blasphemous magick in my presence!" The Bishop rose from his chair, glaring.

"How?" Shugra held his enraged gaze. "That's how."

His robes burst into flames.

The Bishop's arrogant confidence shattered. He screamed and ripped at his robes.

The magistrate, guards, and witnesses bolted for the door. Shugra seized them with a thought and hurled them against the back wall. She held them where they collapsed on the stone floor, drawing their frightened gazes, invading their minds. The men's desperate thoughts in the face of her power were more than sufficient torment in this final moment of their lives. She smiled and set them on fire one by one.

Decker scrambled to his feet, his eyes pleading. "Milady, Ilse, I—"

Shugra ignited the straw around him and turned her back on the inferno.

Immune to the flames, she set the entire dungeon ablaze and left the castle through the same door she had entered.

Xander sat on a chair set just inside the office door with the tranquilizer gun resting on his knees. After Giles had finished relating the horrendous events that had taken place in Castle *Aufklaren*—a tale preserved by a messenger who had escaped the fire—he had finally fallen asleep. He had awakened from a two-hour nap with the remnants of a nightmare branded into his memory.

Hard to forget being naked and burned alive at the Bronze.

He stared at the sleeping werewolf, then at the clock. Only seventy-two minutes until sunrise and no way he was going to doze off. The risk of being shredded by fangs and claws if Oz broke free was all the incentive he needed, but not the only factor keeping him awake. As Giles was leaving to shower and change, he had asked a question expecting a reassuring answer.

"But we know the witch can be killed so there's no problem, right? Assuming we can figure out how to kill her, that is."

Giles had hesitated. "Actually, killing Crystal Gordon's body isn't sufficient. We have to destroy Shugra's essence."

Chapter 10

"THE NUMBERS DEFINITELY INDICATE A TREND," Oz said as Buffy opened her front door.

"Fashion trend? Winning streak? A decline in the Sunnydale death toll?" Buffy had chosen perky for the attitude of the day, mostly for her worried mother's benefit. She and Willow had filled Joyce in on the witch situation over brownies and cocoa last night. The trend for her mom was a downward plunge from constant concern to contained dread.

"Loose werewolf." Xander rocked forward, his nose twitching. "What's cooking?"

"Blueberry pancakes and sausage." Buffy rolled her eyes. Her calorie intake had doubled since her mother had decided food was an appropriate barometer for maternal caring. "My mom's contribution to the current crisis."

"Excellent strategy." Oz glanced at Xander. "Troops with full stomachs have an edge."

"Believe me," Xander said, "we're going to need all the edge we can get."

"You're going to explain that, right?" Buffy stepped back to avoid being trampled by the hungry adolescent males stampeding toward her kitchen. "Xander?"

"Right, but I explain better when my stomach isn't growling louder than I talk."

It took a while because Xander briefed them on Giles's findings between bites. Buffy sipped coffee, relieved because her mom had other mouths to stuff and didn't notice when she passed on seconds. Joyce listened intently between pouring coffee, flipping pancakes, and passing a variety of flavored syrups.

"How can anyone win against someone with that much power?" Joyce hovered over Xander with the last of the blueberry pancakes balanced on a metal spatula.

"Well, we know Crystal can be killed—" Xander pointed at his plate and Joyce deposited the goodies. "—but that's not good enough for Giles. He wants to exterminate Shugra."

"He's right," Oz said. "Otherwise she'll be back in another few hundred years."

"And sooner or later, she'll take over cikgam." Frustrated, Willow stabbed her last piece of sausage.

"Assuming she doesn't take over *cikgam* tonight," Xander added. "Magic even."

"And she's got a shot. She can find someone else to replace Willow in the coven." Oz pushed his plate away. "The *cikgam* number thirteen."

"Ooh!" Willow playfully punched Oz. "It's not funny."

"No, it's not." Joyce exterminated the teasing with her no-nonsense tone and evil mother's eye.

"So, does Giles have any idea how we're supposed to get rid of the personality that won't die?" Buffy asked.

"I'm a little curious about that myself, but I've got to get to the gallery." Joyce picked up her coffee, but didn't sit down.

"He was working on it when we left to come over here." Xander mopped up the last drops of syrup with the last bite of pancake.

The doorbell rang as Buffy started clearing the table.

"I'll get it." Joyce left, cup in hand.

"Great breakfast." Xander sat back with a satisfied sigh. "A man can only survive so long on jelly—"

Breaking glass and a short, strangled cry sounded from the living room.

"Mom!" Dropped dishes clattered into the sink as Buffy sprang to the door with Xander, Oz, and Willow behind her. A four-teen pileup occurred in the doorway when Buffy came to a sudden stop.

Giles and her mother were on the floor picking up pieces of broken cup. Their eyes met for a strained split second, then Joyce pushed Giles's hand away.

"I can get it, Mr. Giles." Joyce's tone was sharp enough to cut tough brisket.

Buffy winced slightly. Her mom was *so* testy around Giles. Obviously, she still wasn't ready to forgive him for his role in her daughter's Slayer life.

"Yes, well—I didn't mean to startle you." Giles nervously pushed on his glasses. "Since, uh, everyone was already here, I thought I'd just, well—drop by instead of waiting for them—to come to the library."

Giles pushed on his glasses again when he stood up. The stammer was more pronounced than usual, too, Buffy noticed. Apparently, Giles wasn't immune to the annoyed-mother whammy, either.

"It's all right, really." With both hands full of coffee cup shards, Joyce wobbled as she started to rise. She flinched when Giles took her arm and avoided looking at him. "Coffee?"

"Yes, please." Giles started when he caught Buffy's eye. "We have some, uh, things to discuss—" Back to Joyce. "—if that's all right with you."

What is with these two? Buffy had to have a Slayer-to-Mom talk soon. Somehow, she had to make Joyce understand that Giles was not responsible her being chosen as the Slayer. Or that she might have died long ago if not for his guidance and grueling training schedules. Her mom was much too jumpy around him. Had been for months.

"It is if you've figured out how to stop Shugra without getting my daughter killed," Joyce said hotly.

Giles's mouth opened, but the protest lodged in his throat.

Just as Buffy was about to enter the ring as referee, Joyce sagged and looked back. "I'm sorry. We were up half the night and—tea?"

"And round one is a draw," Xander muttered as everyone returned to the kitchen.

The tension eased considerably when Joyce set a cup in front of Giles and smiled. "I'd love to sit in, but I've got a prominent buyer coming into the gallery at noon."

"Yes, well—luck with the sale." Giles raised his teacup and visibly relaxed when Joyce dashed out to change.

Buffy sighed with relief. Her mother's attendance at a Slayer planning session was *not* a good idea, especially now that Joyce was expressing her worry in calories.

"Since Xander's told you about Shugra, I won't reiterate." Giles set down his tea. "And let there be no mistake, Crystal *is* Shugra—an ancient being with exceptional cunning, power, and experience."

"And an evil agenda to match," Xander added.

"Yes." Giles glanced at his watch. "And we only have a few hours before the ritual begins."

"Is there a plan yet?" Buffy asked.

"More or less. I have an idea that's theoretically possible." Giles continued before anyone could comment. "The only way to fight magick is with magick."

"Yep," Willow agreed.

"I'm still processing the theoretical part." Xander frowned. "Haven't we been through this before?"

"Actually, it's based on an observation you made last night, Xander," Giles said. "About Shugra being 'zapped' by her own magick at Ephesus."

"I said something brilliant and you didn't tell me?" Xander feigned a pout.

Giles quickly moved on. "The point is that magick functions according to certain laws, and Shugra's been able to protect herself from reprisal for consistently breaking one of the most fundamental of those laws." He slipped into thoughtful silence as he slowly drained his cup.

The others exchanged knowing glances.

A slight smile crept onto Oz's face. "Okay, I'll ask. Which one?"

"Parking her broom in a tow-away zone?" Xander quipped.

"Hmm?" Giles looked up, blinked.

"Magick. Laws. Breaking them," Buffy prompted.

"Oh, yes. Metaphysical order demands eventual balance between good and evil, a process that's in constant flux. Consequently, magick used to harm the innocent comes back on the casting individual three times stronger."

"Oh, yeah!" Willow brightened. "That's a basic principle of ciwac."

"Wicca? Uh—yes, it is. There are exceptions, of course." Giles paused to sip tea. "The most powerful masters of magick can shield themselves from this backlash."

Buffy immediately understood where he was going. "So if we can break through Shugra's shields—"

"Then everything bad she's done for thousands of years will come back on her?" Xander nodded. "I like it."

"The concept is theoretically sound. Turning Shugra's evils against her should destroy her—completely." Giles sighed. "But there are difficulties."

"I'll say," Xander said. "The red lightning didn't destroy her at Ephesus because she can just reincarnate."

"So, why didn't it?" Willow looked at Giles. "The primal gickam destroy her, I mean."

"According to Diomesos, the priests turned a burst of primal magick back on Herostratus—not Shugra. For whatever her reasons, she drew it away from him and absorbed it. Not the same thing as a deliberate attempt to negate her protective wards and balance the cosmic accounts. So her body died, but the perpetual essence that constitutes Shugra survived."

"Then is it possible or not?" Buffy cut to the chase. "To get through her shields?"

"Possible, perhaps," Giles said cautiously. "I have no idea if anyone's ever tried. The problem is that Shugra doesn't simply draw on magick. She's linked to the flow and her spirit can escape into the streams. We'll need a specific spell for a primal witch, which I haven't located yet. And if no such spell exists, we'll have to cobble one together ourselves."

"Cobble?" Xander started. "Is that the magick word for jerry-rig?"

"We may have no choice," Giles said. "And although I'm a more experienced spellcaster, I suspect my natural connection to the primal streams may be significantly lacking compared to Willow's." He met Willow's surprised gaze. "Your spellcasting ability is essential because your affinity for magick is so strong, Willow."

Willow started. "But—I can't say the words. And, well, I don't even want to think about what might happen if I tried to mix a potion."

"Could be interesting," Oz said matter-of-factly.

Xander cocked an eyebrow. "When it comes to mixed-up magic, I've already reached my quota. Thank you, Amy."

Buffy caught herself being sucked into the negative drift. A healthy dose of positive perky was required to get the gang back on track. "A few insurmountable obstacles have never stopped us before. Where do we start?"

"By trying to counter the aphasia spell that's preventing Willow from talking about anything related to magick," Giles said, "and continuing the research. Willow and I will go back to the library."

"And the rest of us will be where?" Xander asked.

"Taking Cordelia's advice, actually." Giles shrugged. "She did have a valid suggestion. Given what Willow heard last night, the members of Shugra's coven don't know they won't be free entities if she succeeds in joining with the source. If their conscious minds and identities aren't destroyed as a result of the ritual, they'll be enslaved to Shugra."

Buffy frowned. "Do you know that for sure?"

"I'm fairly certain. The, uh, brand led me to the personal diary of Amanda Hill, a woman who was accused of practicing witchcraft in Salem in 1692."

"Shugra was in Salem, too?" Willow shook her head. "She really got around."

"Her name then was Miriam Trent," Giles went on. "Just before Amanda was arrested, she went to Miriam and begged her to remove the brand. Miriam refused and taunted the woman for her gullibility. If the source-river had been within reach, which it wasn't, Amanda's last act of free will would have been helping Miriam to catch it."

Willow was horrified. "That's so . . . so heartless."

Oz nodded. "Evil beings usually are."

"And it all fits with Shugra's M.O." Xander said.

"Except no river to the source." Oz's usually placid brow furrowed. "So why Salem? A dry run?"

"Perhaps. Shugra may have been refining her approach to the ritual to avert another failure. The only evidence of the brand in Salem was the mention in Amanda Hill's journal." Giles cupped his chin. "Twenty were convicted and hanged, but none of them bore a mark."

Oz nodded. "So either fewer were branded or most of Shugra's coven escaped detection."

"Or both," Giles said. "Contrary to popular belief, the 'afflicted' in Salem included adults as well as teenagers. That might be relevant, since her new coven is comprised solely of teenagers."

"Except Anya," Willow said. "Although, I guess even she sort of qualifies."

"And maybe if Anya and the others know they've been duped, they'll bail." Buffy stood up, ready to ride. "We only need to convince one. Shugra's ritual is a no-go without a complete coven."

"Wait." Xander held up his hands. "I thought you said Crystal-Shugra, whatever, implanted an 'attendance mandatory' order in their heads."

"Most likely." Giles finished his coffee. "But they'll need to have free will for the ritual itself."

"Let's get to it, then." Fisting his keys, Oz kissed Willow on the cheek.

Dressed for the gallery, Joyce came downstairs just as everyone was leaving. She cornered Giles by the door. "Is there anything I can do to help? Research, perhaps? I *can* read."

"Uh—" Buffy blinked. *Brain freeze.* She didn't want to hurt her mother's feelings by refusing, but Joyce at the library just wouldn't work, especially at sundown when Oz morphed into scruffy, fanged guy. There was only so much she wanted her mother to know.

"Well, uh—" Giles ran his hand over his hair. Her mother's offer had slammed him into a mental stall, too. "That's, uh—something to consider."

When the front door closed behind them, Buffy turned on Giles, eyes flashing. "Why did you tell her it was okay?"

The accusation shocked him. "I didn't. I distinctly said—"

" 'Something to consider' doesn't mean 'no,' which is the same as saying 'yes!' "

"Oh." He paused uncertainly. "Then I should go back—"

"No. Maybe the gallery will be so busy she can't leave." Buffy sighed. "If not, then there's nothing we can do about it now except make things worse."

Giles muttered under his breath as he headed toward his car. "No, what's done is done."

Xander fretted between stops. So far they had tried to connect with five of Shugra's victims and failed. Three either weren't home or weren't answering the door or the phone. Kari and Emanuel had delivered a stern "go away" using their parents as messengers. The cold shoulder routine would have traumatized someone who wasn't used to being A. ignored or B. ridiculed by his peers. *Present company excepted.*

"Looks like we finally got a break." Oz turned into the Havershem driveway. Winston was mowing his lawn. A younger boy was shooting hoops by the garage door.

"I'll go." Buffy, who was provocatively wedged between himself and Oz, nudged Xander to open the van door. "He's a boy. I'm a blonde."

"I can't argue with the logic." Xander slid out and stood back to let Buffy pass. Packed into black pants and a rose-colored, clingy top, she was impossible for any male over the age of ten to ignore. The junior high kid playing basketball missed a rim shot when she smiled and waved.

"Hey, Winston!" Buffy called out as she walked to the edge of the lawn. The lanky boy in black didn't hear her over the roar of the lawn mower. She darted forward and tapped him on the shoulder.

Winston recoiled when he looked back.

Buffy said something Xander couldn't hear, but the effect was like bug repellent. Winston shut off the mower, turned his back on Buffy, and headed for the front door.

Surprised, but undaunted, Buffy followed. "Winston, wait." She paused at the steps. "Winston! I've got to talk to you!"

The kid by the garage stopped dribbling. "You are such a jerk, Winston."

"Stuff it, Sidney." Winston slammed the front door behind him.

Buffy shoved Xander into the middle as she got back into the van.

"Was it something you said?" Xander adjusted so he was closer to Buffy than Oz.

"Doubt it." Buffy sighed, shaking her head. "I'm not sure he even heard me."

"Makes it hard to get the message across." Oz put

the van in gear and pulled back onto the street. "He wasn't deaf to his brother, though."

"So is it just us?" Buffy asked.

"Don't know, but there's not much point in going on, if nobody will even listen," Xander said. "Our time would be better spent brainstorming with Giles."

"I'm not ready to give up, yet." Buffy set her jaw. "Maybe we can get through to Michael."

"Not likely." Oz slowed for a red, accelerated when the light turned green. "Not if Shugra might restore Amy."

"Let's go." Xander stared out the window. Saturday in Sunnydale: sun shining, blue sky, kids playing in parks, dads rummaging through hardware stores. *Sometimes it's hard to believe this town is demon central.*

"Could be we're going to get two birds with one stop." Oz peered out the windshield and parked behind Anya's compact. The slim, pretty girl had locked her car door and was walking toward the house without giving them a glance. Michael was sitting on the porch.

"Hate to say it, Xander, but you've got the best shot here." Buffy opened the door and jumped out.

Xander grunted. Anya's awkward attempts to attract him were flattering, but so far his better judgment had prevailed over hormones on the rebound. He was significantly aware of Buffy's feminine charms as he slipped out the door. "I'm not going into the fray alone, Buff. You're elected."

"Sure. If you get Anya to hold still long enough to listen, maybe Michael will, too."

"We can hope." Xander braced himself and called, "Anya!"

Anya spun, her face lighting up like Christmas when she saw him. "Xander! Hi!"

"Score one," Buffy said through a fixed grin. "She's talking."

"Yeah, but for how long." Xander raised Buffy's fixed grin with a forced smile. "Michael looks petrified."

The shy boy grabbed Anya's arm and tried to haul her up the steps.

"Michael always looks petrified."

"Yeah," Xander agreed, "but this time it's not just because he has layers of make-up hardening on his face."

Anya shook off Michael's hold, her gaze solidly locked on Xander. "Were you looking for me?"

"Actually, no," Xander said. "We stopped to talk to Michael."

"Oh." The light in Anya's eyes dimmed. "He can't talk to you."

Michael stumbled backward, whirled and beat a retreat into the house.

"Michael! Wait!" Buffy bounded up the steps and had the second door of the day slammed in her face.

"Still haven't got the tact thing down, huh?" The only thing Xander liked about Anya was that she didn't get huffy when he was blunt.

"It's not his fault. You're not one of—" Anya frowned like she had suddenly forgotten what she was going to say.

Buffy trotted back down the steps to ground level. "One of what, Anya?"

Anya didn't respond or even glance at Buffy.

"One of what?" Xander asked. "Crystal's coven?"

"No! I mean, what coven?" Anya shrugged and turned her smile back on.

"Let me see if I've got this straight. Michael can't talk to us, but you can talk to me?" Anya didn't have an exclusive on puzzlement. He was thoroughly confused.

"We're talking, aren't we?"

"Yeah, but—" After being shut out by everyone else in Crystal's elite clique, the open line to Anya was unsettling. "Why?"

"Doesn't matter, Xander." Buffy shot him a warning glance.

"Right." Xander breathed in, exhaled. *Gotta go for it while I've got the chance.* "Okay, Anya. Here's the deal. If you go through with this ritual thing for Crystal, you're going to lose your mind. And I don't mean that figuratively."

"I don't know what you're talking about." The newly human Anya hadn't gotten the stone-faced lie down yet, either. She averted her gaze and nervously shifted her weight.

"Yes, you do. You signed on to get your powers back, right? Well, forget it. All you're gonna get—"

Anya made a dash for Michael's front door.

Xander raised his voice. "—is dead or worse! Like being Shugra's puppet 'til the end of time. Anya!"

He flinched when the door slammed. "You know, Buffy, these guys haven't just been brainwashed. They've been run through the wringer and hung out to dry."

"Yeah, well, laundry day isn't over, yet." Buffy headed back to the van like a Slayer bent on some serious staking.

Xander jogged to catch up. Unfortunately, he suspected Buffy's stakes were as useful as a wet match against Shugra.

Crystal retreated from Anya's mind, pleased with her decision to loosen the contact restrictions. The girl had rejected Xander's warning without hesitation. Even with her long experience, Anya was as desperate and rebellious as any normal teenager. While Winston, Michael and the others fought an adolescent war against authority and confinement, she fought against the injustice of her mortal fate. *And the young are so self-absorbed and conscious of social standing, so consumed by the prospect of power, nothing can pry a betrayal from their lips.*

Not even love.

But the boy had called her Shugra.

It was not Anya, but the wild magick that had apparently led the librarian to ancient texts that revealed her name. Annoying, but not troubling. With Willow incapacitated, neither Giles nor the Slayer had the power to stop the ritual. Tomorrow the name Shugra would be known throughout the world.

What's left of it.

There was, however, one last detail to check. Crystal picked up the phone and dialed. When Mrs. Wayne answered, she asked to speak to Lindsey. She had excluded Janice McDonald from Lindsey's list of prohibited contacts before sending her home last night, a necessary concession after Willow's impudent refusal to join them. Janice's name had first come up when Crystal was looking for sympathetic students, but she had eventually been eliminated from the final choices due to her negligible affinity for magick.

"Crystal! Hi!" Lindsey gushed. "This is so weird. I just finished talking to Janice."

"And?" Crystal asked dryly.

"She's coming with me tonight." Lindsey laughed. "She is totally jazzed and no problem with the oath or anything. She hates Harmony so much, she'll do anything to—"

"Enough, Lindsey!" Crystal cut her off sharply, then softened her tone. "It wouldn't do for anyone to overhear."

Assured that Janice would 'guard their secret with her life,' Crystal slowly replaced the receiver. There was nothing about Janice McDonald that made her an outstanding initiate, except that she was willing and available to complete the coven. Unfortunately, since Janice did not yet bear her brand, she couldn't control the new recruit's actions and thoughts. *Unavoidable and unsettling, but not a major problem,* Crystal thought. The girl's youthful priorities guaranteed her silence about an exclusive, invitation-only club.

Satisfied, Crystal darkened her bedroom window to block a shaft of sunlight and smiled. After all these thousands of years, all the proper pieces were in place. Nothing had been overlooked.

Her thoughts drifted back to Ulmdorf. The authorities had been alerted to the presence of witchcraft in the village because she had conscripted too many. Ephesus as well. After venting her rage at Castle *Aufklaren,* she had fled to England where she had spent the remainder of that life calculating the minimum number of initiates necessary to draw the great stream. Although the source-river was far from the cosmic vicinity of Earth in 1692, her sojourn in Salem had been well worth the time. She had proven that twelve were easily bound and controlled and allowed for variables in magickal affinity. With herself as the binding agent, thirteen generated enough psychic and magickal energy to complete the task.

With less risk of loose tongues.

She should have known after witnessing Herr Decker's cowardly collapse and confession in Bishop Steuben's dungeon that adult loyalty could not be trusted. That lesson had not been learned until Amanda Hill had betrayed her.

Salem, Massachusetts: 1692

Miriam sat quietly among the trees, tracking Amanda through the forest. The great fear had swept through the small community like wildfire through dry grass the past several days. In the two centuries since Ilse Pfeiffer had escaped the inquisition in Germany, the rampant persecution of witches in Europe had subsided. However, the practice of witchcraft continued with a significant difference. Many of those smitten by their meager abilities with magick pursued the craft without sufficient discretion.

"Idiots," Miriam muttered under her breath. The loud thrashing of Amanda's reckless plunge through the forest was indicative of the pervasive naiveté and lack of caution in Salem.

Betty Parris and Abigail Williams's childish dabbling

had induced frenzied fits in front of witnesses. Tituba, the Reverend Parris's Indian slave woman, had even been approached to bake a charmed cake to identify the witch responsible for the girls' afflictions. And once again the innocent and the guilty were being accused, questioned, and detained, which is what had sent Amanda running to her in a panic.

"Miriam!" Amanda stumbled into the clearing, her skirt torn and her eyes wild with fright. "You must help me! I've been accused!"

Shugra knew what had transpired, for she had been lurking in the unstable woman's mind. Amanda's arrogance and misplaced confidence in her skills and immunity had prompted close surveillance.

"Accused by whom, Amanda?"

Amanda stammered between breathless sobs. "My neighbor, Matron Clara Smythe, saw the mark and has gone to the meeting house to give testimony against me."

"How did Clara Smythe see under your collar?"

The homely spinster shriveled under her stare and fell to her knees unwilling to answer. She had sworn to keep the secrets of the coven and to guard Miriam Trent's identity in exchange for a handsome, strapping, young husband. Since Shugra was only testing the power of twelve and not attempting a meld, she might have granted the wish. Instead, the thin, angular woman had broken her oath and would be punished.

"Perhaps it was because you were brewing a potion to silence her barking dog. Did Clara come to the door to inquire about the foul odor?"

Hunched over, the wretched woman wrung her hands and wept.

"And when you bade her beware, she scoffed. You showed Clara the brand to frighten her, did you not?"

Amanda nodded.

Shugra sighed. Amanda's blatant disregard for the safety of the coven could not be tolerated, but she had served her purpose. The other eleven had uttered not a word or pursued any magick that endangered Miriam or her quest. They were all under the age of eighteen. Amanda was twenty-eight.

"What would you have me do?" Shugra asked, curious.

"Take it off!" Amanda tore her dress at the shoulder to reveal the red mark signifying Shugra's eternal existence and unlimited power. "Remove it and there will be no proof! Please, I beg you."

"No."

Amanda blanched, then shrieked hysterically. "But how can I serve you in the ritual if I'm dead?"

Shugra had nothing to gain by maintaining the charade. The pitiful woman deserved to suffer. "Your life was forfeit the moment you pledged yourself to me, Amanda Hill. If the source-river was within reach, your last act of free will would have been your participation in the ritual to call it."

Amanda gasped. "But . . . but you said we'd become magick!"

"Yes, quite so." Shugra smiled. "Your energies, consciousness, and your soul would have been absorbed into the magickal streams—mine to use or destroy."

Overwhelmed by terror, Amanda stumbled back into the forest and ran.

Shugra followed at a more leisurely pace, enjoying the

coolness of the night air and the soothing sounds of the wilds. The untamed new world suited her, but like the great valley of her birth, civilization would eventually sweep it away. When she returned three centuries hence, the vast, untouched forests and the pristine lakes and rivers would no longer exist.

Shugra put these thoughts out of her mind as she neared Amanda Hill's small house on the outskirts of town. She saw John Corwin and William Stoughton, two of the magistrates who investigated accusations, leaving Ingersoll's Tavern with Clara Smythe's husband and three other men, all carrying lanterns. Their stride was bold and their demeanors stern with the weight of their duty. The pious were just as intent on eradicating the evils of witchcraft as ever.

The ludicrous words of clergyman writer, Cotton Mather, ran through Shugra's mind as she paced the men toward Amanda's home.

"Witchcraft will not be fully understood until the day when there shall not be one witch in the world."

The man was a pompous fool, but Shugra had no qualms about aiding the good men of Salem by eliminating one witch.

She waited while the law-abiding citizens of Salem broke into Amanda's house. Taught to read and write by her father, another sin in the eyes of dominant men, Amanda was furiously scribbling in her diary when she was rudely interrupted. The journal was confiscated and the stricken woman dragged outside, begging for mercy and blaming Miriam for bewitching her.

Shugra moved out of the darkness, drawing Amanda's gaze.

She invaded the woman's trembling body and stopped her heart.

As Amanda fell dead, she removed the brand and faded back into the shadows.

Crystal checked the minimal wards around the house. Still exhausted from animating the woods last night, she had to conserve her depleted energies for the enormous task ahead. The librarian and his entourage were no doubt developing an attack strategy, but since their efforts could not possibly threaten her magick, there was no reason to tax herself with a mental surveillance.

She drifted back into sleep, secure and confident.

After Miriam Trent removed the brand from her other, sleeping initiates, she had vanished into the virgin wilderness never to be seen again. She had lived in solitude, observing the ways of the natives who shared her respect for the true world, until she had abandoned Miriam's life at age sixty-two.

Like Ilse, Miriam had not been killed.

Crystal Gordon would not die, either.

Chapter 11

WILLOW SCRUNCHED HER EYES SHUT. GILES HAD ALready tried two spells to cure her aphasia. His first attempt had jumbled *all* her words, which was a little disconcerting. The second was a voodoo healing ritual that required a potion made of chicken innards stewed with things she was glad Giles hadn't identified.

"Yes, well—it does look rather vile," Giles had said, "but think of it as chicken soup, which cures everything, doesn't it?"

Almost everything. The tangy gunk had been too salty for her taste, but it had reversed the effects of Giles's first spell. Better than nothing, but she still couldn't say any words relating to magick.

"Just about ready, Willow."

Willow opened one eye. She couldn't hide her trepidation as Giles mixed herbs and undefined animal parts over a Bunsen burner. "If I have to drink that, I'm going to throw up."

Giles looked at her, aghast. "No—don't! This potion isn't ingested."

"Okay, well, that's good, but—it won't make me speak only in ancient Aramaic or anything, will it?"

"Do you speak Aramaic, Willow?"

"No."

"Then I doubt it." Giles smiled gently. "Ready?"

"Whenever you are." Willow straightened in her chair and sighed as he began.

"Hear me, Hecate, goddess of the dark. *Non facere blasphemare verbum maga, et liber magia dicta.* In the name of Hecate—let it be done." Giles added the catalyst with a snap of his hand. Smoke and brilliant green light flared from the bowl with a hefty whoosh.

Willow stopped holding her breath.

"I see we made it for the big finish." Xander walked in with Buffy and Oz.

Buffy glanced warily at the dissipating smoke. "I hope you're having better luck than we did." She took a deep breath and choked.

"I hope we're having better luck than *we've* had." Willow grinned. "Well, I'm still speaking English anyway."

"I won't ask." Oz gripped Willow's hand.

"Okay." Willow smiled tightly as she looked into his eyes. In a few hours Oz would transform into the werewolf, and the elfin twinkle would become glittering rage. They both handled it pretty well, actually. It was kind of amazing, but then, love was like that.

"Perhaps we should test the results, Willow." Giles

cleaned spell residue off his glasses with a handkerchief.

"Does she have to try a spell?" Xander looked around. "We don't have a blast shield handy."

Willow took a deep breath. "All I have to do is try and talk about Lyrscat and kagcim—"

"Guess that answers that." Xander sprawled on the steps. "We were a total failure, too, if that makes you feel any better."

"It doesn't." Giles began pacing.

"Actually, Xander managed to get a few words of warning in to Anya before she closed us down." Buffy shrugged. "Didn't make the impression we were hoping for, though."

"Slamming door being a pretty definite indicator." Xander planted his feet and rested his elbows on his knees.

"So is not being able to say cigmak." Willow shrugged with a sheepish sigh.

Buffy nodded sympathetically. "Just how essential is Willow's spellcasting ability, Giles?"

"Extremely. It's more than a matter of magickal ability. It's a matter of balance. Against an evil as potent as Shugra, Willow's genuine goodness and purity could make a difference."

"But you're a good person, Giles." Willow switched chairs to sit beside Oz at the study table. "Okay, so maybe not so pure because of—well, you *are* an adult and there was that business with Eyghon, but even so. You *are* a better spellcaster than I am. Can't you do it?"

"My expertise has already been factored in, I'm afraid." Giles frowned. "I believe the attack requires two simultaneous and ongoing spells. One to deflect Shugra's magick and one to break down her protective wards. I should be able to handle the wards."

"My memory of that spell to keep the woods at bay last night doesn't lend itself to confidence." Xander shrugged.

Giles didn't take offense. "Circumstances will be more favorable tonight. Relatively speaking."

"Latching on to the 'more favorable' thing—how?" Buffy's eyes tracked Giles to the book cage, which was still lacking a door.

Kicking chains aside, Giles pulled several books from shelves and cartons. "Shugra may have immense power at her disposal, but she's still operating with a human body, which has limitations. Calling the source-river will require huge amounts of psychic, magickal, and *physical* energy. Consequently, she'll have to guard against unduly taxing her physical strength."

"Hey! A ray of hope!" The weight on Willow eased.

"Only to a degree," Giles clarified as he dropped the stack of books on the table. "It won't affect the power of her magick when we launch a direct assault. The best we can hope for is that the woods will be passable."

"Passable." Buffy looked at the librarian askance. "Like take a stroll through without being groped by vines and branches passable? Or watch your step 'cause anything can happen passable?"

"The latter, I'm sure, but that's not our greatest concern." Giles flicked a glance at Willow.

"I know this isn't my fault . . . not being able to

do . . . stuff, but I feel so . . . so . . . victimized!" Willow's temper routed her discouragement. "And, well—there's got to be something we can do. Something Calryst didn't think of. I mean, every diabolical plot has a hole in it somewhere."

"I'm not seeing any leaks," Xander muttered.

"A new plan does seem to be in order, though." Oz draped a comforting arm over the back of Willow's chair.

"I've got an idea." Buffy instantly captured everyone's attention. "It's a little far out, but—what if Willow channeled her power through someone else? Like me."

"Willow power plus Slayer power?" Oz nodded. "Has potential."

"But will it work?" Xander left the dubious comfort of the steps and pulled up a chair.

"It might, but it would require a specific binding spell—one that connects, not contains." Giles shuffled through the books, found the text he was looking for, and opened it. "Excellent idea, Buffy."

"Thank you." Buffy looked pleased. "It was kind of brilliant and innovative—"

"Time!" Xander looked up sharply. "A third spell? At last count we had only one spellcaster in perfect working order—you."

"Yes, well—" Giles concentrated on the book. His voice dropped off as he thumbed through the pages. "Perhaps Angel could manage a binding spell."

"He could." Willow agreed enthusiastically. "Angel made a perfectly fine living flame when Gwendolyn Post tried to steal the Glove of Myhnegon."

"The academic snob who insulted Giles's book collection?" Buffy executed a mock shudder.

"And don't forget the concussion," Xander added.

"If you don't mind, I'd just as soon forget about *Mrs.* Gwendolyn Post entirely." Giles handed each of them a book.

After waking in the late afternoon, Crystal had taken a long bath. Refreshed and revitalized, she slipped into a calf-length black dress with long sleeves that widened dramatically at the wrists. She brushed her short, blond hair back off her face. No make-up. No shoes.

She stared at her reflection in the large, oval antique mirror that had been in the Gordon family for five generations. The Gordon women valued its age and the tradition of handing the finely crafted piece down from one eldest daughter to the next. Although she appreciated the artistry that had gone into carving the cherry wood frame, she mourned the tree. The mirror would not be handed down again.

Tonight I will achieve the destiny I was born to nineteen thousand years ago.

And tomorrow the true world will be restored.

Sunnydale would crumble first. Drawn by her wrath, a storm of primal magick would descend on the small town. The monuments to mankind's vanity would shatter into pristine ores and dust in a crimson blaze. She would rip conduits from the ground, snatch satellites from the sky, and reduce everything to rubble. With all magick hers to wield it would not be long before the Earth's surviving population again lived at the mercy of the elements—and the true and only daughter of earth, wind, water, and fire.

Daylight dimmed, throwing the sparsely furnished bedroom into shadow. Crystal left the house through the back door without bothering to close it. Pine needles and twigs softened underfoot as she headed for the clearing to await the initiates.

The library bustled with pre-attack prep. Xander rolled protection packets and flipped them over his shoulder into a pile on the study table, all the while complaining bitterly about the smell. Giles ran down his checklist for the tenth time, decided he had everything, and zipped the spell bag. Cordelia, armed with pepper spray and the tranquilizer gun, paced and watched the clock. Inside the book cage, Oz tested the chains and manacles for weak links.

Sitting on the upper tier, Buffy read the incantation she had to memorize again. When she tried to repeat it in her mind, she stumbled over the Latin words.

"How are you doing?" Willow sat down.

"Not great. I seem to have a mental block about speaking in dead languages."

"You'll be fine, Buffy. Just don't forget to say it with *feeling* when the time comes." Willow raised a fist to drive home the point. "Remember . . . you're really mad and if you don't get it right, she will be the most powerful entity in the world—and we'll all be toast."

"And don't buckle under the pressure?" Buffy raised an eyebrow. She was a vampire Slayer, not a witch. Driving stakes into the hearts of a dozen vampires during an earthquake seemed like a Sunday social compared to the impending magick-off with Shugra.

"Trust me, Buffy." Smiling, Willow gripped her shoulder. "We can do it."

"Absolutely." Buffy smiled back and took a deep breath. According to Willow, the power of hocus-pocus depended a lot on emotional punch. When it came to the wicked witch in the woods, she had more than enough animosity to make up for her lack of magickal affinity.

"Aren't we pushing the timing a little too close?" Cordelia confronted Giles, assuming a wide stance with the tranq gun resting on her shoulder. In a tank top and jeans with her long dark hair tied back and the pepper spray handy on her belt, she was combat ready.

Giles glanced at his watch. "Yes, we probably should get Oz settled."

"Any time." Oz stood quietly while Giles secured the restraints. Since he had little privacy other than an old blanket stretched across the cage door, he wore old clothes. They wouldn't survive the transformation, but the sacrifice was better than disrobing in front of a crowd with Cordelia in front row center. An extra set of clothes rested on the filing cabinet, a silent statement of his faith in the witch busters. He fully expected to morph back into the same old Sunnydale—sans one primal witch—at sunrise.

"Come on, Buffy. Give the old brain a break." Willow dusted off her knees as she stood. "You probably know it anyway. You just don't know you know."

Buffy ran over the deflection spell in her mind as she bounced down the steps. The foreign words flowed without flaw. She stopped and checked the paper, surprised that she had gotten it right. *Now if I can say it without spacing, we'll be all set.*

"Step right up and get your stinky charms here!" Xander tossed a pungent, leaf-wrapped mass underhand. "There ya go, little lady."

Buffy caught it and pretended to stagger from the stench.

Willow swept up a charm on her way to the book cage. She kissed Oz, quickly stepping back when his head jerked. "Be good."

"He'd better be." Cordelia pulled a chair into position a few feet back from the cage door. "Point blank range. That should do it."

"A trigger-happy GI Cordelia. As if I didn't have enough material for a lifetime of nightmares." Xander diplomatically didn't look as Oz began to change.

"The tranq gun's loaded." Cordelia turned her head slowly. "Keep it up, Xander, and you'll make my day."

"Yes, well, let's forgo the squabbling for now and get moving." Giles picked up the spell bag. "We have to be in position when the moon rises."

The werewolf roared and lunged at the door.

Xander jumped. "You had to mention the moon."

Cordelia braced the tranq gun against her shoulder and aimed.

The chains stopped the beast, but provoked a furious fit of snapping jaws and enraged snarls just as Buffy's mother pushed through the library doors.

Chapter 12

W*HOA!* B*UFFY INHALED SHARPLY AS* J*OYCE ENTERED.* Her brain went numb. This was not a typical Hellmouth threat that she could handle without hesitation. This was her mother walking into Slayer headquarters where they kept a werewolf as a mascot.

Cordelia snapped the tranquilizer gun behind her back, hiding it in plain sight. "Buffy! Your mother's here."

"The gallery was a madhouse—" Joyce sniffed. "What's that—"

Giles was not stunned by Mom-suddenly-shows-up syndrome. Before Joyce came abreast of the cranky, thrashing werewolf, he intercepted, took her arm, and spun her back toward the doors.

"—smell?" Joyce scowled up at the librarian. "What do you think you're—"

"You're just in time," Giles said. "We were just on our way out."

"Right!" Willow and Xander closed ranks behind them.

"Wait a minute!" Buffy barged into the hall and darted ahead of her mother and Giles, blocking their advance. "She's not coming with us."

"Yes, I am." Joyce pulled free of Giles's grasp.

"Mom—" Buffy breathed deeply. Losing her temper would just make her stubborn mother more determined. "Believe me, you don't want to go. Creepy woods, nasty witch, lots of evil magick, very dangerous. If you really want to help me—"

"Actually, she can help, Buffy," Giles said evenly.

"Giles!" Buffy stared at him, appalled. The memory of her mother's kidnapping and ordeal at the hands of Fulcanelli was still too fresh in her mind. The master sorcerer had used Joyce to distract her Slayer daughter while he attacked the Gatekeeper and tried to open the barrier between hell and the human world. Buffy hadn't had a choice about her mother's involvement then, but she did now. "How can you ask me to risk—"

"He's not asking you, Buffy." Joyce matched Giles's even tone with a steady gaze. "And neither am I. I'm in. No arguments."

"I'll explain on the way." Giles strode forward.

"But—" Buffy's protest was ignored as her mother, Willow, and Xander rushed out the doors behind him. She followed, fuming.

After they were in the van and headed toward Angel's mansion, Giles briefed Joyce on the plan. She listened without comment.

"I'm not trying to be difficult, Mom," Buffy said

when he finished. "It's just that my abracadabra quotient isn't exactly off the scale."

"Which is why you need as much support as possible." Giles shifted in the passenger seat to look back. Wedged between him and Xander, Joyce stared straight ahead. "While I was looking for the spell to connect you and Willow, I found another that will bind the rest of us to both of you."

Xander gave him a sidelong glance. "The rest meaning you, me, and Buffy's mom?"

"And Angel," Giles added. "Adding ourselves to the mix will greatly amplify the power of good Willow and Buffy have at their disposal."

"Angel, once the scourge of Europe, will give us good vibes?" Xander scoffed. "Don't you want to re-think that?"

"No." Giles was definite. "Angel, like Joyce, loves Buffy—unconditionally, enough to die for her."

Joyce only nodded.

"Mom, I can't—"

"Let me finish, Buffy," Giles said gently. "Shugra has used and destroyed people with depraved indifference for millennia. She commands wild magick with a malicious intent that's wreaked havoc across the ages and her cunning is as chilling as the restraint she's exercised in her more recent reincarnations. She's waited and learned and grown more powerful than any magickal adversary that's ever walked the face of the Earth. The world has not yet known the extent of her power—or her evil. You and Willow will need all the positive energy we can muster to have any hope of defeating her. Your mother has much to offer in that respect."

Giles pressed closer to the door as Joyce craned about to look back. "Maybe I'll make the difference, Buffy, between winning or losing. Maybe not. I've, uh, always gotten caught up in whatever was going on by accident before."

"Like that time you clobbered Spike with an ax." Willow grinned.

"Yes, but I just happened to be there," Joyce said. "This time, I'm jumping in because I can honestly contribute. I can't walk away, honey. Do you understand?"

"Yeah, I do," Buffy finally said. "If our positions were reversed, I'd feel the same way."

"So, does this make your mom an official Slayerette?" Willow asked, breaking the tension.

"Just for tonight." Buffy smiled to put some positive vibes in the bank, then realized Giles was staring at his lap, hands on the wheel. "And the downside that you haven't mentioned yet, Giles?"

"Well, there is one, yes. If Shugra harms or kills one of us while we're bound, everyone will suffer the same fate."

The evening air turned colder as Anya and her passengers left the parked car and started up the drive. She shivered and pulled her dark sweater closed. The unlit house was a black hole in the woods, an illusion of ominous portent. The trees lining the packed dirt track loomed above, giving credence to the disquiet she had not been able to shake since seeing Xander that afternoon.

Kari and Rebecca whispered between themselves, excited about the mysterious ritual that would begin at moonrise and the promises to follow. Even Michael, always quiet and subdued, seemed charged with energy. Lagging behind, watching the path, Anya recognized the signs of aloof conceit brewing within them. Being singled out as Crystal's chosen bred contempt for the masses that would not share their power.

I should know, Anya thought. *I felt the same way for a thousand years.*

Empowered and assured of continued existence, she had thrived on the misery of others, thinking herself immune. All it had taken to topple her from that lofty pedestal was an educated, fearless man with a heavy object.

Giles had crushed her hollow sense of superiority and condemned her to mortal life when he had smashed the necklace.

Crystal could annihilate her as easily with a look.

Shugra, Xander had said. An image of ancient corruption flashed through her mind. Anya knew from experience that once the witch had what she wanted, she had no reason to give anyone what she had promised.

She stepped over a root.

The flicker of uncertainty fled when Anya's mind blanked.

Crystal shut down Anya's conscious thought. She had anticipated a fluctuation in the girl's resolve and was not concerned, but it would not do to let her brood. Once the preliminary ceremony to complete the coven began, she would restore Anya's free will and the girl would be swept into the fervor generated by the demonstration of her magick, a demonstration to prove she intended to keep her word.

Crystal sat concealed in the thicket behind the tall boulder. The torches lighting the clearing beyond cast flickering patterns on the trees. Eight initiates had already arrived, all of them dressed in shades of gray and black. They spoke softly, with awed reverence, infusing the night with anticipation as they enjoyed the spread of roasted meats, freshly baked breads, and crisp vegetables she had set out. They drank sparkling water from pewter tankards engraved with their names. A New Age CD played on a portable boombox concealed in the brush. The strains of instrumental folk music dating back to the country's Colonial era fit the occasion and soothed taut nerves. The subtle, festive atmosphere was designed to lull them into a sense of security and well-being.

Janice had arrived with Lindsey as promised. She was a coarse-looking girl with bland facial features and limp, blunt-cut, brown hair. Her blue eyes, however, glittered with excitement. Given the nature of modern teenaged society, Crystal was not surprised that she had jumped at the chance to be included among an elite, chosen few or that she wanted revenge on the brutally caustic Harmony Kendall.

Not ideal, but she'll do.

The source-river was so much closer this time she could adjust for the girl's lack of magickal affinity. As soon as the moon began its ascent, Janice would be pledged. After Janice was pledged and the others reaffirmed their vow, the ritual could begin.

"Kari!" Joanna waved as the four latecomers entered

the clearing. Eyes shining and flushed, Kari and Rebecca walked up to the table. "Isn't this great? Are you nervous?"

"A little." Rebecca picked up a chicken leg.

Kari nodded as she looked around. "This isn't what I expected. I mean, I thought it would be more, well—*serious.* Like with candles and black robes—"

"Storybook stuff. Not to worry. I don't think we'll be disappointed." Winston handed Michael a tankard and raised his in salute. "Here's to magick. And Crystal."

Crystal drew Anya toward the thicket. When the girl's eyes were accessible through the twisted branches, she erased the memory of her encounter with Xander and released her to join the celebration.

"—*imperium iussu.*" Giles paused, his hand clamped over Buffy and Willow's bound wrists. When the slight tingling seeping through their skin subsided, he untied the leather thong.

"That's it?" Buffy vigorously shook her hand, glanced at Angel. "My fingers are numb."

"Magick has that effect." Angel held her gaze for a moment and shoved his hands into his coat pockets.

Willow stared at her spread fingers. "So, we don't have to be touching or anything? The magick just leaps from me to Buffy?"

"Yes. Like an electrical arc." Giles dampened the remnants of a smoking potion with oil and packed the mixture into two leather pouches. He gave one to each of the girls, then repacked his bag. As a precaution, the others would not be bound to them until they reached the ritual site—in case someone didn't make it.

"You sure you're okay with this, Mom?" Buffy slipped the potion into the pocket of her leather jacket, then shifted the flashlight to her free hand. She carried the machete in the other.

"Yes." Joyce nodded, smiled tightly. She glanced down at her tailored brown pants and print blouse. "Except that I'm not dressed for skulking around the woods in the dark."

"Your shoes are quite sensible." Giles intended his remark as a compliment and was somewhat chagrined when Joyce, Buffy and Willow eyed him narrowly. "Very . . . appropriate?"

"He's British." Buffy told her mother. "You get used to it."

"Be that as it may—" Giles looked at Joyce. "—your clothes are not a difficulty." Angel was dressed in black as usual, but Buffy, Willow, and Xander wore their usual evil-battling attire. Although Giles had changed into jeans and a dark sweater, night camouflage would make no difference. Shugra could detect them whether she could see them or not.

"When the moon comes up, you'll blend in just fine. Kind of like light filtering through the leaves." Willow hooked a pair of garden pruning shears to her belt. "Unless she turns off the lights again."

"We're packing." Xander held up his large flashlight. "I'm not doing the freaky fun forest in the dark."

"Which works as long as you don't feed it to the swamp." Buffy turned her flashlight on.

"What swamp?" Joyce whispered to Giles.

"Last night's theme." Giles smiled wanly as he moved out behind Buffy and Willow. He had given the girls strict instructions to stay together, regardless of what happened. Joyce seemed to understand that she could distract Buffy and disrupt her concentration. She hung back, walking close behind him, just off his shoulder. He was very aware of her presence and felt responsible for her safety, a burden that was harder to bear because he couldn't guarantee it.

We've done this before. We've united before. It's worked . . . before. He repeated his mantra, steadying his nerves.

However, nothing untoward happened on their brisk walk to the darkened house.

"That was uneventful." Xander shone his flashlight in the windows as they skirted the building. "A delayed reaction to the spell you cast last night, Giles?"

"Not likely. Shugra's conserving her energies, I suspect."

"Or luring us deeper into the woods." Buffy paused to scan her beam back and forth across the worn path they had taken the night before.

"Where we have to go anyway." Joyce's voice was steady in contrast to the trembling Giles felt when she edged nearer.

"I hear them." Angel cocked his head slightly, his acute predatory hearing picking out sounds inaudible to the human ear. "Straight ahead."

Nodding, Buffy started down the path.

"There's a clearing." Willow half skipped, moving sideways to stay up with Buffy while talking to Giles. "I don't remember how far. Maybe a fifteen-minute walk."

"Fifteen minutes if the path doesn't disappear and

the trees don't bite." Xander whipped the flashlight around to shine on Angel. "Just making sure you're still covering my back." He muttered as he closed the gap between himself and Joyce. "I can't believe that makes me feel better."

"We haven't seen any vampires." Joyce's fingers closed around a fold in Giles's sweater. "Besides Angel, I mean."

Angel answered. "According to Willy, the undead are lying low until this is over. One way or another."

Xander exhaled shortly with disgust. "Or that I'm risking my life to make the world a safer place for vampires."

"Silence might be advisable," Giles cautioned. Despite his theory regarding Shugra's limited physical resources, she would not ignore an advancing threat. She would take calculated action—maximum effect with minimal effort.

However, as they pushed farther into the forest, the trees remained firmly rooted. An occasional rustling betrayed the presence of an animal scurrying through the brush, and Xander's flashlight beam jerked when an owl hooted. Giles watched the vines and roots flanking the path, but nothing popped up or curled outward to trip the unwary. He did not find the lack of dastardly activity reassuring and was not surprised when all the flashlights failed at the same time.

The dark swallowed everything.

"Stay close, Joyce," Giles said. "I don't want to risk getting separated."

"Glued." Her hand tightened on his sweater. "Buffy?"

The silence and Joyce's choked gasp wrenched at Giles's heart.

"Willow!" Buffy called anxiously.

"Right here." Willow's hand brushed Buffy's sleeve and she hooked a finger through her belt loop.

"Mom? Giles?"

When they didn't answer, Buffy quickly put the brakes on runaway worry. The tactics were familiar even though the circumstances were different. Shugra had divided them, hoping to throw them into a panic. Wasn't going to work. The apprehension she felt about being Willow's magickal mouthpiece was suppressed as her Slayer instincts took over.

"Are you okay, Willow? I mean, considering we can't see anything and everyone else is gone?"

"Great!" Willow shrugged. "Okay, not great, but—we're together and that's better than being lost out here alone."

"Right." Buffy flicked the switch on the flashlight and started when the beam came on. "That was . . . interesting."

"Uh-huh." Willow didn't let go of the belt loop as she looked over her shoulder. Trees grew across the path where the others had been. "You don't think Shugra could—"

"Turn my mother, Giles, Xander, and Angel into trees?" Buffy panned the light back, being careful not to move her feet. The beam barely penetrated the dense brush and forest. "Maybe, but I'd rather think they've just been cut off to wander aimlessly through witchy wonderland until after the ritual."

"I'd rather think that, too. And that's probably what's happened because, well—*we're* not trees."

"No, but we're on our own." As she moved the beam ahead again, Buffy realized the path curved to the right of the direction her feet pointed, a detour intended to steer them away from the clearing. "Hang on, Willow. We may be in for a rough hike."

Willow plowed into the undergrowth behind Buffy. "Do you know where you're going or just guessing?"

Buffy hacked through a thick vine with the machete. "Just a theory, but Shugra obviously knows we're here, right?"

"Obviously." Willow unhooked her finger from Buffy's belt loop and attacked a huge spider web with her garden sheers.

"And she wants—" A large branch cracked overhead. Buffy grabbed Willow by the front of her jacket and pulled her forward as the limb crashed down. "—to keep us from getting anywhere near the clearing."

"And doing a very good job of it, too." Willow's jacket caught on a tangle of briers. She carefully peeled the barbed stem from her jacket and pulled a thorn from her thumb.

"Right. Watch." Buffy pivoted to the left and took a few steps forward with the light aimed into the woods. No natural obstacles barred her way. She eased back to find the forward route overgrown with vines, which she dispatched with three swift, clean cuts of the sharpened machete. "This is the path of most resistance because we're going in the right direction."

Willow whacked away a dead branch that had suddenly grown thorns. "And I think she's getting a little desperate."

"A little." Buffy jumped to avoid a gnarled root poised to snare her foot and beheaded a giant toadstool.

Shugra was just warming up.

"We should have stayed on the path." Xander ducked under a canted tree that had broken at the base. The top had wedged in the high branches of a tall hardwood nearby, aborting its fall. He stopped to look back. "Being dead for two hundred and forty years doesn't make you an expert on everything."

Angel didn't have time to be annoyed or explain why he had chosen to bushwhack through the thick of the forest. He heard the upper branches of the dead tree shift and bolted forward. He bowled into Xander, flipped the startled boy over his shoulder and raced on through a rain of broken branches that shattered as the massive pine fell.

"But I can't complain about your reflexes," Xander said when Angel stumbled to a halt at the edge of a bubbling spring. Still draped across the broad shoulder, he was quiet for a few blessed seconds. *His apparent limit.* "You can put me down now. Blood's rushing to my head."

Angel thought about dropping him on it, but swung him to the ground instead. Xander's animosity wasn't misplaced, but his cutting remarks were a constant reminder of the weeks he had terrorized Buffy and her friends as Angelus. Giles, who had lost Jenny and been tortured by his demonic persona, had grudgingly accepted him again, as had Willow. Xander would never forgive him or let him forget it.

"Thanks." Xander straightened, his dark hair and dignity ruffled. "I don't suppose it ever occurred to you to just yell 'run!' "

"No more than it occurs to you to shut up."

"Right." Xander crossed his arms. "Giles was better company."

"Fine. When we find him, you can switch partners." Grateful when Xander didn't respond, Angel scoped the surrounding woods with his enhanced senses, relying on sound and scent. Even with night vision, there wasn't much to see in the dense copse except saplings and shrubs packed among trees. He spotted the rabbit by scent. Frightened from its den by the falling tree, it huddled under a bush laden with wild berries. Frogs crouched in the mud around the pool, silent and waiting for the interlopers to move on. He heard the whisper of voices, a muted laugh—and his name as he tried to home in on the sound.

"Angel—"

"Hang on a second, Xander."

"I'm hang—"

Angel spun, saw Xander clawing at a thick vine wrapped around his throat, and lunged. He barely got his fingers under the woody rope before it tightened and pulled upward.

"—urgie!" Xander's eyes bulged with terror as his toes left the ground.

Angel yanked out and hauled down, loosening the plant's stranglehold on Xander's neck and getting the boy's weight back on his feet. Struggling to keep the vine from constricting again with one hand, Angel drew his knife. The vine whipped to avoid the slashing blade, throwing Xander back and forth like a rag doll. When Angel severed the stalk, the boy collapsed in a limp heap. The injured vine shrieked and retreated into the high branches of its host tree, bleeding green sap.

"Sorry." Angel knelt and touched Xander's arm. "I didn't realize—"

Gagging and coughing, Xander nodded.

"Maybe you'd better keep talking." Angel smiled wryly. "Then when you shut up, I'll know if you're in trouble."

"Very funny." Still breathless, Xander dragged himself into a sitting position and rubbed his bruised neck.

A ripple in the gurgling spring drew Angel's eye. Just a frog—that was growing bigger and morphing into something that resembled an amphibious dinosaur.

"I know you're going to find this hard to believe, but at the moment, I can't think of anything to say." Xander coughed again.

"How about this?" Angel hauled Xander up by the wrist. *"Run!"*

"What?" Xander hesitated.

"Never mind." Angel shoved him away as the creature roared and charged. Legs apart, knife fisted, he braced to take the impact of a beast standing eight feet tall and weighing in at four hundred pounds.

Behind him, Xander raised the flashlight.

Yellow, reptilian eyes glittered and long, sharp teeth flashed in snapping jaws. The points grazed Angel's arm as he leaped aside, tearing through leather and raking flesh. Angel tried to shove the knife into the beast's side. The blade glanced off a torso protected by scaly plates covered with slime. The creature whirled, sweeping Angel's feet out from under him with its massive tail.

Xander scurried out of the way.

Nostrils flaring, the creature swiped at Angel. He rolled away from the hooked claws on the beast's upper arm, but didn't escape the huge hind foot that thundered down on the tail of his coat, pinning him.

As he struggled to shed the coat, he saw Xander pick up a large branch, measure it against the adversary, and throw it away. The beast turned, knocking Xander off his feet with its powerful tail.

Angel's jacket tore as he wrenched free and rolled again. Slashing teeth barely missed his shoulder; they slashed again, tearing a long gash in his leg. Angel stabbed at the smaller plates covering the beast's throat. The knife penetrated the leathery connective skin, drawing blood. The creature threw its head, pulling the hilt from Angel's hand.

Angel scrambled clear, stumbled to a crouched position. The knife was still imbedded in the beast's serpentine neck. He couldn't grab it without losing an arm in the wide, snapping mouth. He ducked, jumped back, ducked again, looking for an opening, finding none.

"When in doubt, throw rocks!" Xander heaved a large rock, hitting the back of the beast's head. It bounced off without doing any damage, but it distracted the creature for a few seconds. Angel sprang, pulled the knife free and plunged the blade into a yellow eye.

The creature screamed and thrashed, clawing at its face.

Angel jumped clear and yelled. *"Run!"*

"I'm running!" Xander pounded after him into the woods.

Joyce screamed. She couldn't help it. Her worst nightmares, before she found out her daughter hunted vampires and demons as a matter of routine, were about snakes. The ground in front of her and Giles writhed with hundreds of slithering reptiles. Others twined around tree branches, hissing, baring venomous fangs, and flicking forked tongues.

Giles put his arm around her shoulders and drew her back.

Joyce shuddered, repulsed by the reptiles and embarrassed because she couldn't help reacting like a squeamish female. "I'm sorry, Giles, but I just hate snakes."

"I'm not particularly fond of them, especially when they're masquerading as carpet."

Taking a deep breath, Joyce wrapped her arms around herself and stared at the knots of swarming snakes. Since she and Giles had been separated from Buffy and her friends, they had slogged through a black bog that ruined her sensible shoes, stumbled through piles of bleached bones in an animal graveyard, and fought the local flora for passage. She had borne up well—mostly because Giles was convinced that they would find Buffy and the others waiting at the clearing. Wishful thinking or not, that thought had kept her going. But this was more than she could handle.

"I, uh—I can't go through there. Not through snakes."

"We have to." Giles eased her back a few more steps.

"If we don't, Shugra will know it's our weakness. She'll flood the woods with snakes to force us into retreat."

Joyce hesitated, then nodded. A sea of squirming reptiles would not stop her from helping Buffy. Nothing Shugra could throw at them would stop her. "Okay. Retreat is not an option."

"Unless I can rout the snakes." Giles unzipped his canvas bag and withdrew several plastic bags, two glass vials, a bowl, and a pestle.

Joyce squatted beside him and watched as he quickly ground blue-gray nuggets that looked like dry mold, sifted in shimmering green scales, and added a pinch of black powder. "There's a lot to be said for a man who's handy with a pestle."

"Yes, if one has a yen for tortillas made from scratch." He smiled.

She smiled back, wrapped her arms around her knees and mentally prepared for the ordeal ahead.

"That should do it." He dusted his hands off on his sweater and sighed. "Except for saying a few words to activate the potion."

Fascinated, Joyce didn't pull away when he placed her hands on the sides of the bowl and covered them with his. "Should I close my eyes or anything?"

"Not necessary, but you may, if this . . . bothers you."

"No." Joyce shook her head, grinned. "I'd stand on my head and recite nursery rhymes while twiddling my thumbs if it would get rid of snakes." Something moved near her foot. She shivered, imagining that the awful things were spreading toward them. She breathed in and out slowly.

"Yes, well, let's hold that ritual in reserve and hope this works. Now then—" Giles cleared his throat. "Patrick, blessed of the Emerald Isle, bid these beasts that crawl to vanish from our midst. As it was once done, so let it be done now."

Joyce tensed, waiting. She felt oddly alive and exhilarated, drawn to the understated power of this strange man. Her heart fluttered as Giles lifted his hands, giving her pause. She suppressed the response as Giles quickly repacked his supplies and helped her up.

"Haste would be in order, I believe."

"It worked?" Joyce followed the glow of his flashlight beam. The snakes were gone. "Do you do roaches?"

"Only in the spring." Still holding her hand, Giles dashed through the woods.

Joyce ran without looking at the ground. If a snake or two had escaped the magickal eviction, she didn't want to know. When Giles finally halted, she doubled over to catch her breath. "I'm glad that's over."

"It's not over." Giles looked up. "It's just beginning."

The golden orb of the full moon edged into view through the trees.

Chapter 13

Crystal ignored the quiet music and conversations emanating from the clearing, her attention shifting from one isolated pair of interlopers to another. The Slayer, her mentor, and friends shared a stubborn determination she found both laudable and annoying. If her coven had half the impassioned dedication, her success in melding with the source was assured.

Still concealed in the thicket that rimmed the ritual site, Crystal banned the implied negative from her thoughts. Nothing could stop the joining this time. Having to deal with Giles and the others was a nuisance, but they hardly constituted a serious threat. In fact, toying with them while she waited for the moon to rise had provided an amusing means of passing the time.

She decided to let them continue on, at least until the moon neared optimum position. Smiling, Crystal conjured another obstacle to hinder the Slayer's advance and peered through the eyes of a nearby owl to witness the effects.

If being fighting mad gave her an edge against Shugra, the cards were now stacked in Buffy's favor. She tried not to think about her mother, hoping the missing four were together and not having as much trouble negotiating the witch's wacky world as she and Willow. Scratched, bruised, and filthy after battling through the weird woods, she stood on a rotting log and swore.

"Not a pretty sight, is it?" Willow jumped onto the moss-covered perch holding a burning torch. She wrinkled her nose.

The forest before them was infested with insects. Masses of tiny critters flew, crawled, and skittered across the ground and over trees and brush. Locusts stripped leafy branches clean and termites turned trees to sawdust. The whirring of wings, grinding of mandibles and click of mini-feet multiplied by millions filled the night with an incessant roaring.

"We must be getting close to the clearing."

"Must be." Buffy smiled. Willow's positive attitude, undaunted by an army of maniacal squirrels hurling acorns or steaming tar pits, was contagious. A few million bugs wouldn't dampen their spirits, either. *Shugra, you have grossly underestimated our determination and resourcefulness under fire,* she thought. *And our capacity for cuteness.*

"So, I hope you have an idea how to get by them." Willow brushed her singed hair behind her ear. "I mean, there's too many to stomp."

"Agreed." Buffy's eyes sparkled. "It's crispy critter time."

"It is?" Willow frowned, then nodded slowly when Buffy raised the branches she held in her hand. She dipped them in the nearest tar pit, rolled the tip in dry pine needles, and handed one to Willow. "Gross, but—it's a plan."

Willow scrabbled in her pocket for matches and lit the torch.

Buffy stuffed the flashlight into the waistband of her jeans, lit three more torches off the burning branch, and handed another one to Willow. She hadn't intended to use them as weapons and wasn't even sure fire would disperse bugs, which she didn't mention. If it didn't work, the little beasties would eat them alive.

Which also doesn't need mentioning.

"Ready?" Buffy asked.

Willow took a deep breath. "Faint heart never stopped the wicked witch and I'm itching to kick some evil butt. So since we gotta go through them to get to her—I'm ready."

"Me, too." Buffy swallowed and shortened her grip on the torch shafts. "Swish and run. Fast."

"See Willow run. See Willow run very fast. No problem."

Drawing a deep breath, Buffy leaped into the roaring swarm. Willow squealed as she jumped off the log behind her.

The smoking torches flamed brighter as Buffy ran, waving them to repel the insects around her body and head. The swarm was too thick to chase all the flying bugs out of her way. She bent her head slightly and kept her mouth closed in a frenzied dash around trees and rocks. Bugs hit her face, clung to her clothes and became tangled in her hair. They bit her exposed flesh and buzzed maddeningly in her ears. She ran until the crunch of hard carapaces underfoot faded into the thud of boots on dirt.

Buffy stopped, planted the ends of the torches in the ground, whipped off her jacket and frantically combed dragonflies, moths, and locusts from her hair with her fingers. Willow mimicked her actions, shaking her head and stamping her feet. They pulled bugs with too many legs off each other's clothes and shook others out of their sleeves.

"Did we get them all?" Willow's hands and eyes were clenched shut.

Buffy held the flashlight up to pick through Willow's hair. "All I see are pieces and parts."

Willow shuddered. "As long as they're not moving."

"Not moving." Buffy checked the insides of her jacket sleeves, shook it for good measure, then slipped it back on. Distant thunder boomed. "Rain? I suppose a shower wouldn't—"

Willow muffled Buffy's mouth, held a finger up to hers. She removed her hand when Buffy nodded and pointed toward a dense thicket. Flecks of light and the whisper of voices filtered through the woven branches.

Buffy doused the torches with dirt. They didn't need them or the flashlight in the dim glow cast by the ascending moon.

The trials of the journey were forgotten as they crept silently around the brier patch and settled on their stomachs at the edge of the clearing. Torches on the verge of burning out were spaced around the perimeter and the strains of traditional folk music played softly in the background. The remains of a buffet littered a folding table. Eleven of Shugra's initiates sat on the rocks in a semicircle before the larger stone. One rock was still vacant.

"Am I supposed to start chanting now?" Buffy whispered.

Willow shook her head. "Not until the river ritual starts. Besides, Giles and . . . everyone could still show up."

Buffy nodded. She had been in her element fighting in the forest. Now, as Shugra in the persona of Crystal Gordon emerged from the far side of the clearing, the self-doubt she had felt—and ignored—since the anxiety attack came flooding back.

Sorcery was Willow's territory, not hers. If she stumbled over the alien words or faltered in her conviction, they would all die and Shugra's magick would rule.

Willow tensed as Shugra climbed to the top of the tall stone set behind the ring.

Michael straightened abruptly. Anya gripped his hand and whispered in his ear. The others sat enthralled, tense with expectation, their eyes fastened on the beautiful, blond witch.

Wearing a plain black dress, Shugra looked upward without meeting their eyes and raised her arms.

"Stu da bur gi'st tahr!"

The witch snapped her hands into fists.

The music stopped. The buffet table disappeared and the fizzling torches blazed.

"We could be in trouble," Buffy mumbled.

Crystal closed her eyes, her face a solemn mask as she probed the emotional aura surrounding Buffy and Willow. The obstinate perseverance that had brought them safely through the gauntlet was disturbing, but not alarming. The spells she had cast on the Slayer and the young spellcaster had not been broken. Buffy's uncertainty and fear rendered her ineffectual and Willow could not perform a spell. Their companions had apparently not fared as well in the fierce forest. It was not worth the moment of time or trace of energy it would take to check.

Crystal opened her eyes and stared at the copse where the girls hid. She decided to let them live a while longer. When she unleashed her power to call the river to the source, their terror would add a psychic tang to the proceedings. Besides, killing them as Shugra, her true self, would be so much more satisfying.

She turned her attention to the immediate necessity of completing the thirteen. "Janice McDonald, come forward."

The shy girl stumbled into the circle from the perimeter of the clearing and stood before the stone. She was visibly shaken and nervously wrung her hands.

Cursing Willow for forcing her to settle for the inadequate substitute, Crystal vented her momentary annoyance with a dramatic display of power.

"*I* am magick, the heart and soul of the elements!" Her eyes blazed as she snatched a wild bolt from the sky. The initiates cowered, grabbing onto one another as lightning crackled downward on a lethal trajectory. She dispersed it before it struck.

Janice stared, terrified and rapt.

"I chose you, Janice, as I chose everyone here," Crystal said evenly. "You are of magick, blessed with a great power and connected to the cosmic streams.

Pledge yourself to me and this coven, Janice McDonald, and *become* the magick."

Willow sighed. For a minute there, she thought Janice might be too frightened to buy into Crystal's line, but the promise of more power was too hard to resist. "I've seen this part."

"I haven't." Xander crawled up to rub shoulders with Willow. His face was smeared with dirt and his shirtsleeve was split at the seam. "Anya obviously isn't having second thoughts."

"None of them are," Willow whispered.

"I see that." Xander glanced at Buffy. "Why aren't you two making with the mumbo-jumbo?"

"We were hoping you'd show up." Willow kept her voice low. "And the main event hasn't started yet."

"Where's my mom? And Angel?" Buffy looked back. A disturbing trace of frantic fear infected her voice and expression.

"Angel's lurking in the shadows. Getting in the mood, I guess. For magick," Xander added quickly. "We haven't seen your mom or Giles since the last time we saw you."

"They'll make it, Buffy," Willow said.

"I know." Buffy crept backward into the dark.

Crystal's clear voice cut through the silence. "—and in return you will have what only I can give: power and vengeance on your enemies. Do you so pledge?"

Willow tensed.

"I do." Janice's voice cracked. She cleared her throat. "Yes, I do."

Willow exhaled, shook her head. "Come on, Xander. Shugra's got a coven and we've got a minute or two—

if we're lucky." She eased away from the copse and darted into the forest.

Angel was holding Buffy, his chin resting on her head, his hand smoothing her tangled hair. He let go and stepped back as Willow and Xander approached.

"Sorry to interrupt—well, not really, but it's minus ten and counting." Xander thumbed toward the clearing. "Crystal's go for launch."

Willow noted the absence of Giles and Joyce with a sinking heart. Buffy's confidence in her ability to say the spell was already low. Being sidetracked with worry about her mom wouldn't help her concentration.

"Right." Sighing, Buffy pulled the written spell from her pocket and gripped her flashlight. Her fist closed around the spell as Willow yanked the light away.

"Too late for that now, Buffy. You know the words." Willow gave Buffy an encouraging nod, then motioned to Angel. Xander hung back as the vampire came forward and took Buffy's hand. "You, too, Xander. Hands. Now."

Xander moved into place between Buffy and Willow and did as he was told.

Buffy nervously scanned the dark forest, preoccupied with her missing mother.

"Buffy!" Willow spoke softly but sharply, drawing the Slayer's worried gaze. She was a little amazed at how quickly and easily she had taken charge, but she didn't have time to savor the moment. "I'm sorry your mom isn't here, but you've got to—"

"She's here now." Looking as ragged, dirty, and harried as the rest of the assault force, Joyce broke out of the dark.

"A bit late, but it was rather a rough go." Following close behind, Giles ducked under a branch.

"Mom—" Buffy's smile was relieved, but lacked the usual Slayer spark.

Something was wrong, but Willow couldn't deal with it now. First things first. "Janice McDonald just took Shugra's pledge and joined the coven, Giles. She has her thirteen."

"I see." Giles paused, took a deep breath.

"You didn't happen to think of another spell that might cure Willow's speech problem, did you?" Buffy asked.

"Uh—no, but let's hope that it's only temporary." Giles dropped the spell bag and drew Joyce into the circle. "Meaning that if Shugra dies, all her spells will be voided."

"Really?" Willow flinched as thunder rumbled low overhead and red fire split open the dark. A magickal charge like a physical whisper swept through her hair. Buffy shuddered and Joyce frowned, rubbing her arm. They had felt the mystical pulse, too.

"The binding spell." Giles cast a troubled glance upward as he took Joyce and Xander's hands. "Quickly, Angel."

Grips tightened and steady gazes fixed with resolve.

Willow swallowed, realizing her confidence wasn't at a hundred percent, either. She reminded herself that they had bound themselves to fight the evil Fulcanelli and the Sons of Entropy. The five-hundred-year-old sorcerer had been a seemingly invincible magickal adversary, too. They had prevailed against him, and they would prevail against Shugra.

They had to.

Angel raised his eyes. He spoke quietly, but his throaty voice was infused with power. "Bind these souls against the dark, against the evil! The power flows through one."

Buffy's body jerked and her eyes widened.

With the power—or fear?

"Necto sua animae contra acerbus, contra malum!"

The sound of Angel's voice seemed to recede as a surge of heat shot through Buffy's veins. The roots of her hair tingled as though zapped with static electricity. She trembled and tightened her hold on his hand.

"Imperium iussu una!"

Buffy gasped as another, stronger burst of energy coursed through her, frightening in its intensity. The power was intoxicating, but it was nothing compared to the billions of magickal volts at Shugra's command. Her bravado in the forest hadn't been false. She was angry, incredibly angry—because she was terrified.

Of the witch.

"—contra malum," Angel's voice droned steadily. *"Imperium iussu una!"*

A bolt of red lightning screamed from the sky. The air shimmered with the force of raw magick slicing through the molecular matrix of the atmosphere. Hissing and crackling, crimson sparks and tendrils erupting from its core, the bolt struck with an explosive shriek and obliterated the stand of trees separating them from the clearing.

Angel let go of Buffy's hand and Giles grabbed her by the shoulders. "Now!"

Buffy turned, her ears still ringing from the blast.

Charred ash drifted to the smoking ground where trees had stood a moment before. Her nostrils flared with the acrid stench of incinerated wood and animal flesh.

She froze, her throat constricted and her heart beating like it would burst.

In the clearing, Shugra stood atop the taller rock with the coven gathered around the base. The initiates' faces betrayed emotions ranging from wide-eyed wonder to a savage lust for blood. The witch's face was like stone—unyielding and cruel. Her short blond hair grew into a mane of long, wild curls that streamed out from her head as a gust of wind whipped around her.

The witch lifted her eyes to the night sky, and a blood-red wave washed across the face of the moon.

The initiates looked skyward, empowering Shugra as she reached into the cosmos. Stars blinked out, eclipsed by the river of magick that led to the source.

"Buffy, the spell!" Giles moved his hand in front of her eyes, then glanced at Joyce and shook his head. "She's been bewitched."

Buffy stared through Giles, focused on Shugra. The fear was unlike anything she had ever felt—and it felt wrong. Her insides were ice, her brain numb—but not from within. From without.

"Buffy—" Her mother touched her cheek.

Willow took her hand. "I'm right here, Buffy. Just say the words—"

Bewitched.

Giles pulled a silver censer from the spell bag. He struggled with a long, fireplace match, lit it, and slipped the flaming tip through a hole in the ornamental globe. Wisps of blue smoke wafted from the potion as he swung the vessel by a silver chain and began the incantation to break down Shugra's ancient, protective wards. "Artemis, *domina luna, domina venora.* Let the shield of the sorceress fall and avenge thy name!"

The witch's gaze snapped toward Giles. A smile appeared on her fierce countenance as her arm shot forward to dispense with the interference.

Although paralyzed by terror, Buffy had no trouble interpreting Shugra's expression. Integrated with the immense power of primal magick, the witch's confidence was absolute. That she might fail to instantly vanquish the challengers with a mere flick of her hand never crossed Shugra's mind.

"Uh-oh," Willow muttered.

"Shta doh gru!" Crystal commanded and the elements obeyed.

"I think you touched a nerve, Giles," Xander murmured.

Buffy faltered, almost falling as the ground undulated and cracked. Xander ducked to avoid the fallout of pebbles and splintered wood as trees and boulders exploded around them. Another bolt of red lightning arrowed from the sky.

Chanting and holding onto the censer chain, Giles flung himself at Joyce. She cried out as Giles barreled into her, throwing them both away from the point of impact a split second before the sizzling spear hit.

Anger clawed through Buffy's conjured fear as the earth at ground zero crumbled into a gaping, smoking hole. Fissures radiated outward from the blackened crater.

Shugra had targeted her mother.

Deliberately.

"Come on, Buffy." Willow clung to her hand. "Ho, gihtmy Nap! Rendefed—"

Buffy focused on Shugra's cruel smile and began haltingly. *"Versus om—omnipotens . . . exemplia. Reversus . . . pravus, pravus unde ia-cia."* Her hand tingled as the power within Willow rushed into her. The fear shot through her like a blast of arctic cold to negate it. She fought the immobilizing effect with the force of will. *"Ave, Panus . . . maximus—"*

In the clearing, Shugra's expression shifted in response to the spell. Arrogance segued into a flicker of uncertainty that was abruptly replaced by rage.

Struck a nerve that *time,* Buffy realized when the witch's eyes fixed on her.

Two streams of primal magick shot from Shugra's fingers.

Buffy stood fast. *"Defendeo versus om—nipotens . . . exemplia."*

Willow caught herself bouncing slightly, as though that would make Buffy's words flow more easily. She was staring at the Slayer and didn't see the red lightning coming.

"Reversus pra—vus . . . unde ia—" Buffy staggered as a stream of savage magick struck her in the chest.

"Willow!" Xander rushed toward her, but was tossed aside as the second stream hit her. He fell in a fit of violent convulsions.

Raw, vicious magick flooded Willow, rattling her bones and teeth. Her joints fused and her brain buzzed. For a horrifying instant she was sure she was dead. Then she realized Buffy's spell had worked—sort of.

Shugra's magick hadn't been deflected, but it had been diffused—sort of. But they couldn't take too many hits and stay functional.

Joyce, stricken with the others bound to Buffy and Willow, sat with her arms wrapped around her head, rocking.

Giles recovered quickly. Swinging the smoking censer, he raised his voice to challenge Shugra's thunder. *"—ut punia tua cognomen!"*

Seized with fury, Shugra intensified her assault with guttural words and gestures. Thunder roared through a night sky roiling with red spears and starbursts of wild magick. Trees groaned and shifted into grotesque shapes, reflections of her darkened mood. Smoking crevices opened in the ground and spewed forth foul smelling gases and sprays of molten metals.

Shaky and breathless, Buffy squeezed Willow's hand and forced the incantation through gritted teeth. *"Ave Pan-panus maximus. Defen . . . defen-deo—"*

Behind them, Angel continued to intone the binding spell with practiced ease.

It *was* easy—or should have been—except Buffy was fighting some kind of spell and Willow knew her friend wasn't familiar with Latin or the emphatic cadences that tweaked an incantation. It wasn't her fault the spell wasn't packing the proper punch. Frustrated as Buffy stammered through the spell, Willow ran the words over in her mind. Spellcasting came naturally to her, just like slaying came naturally to Buffy.

Sudden understanding of Buffy's position when she was fighting vampires and the Slayerettes were trying to help hit Willow with a force greater than Shugra's magick. Although they had improved, the gang wasn't nearly as adept at staking vamps and taking out demons as the Slayer. Buffy had to watch out for them in a fight, which only made her job and staying alive harder.

Another bolt hit Willow, short-circuiting her thoughts and her circulation. The power flowing into her from Angel, Giles, Xander, and Joyce fluctuated as they suffered with similar effects. She held on when Buffy dropped to her knees.

"Protect us—from the primal power . . ." Buffy mumbled as a ball of primal lightning smashed into the earth a few feet away, sending a stream of rocks and dirt shooting upward. She bowed her head when gravity dragged the debris down upon her.

"Keep going, Buffy. You're doing great." Willow wiped black ash off her face and winced as the Slayer dragged herself upright. She felt totally helpless as the life force of the others ebbed and waned.

Xander's arms were wrapped around a small tree, his body twitching and his eyes glazed with pain. He cried out when a large rock exploded by his leg, bit his lip to hold the sound back.

Giles cradled Joyce's head in his lap. His face was drenched in sweat and visible spasms coursed through his crumpled legs. The censer dangled from his hand and his voice cracked as he repeated the spell to lower the wards. "Artemis, lady of the moon, mistress of the hunt . . ."

On his knees, Angel held up clenched fists and kept chanting.

"—turn the evil back on she who casts." Buffy twined her fingers through Willow's and swayed on unsteady legs.

Red lightning ripped across the dark sky, cracking and snarling against the tether of Shugra's hold. Small bursts of scarlet magick cast a red sheen on her skin and hair, and her eyes glowed with the fierce light of a wild thing, a vestige of her primitive origin. With a snap of her hand, she released bolts of the red power to strike at random for miles around.

Trees burst into flame and stone shattered or melted. The terrified shrieks of panicked wildlife rose like a demon chorus in the dark. Grit and splinters of rock and wood pelted ground torn apart by internal forces gone berserk and wild magick impacts.

Willow cringed as the witch's malevolent anger surged through the forest, searing the souls of her enemies. A burning fever swept through her, and the energy transmitted from the others weakened suddenly. The full force of Shugra's power was being held at bay by the incantations, but Buffy, Giles, and Angel had to reinforce the spells with constant repetition. It was only a matter of minutes before the primal witch drained their dwindling energies.

"Willow—" Xander cried out as the tree he clung to shattered, driving splinters into his palms. He rolled away, his face contorted with pain.

"—*Panus maximus* . . ." Buffy faltered, her voice a mere whisper.

Outraged and terrified, Willow struggled for calm and forced herself to think rationally. Buffy was doing her best and depending on her for magickal support. However, fighting Shugra with magick alone wasn't enough. The witch was too strong—and knew it.

Willow remembered the torches Buffy had made with the resources at hand.

The only resource she had that Shugra couldn't control was her wits.

And an idea!

A plan sprang full-blown into Willow's mind. It wasn't an *entirely* original idea, but it might work.

They had beaten Catherine Madison's superior magick because of the witch's arrogance. Amy's mom had been so sure they couldn't hurt her she had been taken by surprise twice: first when Giles reversed her spells and again when Buffy's superior reflexes and mental agility brought down the mirror.

The immortal vampire, Veronique, had been duped as well when the Slayerettes had allowed themselves to be possessed by ghosts, which had effectively rendered them "dead" and unfit for demonic consumption. With all Veronique's centuries of planning to bring the Triumvirate into the human world, nothing had prepared her to recognize or deal with an innovative and risky defense.

So there's precedent, Willow thought. Besides which, she didn't have any other options.

Willow braced herself as the witch lashed out with another blast of primal magick. Stronger than the previous bolts, the red lightning burned through every nerve in her body. Wracked with pain, she collapsed.

Chapter 14

"SETTLE DOWN!" CORDELIA'S FINGER FLEXED ON THE trigger as she sighted down the barrel of the tranq gun.

The werewolf howled and lunged against the chains. The restraints held, but the bolts were no longer firmly secured to the floor. They wiggled when he tore at the manacles clamped around his wrists and ankles.

Crimson lightning flashed outside the window, followed by a deafening crack of thunder. The library shuddered.

Shaking bits of falling plaster from her hair, Cordelia aimed. She wanted to do the right thing. The crazed werewolf wasn't just a vicious beast that could rip her apart. It was Oz most of the time. If she put him to sleep and the roof caved in, he'd be crushed. If she didn't shoot him and the roof caved in, he *might* be able to avoid being crushed—but then he'd be loose. She really wasn't up for being buried alive under tons of high school with a man-eating monster.

A flash of red lit up the room when lightning struck nearby.

The werewolf shrieked, then howled with feral terror.

"You're not making this any easier." Cordelia swallowed and adjusted the butt of the gun against her shoulder. Still she hesitated. How could she live with herself if Oz ended up dead? Of course, if she died, that wouldn't be a problem.

Cordelia jumped when another bolt hit just outside the building with a deafening boom. She squeezed the trigger without meaning to. The dart imbedded in the werewolf's torso and he crumpled. *Problem solved.*

Two windowpanes shattered and Cordelia dashed for cover under the study table. The crack of thunder and barrage of weird lightning continued without interruption, getting stronger and closer. Shugra apparently had the upper hand out in the forest.

Cordelia sighed. Her other problems wouldn't matter if she was dead, either. Being broke wasn't a sin.

But it would be a huge pain if she survived.

She covered her ears as a series of strikes strafed the campus. A chunk of ceiling landed on the table. Although it sounded like the Slayer might have met her match, there was a chance Buffy would pull off a victory. The Slayer always did.

Consequently, Cordelia deemed it prudent to protect her assets.

She waited for a lull, then crawled out from under the table. Gripping the mouse in a shaky hand, she clicked on "save," then keyed the computer to shut down. In the seconds it took the machine to whir through the initial phases of the process, a bolt of vicious lightning struck the side of the building.

Cordelia jumped back and stared as crackling arcs of electric red coursed along wire and cord toward the table.

The PC tower melted and the monitor exploded.

Stunned by the magickal surge, a moment passed before Buffy realized that Willow was lying on the ground and not moving. The spell binding them together did more than simply allow for the transfer of power. Buffy felt everything Willow felt on a physical level. The wicca wasn't unconscious and the pain was subsiding.

In the split second this went through her mind, Buffy glanced at Giles. He frowned and shook his head. In another second, she concluded that Willow had a reason for playing possum. Whatever it was, she had to trust the other girl's instincts.

Buffy collapsed and waved the others down amidst a shower of burning coals. A fissure opened under her arm. She lay still when the crack snaked underneath her and a blast of sizzling steam out-gassed around her leg.

Xander, like her mother, was already prone and happy to stay that way. Holding his hands up, he had curled into a ball with his head tucked. He flinched when a barrage of magick missiles struck nearby and coughed quietly when dust and grit enveloped him, but he didn't move.

Giles stopped chanting and stretched out, clutching

the censer. His eyes widened, then closed as a fiery spear ripped through a jagged tree stump behind him. Tongues of flame lapped at his back and scorched his jeans before they subsided. He remained immobile.

Angel maintained the binding spell as he keeled over. Murmuring softly, he ignored the rivulets of molten metal seeping from the rock above his shoulder. The black fabric of his coat sizzled where drops of liquid heat burned through.

Buffy willed her rapid pulse rate to slow, trying to reach the state of inner calm she saw on Willow's face.

Not easy.

The mysterious ploy had left them all vulnerable to instant death at Shugra's hands.

He's not dead. Anya stared at Xander, wishing the knot in her stomach and the lump in her throat would go away. He was hurt, but he'd heal. Human men were incredibly resilient in that department. Being able to take it was a macho thing that hadn't changed since they were wearing bearskin loincloths and clubbing each other to settle territorial disputes.

Xander didn't move. He obviously wasn't taking it very well, but that was his own fault for interfering with the ritual.

A wave of emotion threatened to bring tears to Anya's eyes. She quelled the reaction with a shuddering sigh.

This was all Buffy's fault. She should have known that Crystal would protect herself and the coven, that she would take action against anyone who tried to stop them from reaching the source. Willow had found out the hard way. Anya still couldn't believe the little fool had passed up the chance to join them, or to cure Oz from some awful disease.

It didn't make sense.

Or maybe it did.

The uneasiness nagging at her since Crystal began the attack jabbed Anya pointedly. She was no stranger to death and destruction for the sake of power. She had been a major cause of chaos and pain for too long not to understand the thrilling satisfaction of control over the helpless.

Which probably accounted for her sudden doubt.

"They sleep." Crystal looked down on her initiates, her eyes glinting with a familiar fervor—deep brown, almost black flecked with red. Cascades of long, wavy blond hair billowed around a face that seemed more angular, harder in light composed of flame and crimson explosions. The witch threw her head back and closed her eyes. Her chest rose and fell with deep breaths as she silently communed with the elements and wild magick.

The storm of red lightning abated to weave less frenetic patterns across the dark sky. The surrounding woods were left in smoldering ruin, buried under a blanket of black ash. Not a rock or tree within a hundred yards of the fallen rescue party had survived intact. Smoke and steam poured from impact craters and cracks. Tortured, dead trees crashed to earth beyond the initial devastation. Heated rocks deeper within the forest exploded.

Then all was still.

Unnerved, Anya glanced at the others in the coven. A

few, Winston, Craig, and Greta, seemed unaffected by the brutal pounding the witch had given the intruders. Rebecca, Kari, and Joanna clung to each other, confused and uncertain. Michael scowled.

"Do not be alarmed." Crystal spoke without opening her eyes, as though she knew what was going through their minds.

Anya was alarmed. Willow wasn't a fool. Buffy and Giles were fools, but they were fools dedicated to the destruction of evil.

Which probably explained why they had crashed the ritual to begin with.

To crush Crystal before she became an absolute power and didn't have to pander to anyone. Or keep her promises.

Cursing herself for not realizing what was so blatantly obvious sooner, Anya nudged Michael and drew his gaze. She didn't dare speak, but tried to communicate her anxiety with her eyes. Not hard since she was scared to death. Michael frowned as she glanced toward Crystal, shook her head, then looked at the fallen Xander.

Michael's eyes narrowed with understanding. They had free will. If they withdrew from the ritual—

Anya blinked, her train of thought disrupted, then resumed staring at Xander. *He's not dead.*

After adjusting Anya and Michael's minds, Crystal scanned the emotional matrix around the downed Slayer and her co-conspirators. Calm prevailed—for now. When they awakened, tranquillity would no longer exist.

She closed her eyes and concentrated on the infinite realm beyond the world. The great source-river of wild magick coursed in violent abandon through the orbits of comets so ancient and distant they had never been warmed by the sun. Some evaporated in the roiling rapids of red fire, others were thrown off course to speed through interstellar space. As she touched the raging stream with her mind, she felt the unlimited power emanating from the source.

"I am Shugra!" An elation she had not experienced since Ephesus overwhelmed her as the river responded to her call.

Willow opened one eye, but didn't move. The blood-red moon was directly overhead, the dark sky streaked with wild red magick. Everything around them had been reduced to charred lumps and ashes. In the clearing, Shugra's gullible followers stared upward, entranced by the spectacle. Anya appeared to be watching Xander. Michael was watching her. Focused on the cosmic chaos, the witch shouted her name.

"I am Shugra!"

The ritual had begun.

And we're going to end it.

Closing her eyes again, Willow made sure everyone was still bound. They were, and the power they generated flowed steadily again, revived during the brief but crucial rest. There was another element in the mix as well. Anya's concern for Xander's safety linked her to the group through him. Michael's energies were scattered. He wasn't part of the Slayer's support system, but he wasn't in tune with Shugra's agenda, either.

Willow turned her head slightly. Buffy was staring at her, waiting. She winked and whispered. "You, Giles— Go on."

Buffy stared for another long second, then nodded. Raising her legs, she flipped into a fighting stance. She started to speak before she landed, her voice strong. *"Ave, Panus maximus!"*

Startled, Giles scrambled upright and began swinging the censer. Black organic ash drifted off his clothes and blue smoke billowed around him. Soot and grime streaked his face, and his jeans were singed. "Artemis, lady of the moon, mistress of the hunt—"

The drone of Angel's binding spell continued unbroken as the vampire stood up. He squared his shoulders, his piercing dark gaze boring into the witch. "The power flows through One. *Necto sua animae—*"

Xander crawled over the ground on his elbows, holding his hands up. Dozens of long splinters impaled his palms. His clothes were torn and his cheek sported an oozing red gash. Still, the familiar hint of humor was evident in the harsh rasp of his voice. "Just a glutton for punishment or what, Willow?"

"Just a wicca who wants to win." Willow grinned. She had gambled that Crystal would assume they were beaten. In her arrogance, the primal witch hadn't guessed that the unempowered wicca was setting up an ambush of her own. Shugra's diverted attention had provided the opening they needed.

Willow shivered as a faint arc of green energy appeared between her and Buffy.

"Protect us from the primal power—" Buffy said it and meant it. *"Defendeo versus omnipotens exemplia!"*

Shugra stiffened, turned her head slowly. Her expression darkened as their intent became clear.

"Let the shield of the sorceress fall—"

Willow stared at the censer in Giles's hand, struck with another bold idea. Crystal's aphasia spell was still in effect, but telekinesis didn't rely on words. However, assuming she was still able to move things with her mind, driving pencils into tree trunks was child's play compared to flinging a metal ball across a clearing filled with hostile magick. Still, she had nothing to lose by trying.

Willow concentrated on the pain of Shugra's attacks, feeding her suppressed anger, gathering her strength.

"—and avenge thy name!" Giles's words reverberated through the trees. He staggered, surprised as Willow grabbed the censer from his grasp with a thought and heaved it.

Thrilled, Willow tracked the smoking silver missile as it hurtled through the air. Confident in her shields, Shugra made no move to stop it. Blue fire erupted from the globe as it smashed into the wards.

"Now, Buffy!" The green arc glowed brighter as Willow focused the collective energies on the Slayer.

Every muscle in Buffy's battered body ached. Her throat was raw from eating cinders and her favorite leather jacket was peppered with small holes. Singed hair tangled beyond combing and blood pouring from a deep cut behind her ear fed a furious indignation. Even so, the fear Shugra had planted and cultivated still raged within her, cutting off her air and stopping her heart.

I may be dead, but I'm taking you with me.

Burning with an inner fire all her own, Buffy pointed at the witch and looked her in the eye. "Turn the evil of the ages back on she who casts!"

Shugra's gaze narrowed and her mouth set as she unleashed the storm. A bitter wind tore through the forest, whipping black ash into a blinding, swirling cloud. Thunder rolled and rumbled as the witch's magickal forces amassed for a renewed attack.

"Buffy—" Joyce started toward her. Giles pulled her back.

Xander struggled to his feet, his hands raw and bleeding from the wooden pikes he had pulled out with his teeth.

"Imperium iussu una!" Angel strode forward to stand by Buffy.

In the sky, streaks of red lightning coalesced into a single bolt. Shugra glared and sent the deadly shaft of primal magick driving down toward the Slayer.

"Reversus pravus unde iacia!" Buffy gasped the last word of the spell. Out of oxygen, her heart no longer pumping, she slumped into Angel's arms.

"Buffy?" Angel lowered her to the ground and put his ear on her chest. "Giles! She's not breathing!"

Chapter 15

BLACK SPOTS DANCED IN FRONT OF BUFFY'S EYES BEFORE her heavy lids closed. Her throat and chest constricted as she struggled in vain to breathe. She sensed Angel hovering above her, felt his panicked despair, wished she could reach out and touch his face. She couldn't move her arm. The peace of oblivion enveloped her as she faded out.

Then her mother screamed her name.

"Buffy!"

And Willow yelled. "Yes!"

Buffy gasped again when her lungs suddenly filled with air. Her eyes snapped open as the massive bolt of primal magick zoomed passed her, crackling and spitting on an altered course. It sped into the forest, ripping distant trees out by the roots and burning the brush in its path.

"What's happening?" Buffy whispered.

"Buffy!" Angel folded her into his arms, kissed her lightly on the forehead. "Your spell. It's working."

"It is?" Still dazed from lack of oxygen, Buffy turned her head as the distant bolt reversed direction and arrowed back.

"Not again, please." Joyce grabbed Giles's arm, her voice trembling.

"It's all right," Giles said gently. "If I'm not mistaken, the bolt has homed in on the witch."

Please go after the witch, Buffy silently intoned. Her stomach knotted as the monstrous concentration of lethal magick bore down on them—and sagged as it sped by overhead creating chaos of the debris in its wake.

"No!" Shugra shrieked.

"Sorry about that!" Willow sank to the ground beside Xander, smiling. "No, I'm not."

"Aren't we just a little bit pleased with ourselves?" Xander grinned.

In the clearing, Shugra's coven fell apart. Screaming girls and panicked boys scattered for cover in the remnants of woods around the ritual site.

Anya raced out of the clearing toward the rescue party, ducking as the magick missile streaked by. Puffs of ash marked her pounding feet until she stopped a few feet in front of Xander. She stared at him for a long moment, then shrugged.

Joyce swayed slightly and didn't argue when Giles urged her to sit down. Her stylish business clothes were already destined for the trash and she was beyond caring that her hair and face were coated in black gunk.

Weak and still breathless, Buffy shifted position. Propped against Angel's broad chest, she watched the witch.

Shugra shot her hands forward to repel the renegade

bolt. No red fire exploded from her fingers. Outraged, she screamed at the moon. *"Tah gru da, Duhn che!"*

The bolt struck her in the chest and lifted her off the stone. Impaled by the magickal spear and suspended in midair, Shugra flailed as a web of red energy formed a cage around her.

The temperature dropped abruptly. Buffy shivered and pressed against Angel's cold body without taking her eyes off the unfolding drama.

The low, staccato sound of galloping horses began as a faint tapping and grew louder as the ghostly images of a hundred mounted warriors rode across the dark sky.

"Now the cavalry shows up," Xander quipped.

"The army of Ramses the Great led by Akmontep, actually." Giles's eyes widened in awe as he looked up at the phantom spectacle. Translucent Arabian mounts snorted and bucked as riders carrying sword and shield rode in a wide circle around the imprisoned Shugra.

The witch glared at the ancient forces, spit, and shouted a primitive curse. *"Kot bec!"*

"Who?" Joyce asked.

"Akmontep was a priest in Pharaoh's court. Shugra slaughtered his Egyptian troops by the hundreds around thirteen hundred B.C. Her evil is revisited upon her." Giles flinched as one of the riders broke ranks.

Shugra screamed with rage and fear as the warrior rode forward and neatly beheaded her with a short sword. Her severed head screamed in agony for several seconds before it rejoined her body to be severed again. And again until the last of the riders had taken his revenge and the long dead army vanished back into the ether.

"Revenge is better late than never," Buffy said.

"And that was just the first act," Xander said. "All we're missing is the popcorn."

"Like at the movies, right?" Anya glanced at Xander expectantly.

Xander didn't answer. His gaze was fastened on the witch.

Shugra no longer looked like Crystal Gordon. She wore the stark gray dress, apron, and cap of a Colonial American woman. Miriam was plainer than Crystal, rounder of face and shorter, but the arrogant defiance that was Shugra still blazed from her dark eyes.

"Double feature." Willow pointed at the moon.

The black silhouette of a gallows appeared as the red sheen faded and the moon glowed golden. The noose flew outward like a lasso turning ghostly gray against the night. It snared the captive Shugra around the neck and suddenly grew taut. She clawed at the noose with her fingers, then fell as though the floor had been dropped out from under her. Her body jerked violently for several minutes before she went limp.

"For Salem, I bet." Willow glanced at Giles.

"Yes, most likely."

They watched in silence as Shugra was repeatedly hung, drowned, burned, tortured on the strappado, and stoned by the ghosts of her victims.

After each group had its long-awaited moment of revenge, she reappeared in the persona of her previous reincarnation.

The forces of nature she had used as weapons retaliated next. Wind and rain battered her. Ice froze her. Stone crushed her and a swarm of phantom locusts ripped the flesh from her bones. Then the body into which Shugra had been born materialized.

The primitive female had coarse, dark hair that gripped a round, blunt head in filthy snarls. Broken, discolored teeth filled a thin-lipped mouth in a flat face. Corded muscles covered stubby arms and legs attached to a squat body clothed in ragged animal fur and coarse cloth.

"Not exactly elegant," Xander muttered.

Buffy tensed as the ancient being turned her head and captured the Slayer's gaze.

Shugra's dark eyes burned with savage passion.

Then the red web dissipated and the crimson spear withdrew.

Shugra's body fell back onto the large stone. She moaned and struggled to rise as red lightning exploded from the sky. On her knees, she looked up and stretched out her arms. "Chit, *doh mei!*"

Magick had the last revenge.

The bolt struck her chest, sizzling, crackling and shortening until it was completely absorbed. The red glow burning within Shugra brightened and expanded until she burst into flames. The fire flared for a brilliant instant, then died.

The wind swept the ashes from the stone.

Chapter 16

Buffy leaned on the open window of her mother's car in the school parking lot. Filthy and weary, Joyce sat on a towel she had retrieved from the trunk. She hadn't argued when Buffy had urged her to go straight home and take a long, hot bath. Meeting a werewolf was probably more than her mom could deal with in one night.

"You're sure you're all right?" Buffy asked.

Joyce nodded and turned the ignition key. "I can honestly say this has been one of the more . . . *unusual* nights of my life."

"Pretty awful, huh?" Buffy hadn't meant to sound hopeful, but having her mother too close to the action was just too distracting. Couldn't be helped when the evil forces tried to get to her through her mom, but with luck she wouldn't volunteer again any time soon.

"Well, yes." Joyce sighed. "I know Crystal—or Shugra—was evil, but what that spell did—"

"Mom," Buffy said patiently, "the spell just gave back everything she dished out over several thousand years."

"Three-fold." Willow leaned over Buffy's shoulder and waved. "That's the rule."

"There's a rule?" Anya frowned. "For demons, too?"

"If there's justice in the universe," Xander said, coming up behind her.

"Actually—" Willow turned and started strolling leisurely toward the library. Anya and Xander followed. "Anya helped us tonight. A little."

"A little?" Xander laughed shortly. "We *told* her Crystal was a very bad person and she went out there anyway."

"But I didn't remember talking to you this afternoon!" Anya pouted. "Not until Buffy's spell kicked in."

"A likely story." Xander sighed. "So how did she help?"

"She was worried about you," Willow said. "Because you were hurt. So doesn't that give her points on the good side?"

"Maybe." Xander reluctantly conceded. "But it'll take a thousand years to balance the books."

Buffy smiled as her friends moved off. "It's nice to have things back to normal. Weird normal, but—that's Sunnydale." She glanced over her shoulder when Giles paused behind her. "Hey, Giles. You look like you just battled the worst witch in the known world."

"Yes, I'm sure I do." He smoothed back his hair and cleared his throat with a nervous glance at Joyce. "I do hope events weren't too . . . traumatic for you."

"Not at all." Joyce put the car in gear. "I don't think I'll dream about snakes anymore."

"Snakes?" Buffy stepped back as her mother waved and pulled away. "You dream about snakes?" She turned on Giles. "Dreaming about snakes means—well, you know—sex. So why is my mother dreaming about *that?*"

"Snakes?" Giles started walking. "I suppose you'll have to ask her."

"Don't think so." Buffy shoved her hands into her pockets and lengthened her stride to keep up.

"Shouldn't you make sure she gets home all right?" Giles asked.

"Angel's on it." Buffy took a long, deep breath and exhaled slowly, relishing the chilly air. Her heart was beating normally and her lungs worked. She had even faced off Shugra while the fear spell was still in effect, but she couldn't shake a lingering doubt. "So the whole anxiety attack thing was a spell, right?"

"Yes, apparently." Giles opened the back door into the library. "Shugra probably implanted a fear response to her magick while she was testing your reactions in history class."

"Apparently?" Buffy followed him in the door. *"Probably?* Those aren't the right answers."

Giles paused. "I don't have a definite answer because I don't know. The important thing is that you handled it, Buffy. Admirably, I might add."

"I can accept an admirably." Buffy smiled as she descended the steps, satisfied. She had beaten the witch in spite of the terror and, whether magickal or real, she had beaten the fear, too.

Giles paused by the study table where Cordelia sat with a paperback novel open in front of her. His gaze wandered from the chunk of plaster on the table to the broken window. A layer of grit covered the floor. "Well, I suppose this could have been worse."

Cordelia smiled tightly. "Compliments of the freaky lightning storm. Not fun."

"Quite." Giles sighed and ran his hand through his matted hair. He dropped the spell bag on a chair and grumbled as he went to inspect the damage. "I might as well schedule regular monthly meetings with the School Board budget committee to discuss funds for library repairs."

Cordelia glanced at Buffy and grimaced. "But I'm glad I wasn't with you guys."

"Good call." Dirty, tired, and aching, Buffy wasn't in the mood to trade barbed comments.

Across the room, Anya returned from the nurse's office with a first-aid kit. Xander objected strenuously, but gave in when she insisted on doctoring his wounded hands and face.

Willow stared at the still form of the werewolf lying half in and half out of the book cage. "What happened to Oz?"

"I shot him." Cordelia said blithely. "By accident. With the tranq gun. For a big, scary monster he sure acts like a wimp in a thunderstorm."

"But I'm *not* used to dealing with the supernatural as a mortal!" Anya followed Xander as he stomped to the table. "I'm not used to *being* a mortal."

"And that's supposed to be an excuse?" Xander raised an eyebrow, daring her to counter. Red antiseptic dripped from his hands.

"Well, yeah." Anya's frowned deepened. "It's the only one I've got."

"I think a truce is in order." Willow sank into a chair. "Just for tonight."

Xander rolled his eyes and nodded, resigned. "Fine. For tonight only."

"Great!" Grinning, Anya dragged him back to the counter to finish playing nurse. "Are you up for going to the Bronze?"

Xander held up an orange finger. "Don't push it, Anya."

Buffy sighed. Hanging at the Bronze for a while sounded like a good idea—if they didn't all look like hurricane refugees.

"A celebration is definitely in order," Willow piped up. "I mean, we wiped out the wickedest witch of all time and—I can say magick again." A small cricket crawled out of a tangle in her auburn hair.

"I'm game—after a shower," Buffy said.

"You were quite spectacular tonight, Willow." Giles wandered back from the window with his glasses in hand and pulled a handkerchief from his pocket. He glanced at the useless, dirt-streaked cloth, then stuffed it back into his pocket.

"I was, wasn't I?" Willow bubbled with pride.

"I'll watch Oz for the rest of the night, if you want to go out," Giles offered.

"How is Oz?" Buffy touched the cut behind her ear and winced. A little antiseptic wouldn't hurt her, either.

"Sleeping it off—again." Willow shot Cordelia a disapproving look.

Cordelia huffed. "*I* didn't make the doors vanish last night or—"

"The computer!" Willow shot out of her chair, the blood draining from her face when she saw the blackened mass of melted plastic and pile of glass, electronics, and broken casing pieces at the end of the table.

"Power surge," Cordelia said, closing the book. "Big power surge. You really should get a surge protector for that."

"And the Slayer program?" Giles asked without hope.

"Gone." Closing her book, Cordelia picked up her jacket and bag. "We can settle up tomorrow."

"Uh, right. Tomorrow then." Grabbing the spell bag, Giles quickly retreated into his office as Cordelia left.

Leaving Willow to mourn the dead computer, Buffy sauntered after him. She paused in the doorway, leaned against the jamb, and folded her arms. "Settle up? You've been *paying* Cordelia?"

Giles pulled her inside and closed the door. "Cordelia was the only person willing to work on the Slayer database."

"Sure. For a *fee!*" Buffy threw up her hands. "And all for nothing because the computer crashed and burned."

Giles deflated. "Yes, well, I'd greatly appreciate it if you'd keep this . . . secret. Especially from Willow."

"Okay, but you owe Willow one. Maybe two or three." Buffy was thoroughly enjoying having Giles over a barrel. "She's been wanting to get into some more advanced wicca studies—"

"Done." Exhaling wearily, Giles fell into his desk chair.

"But I have to wonder—" Buffy sat, eyeing him curiously. "What other secrets have you been keeping from me?"

"Secrets?" Giles stiffened, blinked. "Me? None!"

Buffy just nodded and smiled. Whatever they were, she'd find out—eventually.

About the Author

Diana G. Gallagher lives in Florida with her husband, Marty Burke, three dogs, three cats, and a cranky parrot. A Hugo Award–winning artist, she is best known for her series *Woof: The House Dragon.* Dedicated to the development of the solar system's resources, she has written and recorded songs that promote and encourage humanity's movement into space.

Her first adult science fiction novel, *The Alien Dark,* appeared in 1990. She and Marty co-authored *The Chance Factor,* a *Starfleet Academy Voyager* novel for intermediate readers. Diana has contributed to several other series published by Minstrel Books, including *The Secret World of Alex Mack, Are You Afraid of the Dark?* and *The Journey of Allen Strange.* She has also written original young adult novels for the Archway Paperback series *Sabrina the Teenage Witch* and is currently working on another *Buffy the Vampire Slayer* novel for Pocket Pulse.